TO KNOW A WOMAN

TO KNOW A WOMAN

AMOS OZ

Translated from the Hebrew
by Nicholas de Lange

A Harvest Book
A Helen & Kurt Wolff Book
Harcourt, Inc.
Orlando Austin New York
San Diego Toronto London

Requests for permission to make copies of any part of
the work should be mailed to the following address:
Permissions Department, Harcourt, Inc.,
6277 Sea Harbor Drive,
Orlando, Florida 32887-6777.

Translation of La-da'at ishah.

Library of Congress Cataloging-in-Publication Data
Oz, Amos.
  [La-da'at ishah. English]
  To know a woman / Amos Oz; translated from the
  Hebrew by Nicholas de Lange. — 1st ed.
p. cm.
ISBN 978-0-15-690680-7

Translation of La-da'at ishah.
"A Helen and Kurt Wolff book."
I. Title
PJ5054.09L2913   1991
892.4'36—dc20   90-5196

Text set in Sabon.
Printed in the United States of America
First Harvest edition 1992

DOH 16 15 14 13 12 11

TO
KNOW
A
WOMAN

Yoel picked the object up from the shelf and inspected it closely. His eyes ached. The real-estate agent, thinking he had not heard the question, repeated it: "Shall we go and take a look around the back?" Even though he had already made up his mind, Yoel was in no hurry to reply. He was in the habit of pausing before answering, even simple questions such as "How are you?" or "What did it say on the news?" As though words were personal possessions that should not be parted with lightly.

The agent waited. In the meantime there was a silence in the room, which was stylishly furnished: a wide, deep-pile, dark-blue rug, armchairs, a sofa, a mahogany coffee table, an imported television set, a huge philodendron in the appropriate corner, a red-brick fireplace with half a dozen logs arranged in crisscross fashion, for show rather than use. Next to the passthrough to the kitchen, a dark dining table with six matching high-backed dining chairs. Only pictures were missing, where pale rectangles were visible on the walls. The kitchen, seen through the open door, was Scandinavian and full of the latest electrical gadgets. The four bedrooms, which he had already seen, had also met with his approval.

With his eyes and fingers Yoel explored the thing he had taken off the shelf. It was a carving, a figurine, the work of an amateur: a feline predator, carved in brown olivewood and coated with several layers of lacquer. Its jaws were gaping wide and the teeth were pointed. The two front legs were extended in the air in a spectacular leap; the right hind leg was also in the air, still contracted and bulging with muscles from the effort of jumping, only the left hind leg preventing the takeoff and grounding the beast on a stainless-steel stand. The body rose at an angle of forty-five degrees, and the tension was so powerful that Yoel could almost feel in his own flesh the pain of the confined paw and the desperation of the interrupted leap. He found the statuette unnatural and unconvincing, even though the artist had succeeded in imposing on the wood an excellent feline litheness. This was not the work of an amateur, after all. The detail of the jaws and the paws, the twist of the springlike spine, the tension of the muscles, the arching of the belly, the fullness of the diaphragm inside the strong rib cage, and even the angle of the beast's ears—swept back, almost flattened toward the back of the head—all the detailed work was excellent and evinced a mastery of the secret of defying the limitations of matter. This was evidently an accomplished piece of carving, liberated from its woodenness and achieving a cruel, fierce, almost sexual vitality.

Yet, even so, something had not come out right. Something or other was awry, obtrusive: either too finished, as it were, or not finished enough. What it was, Yoel could not discover. His eyes ached. Again he nursed a suspicion that this was the work of an amateur. But where was the defect? A faint, physical anger stirred inside him, with a certain momentary urge to stretch up on the tips of his toes.

Perhaps it was also because the figurine with its hidden flaw seemed to be flouting the laws of gravity. The weight of the predator in his hand seemed to be greater than that of the steel base that the creature was straining to break away from, and to which it remained attached by only a tiny point of contact between the hind paw and the base. It was on this very point that Yoel now focused his attention. He discovered that the paw was sunk in an infinitesimal depression in the surface of the steel. But how?

His vague anger intensified when he turned the object over and to his astonishment found no sign of the screw that he had supposed would have to be there, to attach the paw to the base. He turned the figurine over again: there was no sign of any screw in the beast's flesh either, between the claws of that hind paw. Then what was it that was restraining the animal's murderous leap? Certainly not glue. The weight of the figurine would not allow any adhesive known to Yoel to attach the beast to the ground by such a minute point of contact for any length of time with the body of the animal projecting forward from the base at such an acute angle. Perhaps it was time to admit defeat and start wearing glasses. Here he was, a widower, forty-seven years old, already enjoying early retirement, a free man in almost every sense of the word: what point was there in his stubbornly denying the plain truth: that he was tired. He had earned a rest and he needed one. His eyes burned sometimes, and occasionally print became blurred, particularly by the light of his bedside lamp at night. And yet the main questions were still unresolved. If the predator was heavier than the base and projected almost entirely beyond it, the thing ought to overbalance. If the joint was secured with glue, it should have come apart ages ago. If the beast was complete, what was the invisible defect? What was the source of his feeling that there was some flaw? If there was a hidden trick, what was it?

Finally, in a vague rage—Yoel was angry even at the fury that was stirring within him, because he liked to see himself as a calm, self-contained man—he took hold of the animal by the neck and endeavored, not by force, to break the spell and release the magnificent beast from the torment of the mysterious grip. Perhaps then the invisible flaw would also vanish.

"Come on," said the agent. "It would be a pity to break it. Shall we go and look at the garden shed? The garden may look a bit neglected but a morning's work would get it right as rain."

Delicately, with a slow caress, Yoel ran a cautious finger around the secret join between the living and the inanimate. The statuette was not the work of an amateur, after all, but of an artist gifted with cunning and power. There flickered for an instant in his mind the faint recollection of a Byzantine crucifixion scene: that too had had something implausible about it and yet filled with pain. He nodded twice as though agreeing with himself at last at the end of an inner debate. He blew on the figurine to remove an invisible speck of dust, or perhaps his own fingerprints, then sadly replaced it on the shelf of ornaments between a blue glass vase and a brass censer.

"Fine," he said, "I'll take it."

"Pardon?"

"I've decided to take it."

"Take what?" asked the agent, confused, peering somewhat suspiciously at his client. The man appeared compact, tough, deeply entrenched in the inner recesses of his being, insistent yet also abstracted. He stood immobile, with his face toward the shelf and his back to the agent.

"The house," he answered quietly.

"Just like that? Don't you want to see the garden? Or the shed?"

"I said I'll take it."

"And do you agree to a rent of nine hundred dollars per month, payable half-yearly in advance? Repairs and all taxes to be your responsibility?"

"Done."

"If only all my clients were like you." The agent chuckled. "I'd be able to spend all day at sea. My hobby happens to be sailing. Want to check the washing machine and the stove first?"

"I'll take your word for it. If there are any problems, we can always find each other. Take me to your office and let's get the paperwork out of the way."

2

In the car on the way back from the suburb, which was named Ramat Lotan, to the office in the center, on Ibn Gabirol Street, the agent delivered himself of a monologue. He spoke of the housing market, the collapse of the stock market, the new economic policy, which seemed to him to be completely screwed up, and this government that deserved to be you-know-whatted. He explained to Yoel that the owner of the property, a personal acquaintance of his, Yosi Kramer, was a section manager for El Al, who had been suddenly sent off to New York for three years at barely a fortnight's notice, just time to grab the wife and kids and rush off to snatch the apartment of another Israeli, who was moving from Queens to Miami.

The man sitting on his right did not look to him like someone who was likely to change his mind at the last minute: a client who looks at two properties in the space of an hour and a half and then takes the third twenty minutes after setting foot in it, without haggling over the price, wouldn't slip off the hook now. Nevertheless the agent felt a professional duty to continue to convince the silent man sitting beside him that he had got a good bargain. He was also curious to know something about the stranger with the slow movements and the little wrinkles at the corners of his eyes that suggested a faintly derisive smile, even though the thin lips did not express so much as the ghost of a smile. And so the agent sang the praises of the property, the advantages of this semidetached house in an exclusive suburb that had been built the way it should be, "state of the art," as they say. The next-door neighbors are a couple of Americans, brother and sister, good solid people who apparently were sent over to represent some charitable foundation in Detroit. So, peace and quiet are guaranteed. The whole street consists of well-cared-for homes; there is a carport to park the car in; there is a shopping center and a school just a couple of hundred yards from the front door, the sea is a mere twenty minutes away, and the whole city is at your fingertips. The house, as you saw for yourself, is fully furnished and equipped, because the Kramers, the owners, are people who know what quality is, and anyway, with a manager for El Al you can be certain that everything was bought abroad and that it's all a hundred percent, including all the fittings and the gadgets. Anyone can see that you're a man of discernment and also that you know how to make your mind up quickly. If only all my clients were like you—but I've already said that. And what's your line of business, if you don't mind my asking?

Yoel thought about it, as though selecting his words with tweezers. Then he replied:

"I work for the government."

And he went on with what he was doing: placing his fingers over and over again on the glove compartment in front of him, letting them rest for a moment on the dark-blue plastic surface, and removing them, now abruptly, now gently, now steathily. Then starting all over again. But the motion of the car prevented him from reaching any conclusion. And in fact he did not know what the question was. The crucified figure in the Byzantine icon, despite the beard, had had a girl's face.

"And your wife? Is she working?"

"She's dead."

"I'm sorry," the agent replied politely. And in his embarrassment he saw fit to add: "My wife also has problems. Splitting headaches, and the doctors can't get to the bottom of it. So what ages are the children?"

Once again Yoel seemed to be checking in his mind the accuracy of the facts and choosing a carefully planned reply:

6

"Just one daughter. Sixteen and a half."

The agent let out a chuckle and said in a tone of intimacy, eager to forge a bond of male camaraderie with the stranger:

"Not an easy age, eh? Boyfriends, crises, money for clothes, and so on?" And he went on to ask, if it wasn't rude of him, why in that case they needed four bedrooms. Yoel did not answer. The agent apologized; of course he knew it was none of his business, it was just, how should he say, idle curiosity. He himself had two boys, aged nineteen and twenty, barely a year and a half between them. Quite a problem. Both in the army, both in combat units. Just as well that screwed-up business in Lebanon's over, assuming it is, only a pity it ended in such a mess, and he says this although he personally is a long way from being a leftist or anything like that. And where do you stand on that business?

"We also have two old ladies." Yoel answered the previous question in his low, even voice. "The grandmothers will be living with us." As though that concluded the conversation, he closed his eyes. Which was where his tiredness had concentrated itself. In his mind for some reason he repeated words the agent had spoken. Boyfriends. Crises. The sea. And the whole city at your fingertips.

The agent said:

"Why don't we introduce your daughter to my boys? Maybe one of them would hit it off with her. I always come this way into town and not the way everyone goes. It's a bit of a detour, but we miss four or five god-awful traffic lights. By the way, I live in Ramat Lotan too. Not far from you. I mean, from the house you've chosen. I'll give you my home phone number, then you can give me a ring if you have any problems. Not that there will be. Just give me a ring anyway anytime you feel like it. It'll be a pleasure to show you around the neighborhood and explain where everything is. The main thing to remember is when you go into town during the rush hour, always go in this way. I had a regimental commander when I was in the army, in the artillery, Jimmy Gal, he had an ear missing; you must have heard of him;

he always used to say that between any two points there is only one straight line, and that that line is always full of imbeciles. Have you heard that one before?"

Yoel said:

"Thank you."

The agent muttered something more about the army then and the army now, then gave up and switched on the radio in the middle of an idiotic commercial on the pop station. All of a sudden, as though at last a whiff of sadness from the man sitting next to him had forced its way through to him, he reached out and switched the dial to the classical-music station.

They drove without speaking. Tel Aviv at 4:30 on a humid summer afternoon seemed angry and sweaty to Yoel. Jerusalem by comparison sketched itself in his mind in a wintry light, swathed in rain clouds, glimmering in a grayish twilight.

The program was baroque music. Yoel too gave up, and withdrew his fingers, resting his hands between his knees as though seeking warmth. He felt suddenly relieved, because at last, so it seemed to him, he had found what he was looking for: the predator had no eyes. The artist—an amateur after all—had forgotten to give it eyes. Or perhaps it had eyes but in the wrong place. Or of unequal size. He'd have to take another look. In any case, it was too soon to despair.

3

Ivria died on the sixteenth of February, on a day of driving rain in Jerusalem. At 8:30 in the morning, while she was sitting with her coffee cup at the desk facing the window, in her little cell, the electricity suddenly failed. Yoel had purchased this room for her some two years previously from the next-door neighbor and annexed it to their apartment in Talbiyeh. An opening had been cut in the back wall of the kitchen and a heavy brown door had been fitted in it. This door Ivria had been in the habit of locking when she was working, and also when she was sleeping. The old door that had formerly joined this cubbyhole to the neighbor's living room had been bricked up, plastered, and whitewashed twice, but its outline could still be made out on the wall behind Ivria's bed. She had chosen to furnish her new room with monastic austerity. She called it her study. Besides the narrow iron bedstead, it contained her wardrobe and the deep, heavy armchair that had belonged to her late father, who was born, lived, and died in the northern town of Metullah. Ivria too had been born and raised in Metullah.

Between the armchair and the bed she had a wrought-iron standard lamp. On the wall that separated her from the kitchen she had hung a map of Yorkshire. The floor was bare. There was also an office desk made of metal, two metal chairs, and some metal bookshelves. Above the desk she had hung some small black-and-white photographs of ruined Romanesque abbeys of the ninth or tenth century. On the desk stood a framed photograph of her father, Shealtiel Lublin, a thickset man with a walrus mustache, in the uniform of a British policeman. It was here that she had decided to dig herself in against the household chores and finally complete her thesis for an MA in English Literature. The topic she had selected was "The Shame in the Attic: Sex, Love, and Money in the Work of the Brontë Sisters." Every morning, when Netta had gone off to school, Ivria used to put a quiet jazz or ragtime record on the record player, put on her square frameless eyeglasses, which made her look like a stern family doctor of an earlier generation, switch on the desk lamp, and, with a coffee cup in front of her, burrow among her books and notes. Since her childhood she had been used to writing with a pen that had to be dipped in the inkwell every ten words or so. She was a slim, gentle woman, with paper-thin skin and clear eyes with long lashes. Her fair hair cascaded over her shoulders, though half of it had turned gray by then. She almost always wore a plain white blouse and white long pants. She wore no makeup and no jewelry apart from her wedding ring, which for some reason she wore on the little finger of her right hand. Her childlike fingers were always cold, summer and winter alike, and Yoel loved their cold touch on his naked back. He also loved enfolding them within his broad, ugly hands as though he were warming frozen chicks. Even from three rooms away and through three closed doors he sometimes imagined his ears could pick up the rustle of her papers. At times she would get up and stand for a while at her window, which overlooked only a neglected back garden and a high wall of Jerusalem stone. In the evenings she would sit at her desk with the door locked, crossing out and rewriting what she had written in the morning, scrabbling in various dictionaries to establish the meaning of an English word of a century or more ago. Most of the time Yoel was away from home. On the nights when he was not, they used to meet in the kitchen and drink tea with ice cubes in it in the summer or a mug of cocoa in the winter before separating to sleep in their respective bedrooms. She had a tacit agreement with him and with Netta: there was no entry to her room unless it was strictly necessary. Here, beyond the kitchen, in the eastern extension of their home, was her territory. Always defended by its heavy brown door.

The bedroom with its wide double bed, with the chest of drawers and the two identical mirrors, was inherited by Netta, who adorned the walls with photographs of her favorite Hebrew poets: Alterman, Lea Goldberg, Steinberg, and Amir Gilboa. On the tables on either side of what had been her parents' bed she placed vases containing dried thistles she had gathered at the end of the summer in the empty field on the slope beside the leper hospital. On the shelf she had a collection of sheet music that she liked to read, even though she did not play an instrument.

As for Yoel, he settled into his daughter's nursery, its little window overlooking the German Colony and the Hill of Evil Counsel. He hardly took the trouble to change anything in the room. In any case, most days he was away traveling. A dozen dolls of different sizes kept watch over his sleep when he was home for the night. And a large colored poster of a sleeping kitten snuggling up to an Alsatian dog, which wore the reliable expression of a middle-aged banker. The only change was that Yoel removed eight tiles from a corner of the floor in the girl's room and installed his safe there, embedded in concrete. In this safe he kept two handguns, a collection of detailed plans of capital cities and provincial towns, six passports and five driving licenses, a yellowing English booklet entitled *Bangkok by Night*, a small case containing an assortment of simple medicines, a couple of wigs, several toilet kits for his journeys, a few hats, a folding umbrella and a raincoat, two fake mustaches, stationery from various hotels and institutions, a pocket calculator, a tiny alarm clock, plane and train timetables, and notebooks containing telephone numbers with their last three digits reversed.

Ever since the changes, it was the kitchen that served all three as their meeting place. This was where they held their summit conferences. Especially on weekends. The living room, which Ivria had furnished in quiet colors, in the style of early 1960s Jerusalem, served mainly as their television room. When Yoel was at home, sometimes the three of them would converge on the living room at nine o'clock in the evening to watch the news and occasionally also a British drama in the "Armchair Theatre" series.

Only when the grandmothers came to visit, always together, did the living room fulfill its intended role. Lemon tea was served in tall glasses on a tray with fruit, and they ate the cake that the grandmothers brought. Once every few weeks Ivria and Yoel made dinner for the two mothers-in-law. Yoel's contribution was the rich, finely shredded, highly seasoned mixed salad that had been his specialty long ago, when he was still a young man on the kibbutz. They would chat about the news and other matters. The grandmothers' favorite subjects of conversation were literature and art. Family affairs were never discussed.

Ivria's mother, Avigail, and Yoel's mother, Lisa, were both straight-backed, elegant women, with similar hairstyles reminiscent of a Japanese flower arrangement. Over the years they had grown more alike, at least at first glance. Lisa wore delicate earrings and a fine silver chain around her neck, and was made up with restraint. Avigail liked to tie a young-looking silk scarf around her neck, which enlivened her gray suits like a border of flowers beside a concrete path. On her breast she wore a little ivory brooch in the shape of an inverted flask. At a second glance one could see the first signs in Avigail of a tendency to rotundity and a Slavic ruddiness, whereas Lisa looked as though she might shrivel away. For six years they had lived together in Lisa's two-room apartment in Radak Street on the respectable slopes of Rehavia. Lisa was active in a branch of the Soldiers' Aid Association, whereas Avigail did voluntary work with the Committee for Retarded Children.

Other visitors arrived infrequently. Netta, because of her condition, had no close girlfriends. When she was not at school, she went to the city library. Or lay in her bedroom reading. She would lie and read for half the night. Occasionally she went out with her mother to the cinema or the theater. The two grandmothers took her to concerts at the National Auditorium or the YMCA. Sometimes she went out on her own to gather thistles in the field by the leper hospital. Sometimes she went to musical soirees or literary discussions. Ivria hardly ever left the house. Her delayed thesis occupied most of her time. Yoel arranged for a cleaner to come in once a week, which was sufficient to ensure that the apartment was always clean and tidy. Twice a week Ivria took the car and went on a comprehensive shopping expedition. They did not purchase many clothes. Yoel was not in the habit of bringing booty back with him from his travels. But he never forgot a birthday, or their wedding anniversary on the first of March. He had a discerning eye, and always managed to select, in Paris, New York, or Stockholm, sweaters of excellent quality at a reasonable price, a blouse in exquisite taste for his daughter, white pants for his wife, a scarf or a belt or a kerchief for his mother-in-law and his mother.

Sometimes after lunch an acquaintance of Ivria's would drop in for a cup of coffee and a quiet chat. Sometimes their neighbor, Itamar Vitkin, came in "looking for signs of life" or "to take a look at my old storeroom." He would stay to talk to Ivria about what life had been like in the days of the British Mandate. Not a voice had been raised in the apartment for several years. Father, mother, and daughter were always attentively careful not to disturb one another. Whenever they talked, they did so politely. They all knew their boundaries. When they met together on weekends in the kitchen, they talked of remote matters of common interest, such as theories about the existence of intelligent life in space, or whether there was some way of safeguarding the ecological balance without forfeiting the benefits of technology. On subjects such as these they conversed with animation, although without ever interrupting one another. Sometimes there was a brief conference about some practical matter, such as buying new shoes for the winter, getting the dishwasher repaired, the relative cost of different forms of heating, or whether to replace the medicine cabinet in the bathroom with a newer type. They rarely talked about music, because of their discrepant tastes. Politics, Netta's condition, Ivria's thesis, and Yoel's work were never mentioned.

Although Yoel was absent a good deal, he was careful so far

as possible always to give notice of his return. Beyond the single word "abroad" he never gave any particulars. Except for weekends, they ate separately, at the time that suited each of them best. Their neighbors in the small block of apartments in Talbiyeh understood, thanks to some rumor or other, that Yoel dealt with overseas investors, which explained the suitcase, and the winter coat that could be seen draped over his arm in summer, and the comings and goings by taxi to the airport in the early hours. His mother-in-law and his mother believed, or affected to believe, that Yoel traveled on behalf of the government to procure military equipment. They rarely asked questions like Where did you catch that cold? or, Where did you get that tan? because they knew well that the only answer they would get would be something offhand, such as "In Europe" or "In the sun."

Ivria knew. Details did not interest her.

What Netta understood or guessed was impossible to tell.

There were three stereo systems in the apartment, one in Ivria's study, one in Yoel's nursery, and the third at the head of Netta's double bed. Hence the doors in the apartment were almost always closed, and the different types of music, out of constant consideration, were played at low volume. So as not to disturb.

Only in the living room was there sometimes a strange mixture of sounds. But there was no one in the living room. For several years it had been tidy, clean, and empty. Except when the grandmothers came to visit, when they all assembled there from their various rooms.

14

4

This is how the disaster happened. The autumn came and went, and then it was winter. A half-frozen bird appeared on the kitchen balcony. Netta took it to her bedroom and tried to warm it. She boiled maize and fed it the water from a dropper. Toward evening the bird recovered its strength and began to flutter around the room emitting desperate chirps. Netta opened the window and the bird flew away. Next morning there were more birds on the branches of the bare trees. Perhaps the bird was among them. How could one tell? When the electricity went off at 8:30 in the morning on that day of driving rain, Netta was at school and Yoel in another country. It would appear that Ivria found she did not have enough light. Jerusalem was darkened by low clouds and mist. She went outside and down the steps to the car, which was parked in the open basement of the building. Apparently she was intending to fetch from the trunk of the car the powerful flashlight that Yoel had bought in Rome. On her way down she noticed her nightdress on the garden wall, snatched by the wind from the clotheshorse on the balcony. She went across to pick it up. That was how she came upon the high-tension wire. No doubt she mistook it for a clothesline. Or perhaps she correctly identified it as an electric wire but reasonably assumed that since there was a power cut it would be dead. She reached out to lift it up so that she could cross underneath it. Or perhaps she tripped and stumbled against it. How can one know? But the power cut was not a real power cut; it was only their building that was affected. The cable was live. Because of the humidity it is almost certain that she was electrocuted on the spot and felt no pain. There was another victim too; Itamar Vitkin, the next-door neighbor, the one from whom Yoel had purchased the room a couple of years before. He was a man in his sixties, who owned a refrigerated truck and had lived alone for several years. His children had grown and moved away and his wife had left him and Jerusalem (which is why he had had no further use for the room and sold it to Yoel). It is conceivable that Itamar Vitkin saw the disaster from his window and hurried downstairs to help. They were found lying in a puddle almost in each other's arms. The man was still alive. At first they tried to apply artificial respiration and even smacked his face hard. He expired in the ambulance on the way to the Hadassah hospital. Among the neighbors an alternative version circulated; Yoel took no notice of it.

The neighbors considered Vitkin rather strange. He would sometimes climb into the cab of his truck at twilight, stick his head and half his clumsy body out the window, and play the guitar for a quarter of an hour to passersby. They were not numerous, since it was a side street. People would stop to listen, and after a couple of minutes they would shrug their shoulders and go on their way. He always worked at night, delivering dairy products to the shops, and came home at seven o'clock in the morning. Summer and winter alike. Through the party wall his voice could be heard sometimes, lecturing the guitar as he played it. His voice was gentle, as though he were wooing a reluctant woman. He was a fat, flabby man, who walked around most of the time in an undershirt and khaki trousers that were too loose for him. He looked like someone who lived in constant fear of having just accidentally done or said something unspeakable. After his meals he used to stand on his balcony and throw crumbs to the birds. He used to coax them softly too. Sometimes, on summer evenings, he would sit in his gray undershirt on a wicker chair on his balcony playing heartrending Russian tunes that were perhaps originally intended for the balalaika rather than the guitar.

Despite all these eccentricities he was considered a good neighbor. He never stood for election to the Residents' Committee, yet he volunteered to be a sort of regular duty officer for the entrance hall and stairs. He even bought a pair of potted geraniums out of his own pocket and stood them on either side of the front entrance. If ever anyone spoke to him, asked him the time, a sweet expression would spread over his face, like a child surprised by a wonderful present. All of which merely aroused a faint impatience in Yoel.

When he died, his three grown-up sons arrived with their wives and lawyers. All those years they had never taken the trouble to visit him. Now they had apparently come to divide the contents of his apartment and to get it ready to be sold. On their return from the funeral an altercation broke out. Two of the wives raised their voices, so loudly that the neighbors could hear. Then two or three lawyers arrived, on their own or with a professional assessor. Four months after the calamity, when Yoel had already begun to prepare to leave Jerusalem, the neighbor's apartment was still locked and shuttered and empty. One night Netta imagined she heard sounds of soft music through the wall—not a guitar but, so she said, perhaps a cello. In the morning she told Yoel, who chose to pass over it in silence. As he often did with things his daughter told him.

In the entrance hall of the building, above the mailboxes, the notice of condolence from the Residents' Committee faded to yellow. Several times Yoel meant to take it down, but he never did. There was a spelling mistake in it. It said that the residents were shocked and shared the sorrow of the respective families on the tragic and premature oss of our dear neighbors Mrs. Ivria Raviv and Mr. Eviatar Vitkin. Raviv was the surname that Yoel used in everyday life. When he rented the new house in Ramat Lotan he chose to call himself Ravid, although there was no logical reason for it. Netta was always Netta Raviv, apart from one year when the three of them had lived in London in connection with Yoel's work under a different name altogether. His mother's name was Lisa Rabinovich. Ivria, for the fifteen years that she had studied, intermittently, at the university, had always used her maiden name, Lublin. The day before the disaster Yoel had checked in at the Hotel Europa in Helsinki with the name Lionel Hart. However, the middle-aged guitar-loving neighbor whose death in the yard in the rain in the arms of Mrs. Raviv had given rise to various rumors was named Itamar Vitkin. Not Eviatar Vitkin, as the printed notice had it. But Netta said she actually preferred the name Eviatar, and anyway, what difference did it make?

5

He was disappointed and tired when he returned by taxi to the Hotel Europa at 10:30 P.M. on the sixteenth of February. His intention was to linger for a few minutes in the bar, drink a gin-and-tonic, and analyze the meeting before going up to his room. The Tunisian engineer on whose account he had come to Helsinki and whom he had met earlier in the evening in the restaurant at the railroad station had struck him as small fry: he was asking disproportionate favors and offering trivial goods in exchange. The material he had handed over at the end of their meeting, as a sample, had been almost banal. Even though in the course of their conversation the man had striven to convey the impression that at the next meeting, if there were one, he would bring along a regular Aladdin's cave. And actually along lines that Yoel had been hankering after for ages.

But the favors the man was asking in return were not financial. With judicious use of the word "bonus," Yoel had put out feelers for signs of greed, but in vain. In this matter, and this alone, the Tunisian had not been evasive: he had no need of money. It was a question of certain nonfinancial favors. Which Yoel, in his heart of hearts, was not certain they could grant. Certainly not without authorization at a higher level. Even if it transpired that the man was in possession of first-rate goods, which Yoel was inclined to doubt. He had therefore taken his leave of the Tunisian engineer for the time being with a promise that he would get in touch again the next day to arrange for further contact.

This evening he intended to turn in early. His eyes were tired:

19

they almost hurt him. The cripple he had seen in the street in a wheelchair intruded several times on his thoughts: he seemed familiar. Not so much familiar as not entirely unfamiliar. Involved, somehow, in something he ought to remember.

But that was what he could not do.

The desk clerk caught up with him at the entrance to the bar. Excuse me, sir, somebody called Mrs. Schiller has been trying to get hold of you several times in the past few hours. She left an urgent message for Mr. Hart that the moment he returned to the hotel he should get in touch with his brother.

Yoel thanked him. He gave up the idea of the bar. Still wearing his winter coat he turned and walked out into the snowbound street, where there were few pedestrians and not many cars at this time of night. He headed down the street, glancing over his shoulder and seeing only puddles of yellow light in the snow. He decided to turn right and then changed his mind and turned left, shuffling in the soft snow for two blocks until he found what he was looking for: a public telephone. Again he looked around. There was not a living soul. The snow turned blue or pink like a skin disease wherever the light struck it. He called collect to the office in Israel. His brother, for the purpose of emergency contact, was the man they all called Le Patron. In Israel it was nearly midnight. One of Le Patron's assistants instructed him to return at once. He added nothing and Yoel did not ask anything. At 1:00 A.M. he flew from Helsinki to Vienna. There he waited for seven hours for a flight to Israel. In the morning the man from the Vienna Station came and drank a coffee with him in the departure lounge. He could not tell Yoel what had happened, or else he could but had been ordered to say nothing. They spoke a little about business. Then they talked about the economy.

That evening, at Ben-Gurion airport, Le Patron was waiting for him in person. Without preamble he told him that Ivria had been accidentally electrocuted the previous day. To Yoel's two questions he replied precisely and without embellishment. He took Yoel's small suitcase out of his hand, led him through a side entrance to the car, and announced that he would drive Yoel to

Jerusalem personally. Apart from a few words about the Tunisian engineer they drove the whole way in silence. The rain had not stopped since the previous day; it had merely changed into a fine, penetrating drizzle. In the headlights of the oncoming cars the rain seemed to be not falling but rising from the ground. An overturned truck, lying with its wheels still spinning by the roadside at the beginning of the winding ascent to Jerusalem, reminded him again of the cripple in Helsinki, and he still felt the nagging worry that there was some discrepancy, some implausibility, some irregularity. What it was, he could not tell. As they were driving up Mount Castel he took a small battery-powered shaver out of his briefcase and shaved by heart in the dark. As he always did. He did not want to appear at home unshaven.

At ten o'clock the next morning the two funeral corteges set out. Ivria was buried at Sanhedriya, while the neighbor was taken to a different cemetery. Ivria's older brother, a stocky farmer from Metullah named Nakdimon Lublin, mumbled the memorial prayer, stumbling over the unfamiliar Aramaic words. Then he and his four sons took turns supporting Avigail, who was feeling faint.

As they left the cemetery Yoel walked next to his mother. They walked very close together but they did not touch, except once, as they went through the gateway and they were pressed together and two black umbrellas tangled in the wind. Suddenly he recalled that he had left *Mrs. Dalloway* in his hotel room in Helsinki and the woolen scarf that his wife had bought him in the departure lounge at Vienna. And he reconciled himself to their loss. But how had he never noticed how much his mother-in-law and his mother were growing to resemble each other since they had been living together? Would he start looking like his daughter from now on? His eyes burned. He remembered that he had promised the Tunisian engineer to call him today and he had not kept his promise, nor would he be able to. He still could not see the connection between this promise and the cripple, although he sensed there was one. It troubled him.

21

6

Netta did not go to the funeral. Nor did Le Patron. Not because
he was busy somewhere else but because, as usual, he had changed
his mind at the last minute and decided to stay behind in the
apartment and wait with Netta for them to come back from the
cemetery. When the family returned with a few acquaintances
and neighbors who had joined them, they found the man and
Netta sitting facing each other in the living room, playing checkers. Nakdimon Lublin and the rest of them did not approve, but
they took Netta's condition into account and chose to be indul-
gent. Or at least to say nothing. Yoel could not have cared less.
While they were away, the man had taught Netta to make strong
black coffee laced with brandy, which she served to all of them.
He stayed till early evening. Then he got up and left. The acquaintances and relations dispersed. Nakdimon Lublin and his
sons went to stay somewhere else in Jerusalem, promising to return in the morning. Yoel was left alone with the women. When
it grew dark outside Avigail began to sob in the kitchen, a loud,
broken noise that sounded like an attack of hiccoughs. Lisa calmed
her with valerian drops, an old-fashioned remedy that nevertheless brought her some relief after a while. The two old women
sat in the kitchen, with Lisa's arm around Avigail's shoulders and
the two of them wrapped in a gray woolen shawl that Lisa must
have found in a closet. Every now and again it slipped off, and
Lisa bent down to pick it up, then raised it like a bat spreading
its wings to wrap them in it again. After the valerian drops Avigail's crying became quieter and more even. Like a child crying

in its sleep. But outside there suddenly rose the wailing of cats in heat, a strange, evil, piercing sound at times like barking. He and his daughter sat in the living room on either side of the low table that Ivria had bought in Jaffa ten years before. On the table was the game board, surrounded by checkers and a few empty coffee cups. Netta asked if she should make him an omelette and a salad; Yoel said "I'm not hungry" and she replied "Neither am I." At 8:30 the phone rang, but when he lifted the receiver he heard nothing. Out of professional habit he asked himself who would be interested in simply knowing if he was at home. But he could make no guess. Then Netta got up and closed the shutters and the windows and drew the curtains. At nine o'clock she said, "If you want to watch the news, suit yourself." Yoel said, "Fine." But they remained sitting; neither of them approached the television. And again by dint of professional habit he remembered the phone number in Helsinki and it occurred to him to call the Tunisian engineer now, from here. He decided not to because he did not know what to say to him. Soon after ten he got up and made them all open sandwiches with some cheese and sausage he found in the refrigerator; the sausage was the spicy kind coated with black pepper that was Ivria's favorite. Then the kettle boiled and he made four glasses of lemon tea. His mother said: "Leave all that to me." He said: "Never mind. It's all right." They drank the tea but nobody touched the sandwiches. It was nearly one o'clock in the morning before Lisa managed to persuade Avigail to take a couple of Valium tablets and put her to bed fully dressed in the double bed in Netta's room. She lay down next to her without switching off the bedside lamp. At 2:15 Yoel peeped in and found them both asleep. Avigail woke up three times and cried, then stopped, and all was quiet again. At three Netta suggested a game of checkers to help pass the time. Yoel agreed, but tiredness suddenly overcame him, his eyes were burning, and he went off to have a doze in his nursery. Netta went with him as far as his bedroom door, and there, as he stood and unbuttoned his shirt, he told her that he had decided to exercise his right to take early retirement. He would write a letter of resignation that same week, and would not wait for them to appoint his successor. At the end of the school year they'd leave Jerusalem.

Netta said: "Suit yourself." And left it at that.

Without closing the door he lay down on the bed, with his hands under his head and his burning eyes on the ceiling. Ivria Lublin had been his only love, but that had been a long time ago. Sharply, in every detail, he recalled a time they had made love many years before. After a violent argument. From the first caress to the final shudder they had both been weeping, and afterward they had lain huddled for several hours, less like a man and a woman than like two people freezing in the snow at night. And he had stayed inside her body even when there was no more desire left and almost for the whole of that night. Now with the recollection there stirred in him a desire for her body. He placed his broad, ugly hand on his organ, as though to calm it, careful not to move either his hand or his organ. Because the door was open, he put out the light with his other hand. When he had put the light out he realized that the body he desired was encased in earth and would always remain so. Including the childlike knees, including the left breast that was slightly fuller and more attractive than the right one, including the brown birthmark that was sometimes visible and sometimes hidden in the pubic hair. And then he saw himself imprisoned in her cell in total darkness and saw her laid naked beneath the slabs of concrete beneath the little mound of earth in the rain that fell in the dark and he remembered her claustrophobia and reminded himself that the dead are not buried naked and reached out again and switched on the light in alarm. His desire had vanished. He closed his eyes and lay motionless on his back and waited for the tears. But the tears would not come, nor would sleep, and his hand groped on the bedside table for his book. Which had been left behind in Helsinki.

Through his open door, to the accompaniment of the wind and the rain, he saw far away his daughter, plain, spare, stooped, picking up the empty coffee cups and glasses and putting them on a tray. She took them all out to the kitchen and washed them unhurriedly. The dish of cheese and sausage sandwiches she covered with plastic wrap and carefully put away in the refrigerator. She turned most of the lights out and made sure the apartment was locked. Then she knocked twice on the door of her mother's study before opening and entering. On the desk lay Ivria's dippen and the inkwell, which had been left open. Netta closed the inkwell and put the top on the pen. She picked up from the desk the square frameless glasses that suggested a stern family doctor of an earlier generation. She picked them up from the desk as though intending to try them on. But she restrained herself, polished them lightly with the bottom of her blouse, folded them, and put them away in their case, which she found under the papers. She picked up the coffee cup that Ivria had left on the desk when she went out to fetch the flashlight, turned the light out, left the study, and closed the door behind her. Having washed this last cup she returned to the living room and sat alone in front of the checkerboard. On the other side of the wall Avigail was crying again and Lisa comforted her in a whisper. So deep was the silence that even through the closed and shuttered windows there could be heard the sound of cocks crowing in the distance and dogs barking; then the long-drawn-out sound of a muezzin's call to morning prayer insinuated itself indistinctly. And now what? Yoel asked himself. How ridiculous, how irritating, how unnecessary to have shaved in Le Patron's car on the way home from the airport. The cripple in the wheelchair in Helsinki had been young, very pale, and Yoel seemed to remember that he had had delicate, feminine features. He had no arms or legs. From birth? An accident? It rained in Jerusalem all through the night. The electricity had been restored less than an hour after the disaster.

7

In the late afternoon of a summer day, Yoel was standing barefoot in a corner of the lawn, trimming the hedge. In the little street in Ramat Lotan there were agricultural smells, mown lawns, manured flower beds, and a light soil that soaked up the water from the sprinklers. There were many sprinklers revolving in the little front and back gardens. It was quarter past five. Occasionally a neighbor would come home from work, park his car, get out unhurriedly, stretch his arms, and loosen his tie even before reaching his paved garden path.

Through the garden doors of the houses opposite could be heard the voice of the man reading the news on television. Here and there neighbors were sitting on the lawn staring indoors at the television in their living room. With a small effort Yoel could catch the man's words. But his thoughts were distracted. At times he would stop clipping and watch three little girls playing on the street with an Alsatian they called Ironside, perhaps after the detective in a wheelchair in a television series a few years back, which Yoel had happened to watch by himself in hotel rooms in various cities. Once he had watched an episode dubbed into Portuguese, and had still managed to follow the plot. Which was a simple one.

All around, birds were singing in the treetops, hopping along the walls, flitting from one garden to the next as though they were intoxicated with joy. Even though Yoel knew that birds do not flit for joy but for other reasons. Far away like the sighing of the sea sounded the din of heavy traffic on the highway that ran below Ramat Lotan. In a hammock behind him lay his mother, wearing a housecoat, reading the evening paper. Once, years before, she had told him how when he was three years old she had trundled him, in a squeaking carriage, completely buried and hidden under packages and bundles hastily thrown together, for hundreds of miles from Bucharest to the port of Varna. Most of the way she had fled along remote side roads. Nothing remained in his memory, but he had a faded image of a dark dormitory in the bowels of a ship, packed with tier upon tier of iron beds crammed with men and women groaning, spitting, perhaps vomiting over each other, or over him. And a vague picture of a fight, scratching and biting till the blood ran, between his shrieking mother and a bald, unshaven man on that same terrible voyage. His father he could not remember at all, even though he knew what he looked like from the two sepia pictures in his mother's old photograph album and he knew, or had inferred, that his father was not a Jew, but a Christian Romanian who had walked out of his life and his mother's even before the Germans arrived. But in his thoughts the father took on the appearance of the bald, unkempt man in the ship who had hit his mother.

On the other side of the hedge, which he was trimming slowly and precisely, his neighbors, the American brother and sister who occupied the other half of the double house, were sitting on white garden chairs drinking iced coffee. Several times during the weeks since their arrival the Vermonts had invited him to drop in with the ladies one afternoon for iced coffee or else to watch a comedy on their VCR one evening after the nine o'clock news. Yoel had said: "We'd like that." Meanwhile he had not done so. Vermont was a fresh-looking, pink, heavy man, with the rough manner of a farmer. He looked like a healthy, wealthy Dutchman in an advertisement for expensive cigars. He was jovial and loud. Loud perhaps because he was hard of hearing. His sister was at least ten years younger than he, Annemarie or Rosemarie; Yoel could not remember which. A petite, attractive woman, with childlike laughing blue eyes and pointed breasts. "Hi," she said cheerily when she noticed Yoel eyeing her body over the hedge. Her brother repeated the same syllable, a split-second later and a touch less cheerily. Yoel wished them good afternoon. The woman came over to the hedge, her nipples visible under a light cotton blouse. When she got close to him, delightedly intercepting the look that was fixed on her, she added in English, speaking quickly in a low voice: "Tough life, huh?" Louder, in Hebrew, she asked if she could borrow his shears later so that she could trim the ligustrum hedge on their side too. Yoel said: "Why not?" And after a slight hesitation he offered to do it himself. "Careful." She laughed. "I might say yes."

The late-afternoon light was gentle, honeyed, casting a strange golden glow on a few semitransparent clouds that were passing overhead on their way from the sea to the mountains. For a slight breeze had blown up from the sea, bringing a salty tang and a faint shade of melancholy. Which Yoel did not reject. The breeze rustled in the foliage of the ornamental and fruit trees, caressed the well-kept lawns, and splashed his bare chest with tiny droplets from a sprinkler in another garden.

Instead of finishing his side of the hedge and going next door, as he had promised, to trim the other side, Yoel put the shears down on the edge of the lawn and went for a little stroll, as far as the point where the street was blocked by a fenced citrus grove. He stood there for a few minutes, staring at the dense foliage, vainly straining to decipher a silent movement that he imagined he could discern in the depths of the grove. Until his eyes ached again. Then he turned around and walked home. It was a tender evening. From a window of one of the other houses he heard a woman saying, "So what; tomorrow is another day." Yoel checked this sentence in his mind and found no error in it. At the entrances to the gardens were stylish, occasionally even ostentatious, mailboxes. Some of the parked cars still gave off residual heat from the engine and a faint smell of burned gasoline. Even the street, made of precast squares of concrete, radiated a warmth, which was pleasing under his bare feet. Each square bore a stamp in the form of two arrows flanking the inscription SCHARFSTEIN LTD RAMAT GAN.

Some time after six o'clock Avigail and Netta returned in the car from the hairdresser's. Avigail, despite her mourning, struck him as healthy and applelike: her round face and sturdy body suggested a prosperous Slavic peasant woman. She was so unlike Ivria that for a moment he had difficulty remembering what his connection was with this woman. His daughter had had her hair cut boyishly short, bristly like a hedgehog, as though to defy him. She did not ask what he thought, and Yoel decided not to say a word this time either. When they were both indoors, Yoel went over to the car, which Avigail had parked sloppily, started it, reversed out of the drive, turned around at the bottom of the street, and backed into the drive so that the car now stood precisely in the center of the carport, facing the street, ready to go. He stood for a few minutes at the gate of his house as though waiting to see who else would turn up. Softly he whistled an old tune. He could not remember precisely where it came from but he vaguely remembered that it was from a well-known musical, and he turned to go indoors to ask but recalled that Ivria was not here and that was why they were here. Because for a moment it had not been clear to him what he was actually doing in this strange place.

By now it was seven o'clock. Time for a brandy. Tomorrow, he reminded himself, was another day. Enough.

He went inside and had a leisurely shower. Meanwhile his mother-in-law and his mother prepared the supper. Netta was reading in her room and did not join them. Through her closed door she answered that she would eat something later.

By half past seven the dusk was beginning to spread. Shortly before eight he went outside to lie on the glider, clutching a transistor radio and a book and the new reading glasses that he had been using for a few weeks now. He had chosen a pair of ridiculous round black-framed glasses that made him look like an elderly French priest. In the sky strange reflections were still flickering, the last remnant of the day that was ending, while a cruel red moon suddenly rose beyond the citrus grove. Opposite, behind the cypress trees and tiled roofs, the sky reflected the glare of the lights of Tel Aviv and for a moment Yoel felt that he must get up and go there now, right away, to bring his daughter back. But she was in her room. The light of her bedside lamp shining through her window into the garden cast a shape onto the lawn, which Yoel, contemplating it for several minutes, attempted in vain to define. Perhaps because it was not a geometric shape.

The mosquitoes were beginning to bother him. He went indoors, remembering to take with him the transistor, the book, the round black-framed glasses, aware that he had forgotten something but unable to recall what it was.

In the living room, still barefoot, he poured himself a brandy and sat down with his mother and his mother-in-law to watch the nine o'clock news. It would be possible to sever the predator from its metal base with a single moderate jerk, and so, if not to decipher, at least to silence it, but afterward, he knew, he would have to mend it. And that he could do only by drilling into the paw and putting a screw through it. Perhaps it would be better not to touch it.

He stood up and went out onto the terrace. Outside the crickets were already chirruping. The breeze had dropped. Choruses of frogs filled the grove down the street, a child was crying, a woman laughed, a mouth organ spread sadness, water roared in a bathroom. The houses had been built very close together and the gardens between them were small. Ivria had had a dream: when she completed her thesis and Netta finished school and Yoel was discharged from the service, they could sell the apartment in Talbiyeh and the grandmothers' apartment in Rehavia and buy themselves a house at the edge of a village in the Judaean Hills, not too far from Jerusalem. It had to be an end house; that was important. So that at least on one side the windows would look out only onto wooded hills with no sign of life. Now he had managed to realize at least some of the components of this plan. Even though the two apartments in Jerusalem had been rented, not sold. The income was sufficient to pay the rent of this house in Ramat Lotan, and there was even a little to spare. There was also his monthly pension and the old ladies' savings and their

National Security money. And there was Ivria's inheritance too, an extensive plot of land in the township of Metullah on which Nakdimon Lublin and his sons grew fruit, and had recently also built a small guesthouse. Every month they transferred a third of the proceeds to his account. It was among those fruit trees that he had first had Ivria, in 1960, when he was a soldier who had lost his way on an orienteering exercise during a section commander's training course and she was a farmer's daughter two years older than he who had gone out in the dark to turn off the irrigation taps. Both of them were startled, but, total strangers to each other, they had barely exchanged ten words in the darkness before their bodies suddenly clung, groping, rolling in the mud fully dressed, panting, burrowing into each other like a pair of blind puppies, hurting each other, finishing almost before they had begun and then fleeing almost without a word and going their separate ways. And it was also there among the fruit trees that he had had her for the second time, when, as though bewitched, he had returned to Metullah a few months later and lain in wait for her for two nights by the irrigation taps, until they met and fell on each other again and he asked for her hand and she said, Are you out of your mind. After that they used to meet at the cafeteria in the bus station at Kiryat Shmonah and make love in an abandoned tin shack he had discovered in a place where there had once been an immigrant transit camp. After six months or so she gave in and married him without reciprocating love but devotedly, honestly, determined to give her full share and to try hard to give more. They were both capable of compassion and gentleness. When they made love they no longer hurt each other but strove to be attentive and generous. Teaching and learning. Getting close. Not pretending. Yet there were times, even after ten years, when they made love again fully dressed in some field in Jerusalem, on the hard earth in places from which they could see only stars and shadows of trees. So whence this feeling that had been with him all evening that he had forgotten something?

After the news he tapped gently on Netta's door again. There was no answer, so he waited and tried again. Here too, as in

31

Jerusalem, it was Netta who had been given the master bedroom with its double bed. Here she had hung her pictures of poets and installed her musical scores and vases of thistles. It was he who had decided on this arrangement, because he had difficulty getting to sleep in a double bed, whereas it was good for Netta, with her condition, to sleep on a wide bed.

The two grandmothers had settled into the two children's bedrooms, which were joined by a communicating door. And he had taken for himself the room at the back of the house that had been Mr. Kramer's study. There was a Spartan sofa bed and a desk and a picture of the graduation parade of the Armored Corps School, class of '71, with tanks drawn up in a semicircle and colorful pennants on the ends of their antennas. There was also a photograph of the landlord in uniform, wearing the bars of a captain, shaking hands with the Chief of Staff, David Elazar. In the bookcase Yoel found some books in Hebrew and English on business management, commemorative picture books of the victories, a Bible with Cassuto's commentary, a set of the *World of Learning*, the memoirs of Ben-Gurion and Moshe Dayan, travel guides from several countries, and a whole shelf of thrillers in English. In the built-in wardrobe, he hung up his clothes and some of Ivria's, whatever he had not donated after her death to the leper hospital next to their apartment in Jerusalem. He put his safe in this room too, without bothering to fix it into the floor, because there was almost nothing left in it now: when he retired from the service he had been careful to return the guns and the rest of the stuff to the office. Including his own handgun. The lists of telephone numbers he had destroyed. Only the town plans and his real passport remained, for some reason, locked in the safe.

He knocked a third time and, receiving no answer, he opened the door and went in. His daughter, angular, gaunt, her hair cropped almost to the skull, with one of her legs dangling to the floor as though she meant to stand up, exposing her bony knee, was lying asleep with her open book concealing her face. He carefully removed the book. He managed to take off her glasses without waking her, folded them, and put them down on the bedside table. They had transparent plastic frames. Gently, very patiently, he raised the dangling leg and laid it straight on the bed. Then he covered the frail, angular body with a sheet. He lingered for a moment to inspect the pictures of poets on the wall. Amir Gilboa offered him the ghost of a smile. Yoel turned his back and put out the light and left the room. As he did so he heard her drowsy voice in the darkness. She said: "Turn the light out, for God's sake." And although there was no light left in the room to turn out, Yoel did not remonstrate, but soundlessly pulled the door to behind him. Only then did he remember what it was that had been bothering him vaguely all evening: when he had stopped clipping the hedge and gone out for his walk, he had left the garden shears outside on the edge of the lawn. It would not do them any good to be out all night in the dew. He put his sandals on and went out into the garden and saw a pale ring around the full moon, whose color now was not purply red but silvery white. He could hear the chorus of crickets and frogs from the direction of the citrus grove. And the bloodcurdling shriek that burst simultaneously from every television set on the street. Then he noted the swish of sprinklers and the hum of distant traffic on the main road and a door slamming in one of the other houses. Quietly he said to himself, in English, the words he had heard from his neighbor: "Tough life, huh?" Instead of going back indoors he put his hand in his pocket. Because he found the keys there he got into the car and drove off. When he returned at one o'clock in the morning the street was quiet and his house too was dark and silent. He got undressed and lay down, put on the stereophonic earphones, and until two or half past listened to a sequence of short baroque pieces and read a few pages of the unfinished thesis. The three Brontë sisters, he discovered, had had two older sisters, who both died in 1825. There was also a consumptive, alcoholic brother by the name of Patrick Branwell. He read until his eyes closed. In the morning it was his mother who went out to pick up the morning paper from the garden path and put the shears back in their place in the shed.

8

Because the days and nights were empty and vacant Yoel fell into the habit of watching television almost every evening until the programs ended at midnight. Generally his mother sat opposite him in an armchair, embroidering or knitting, with her narrow gray eyes and her tight sunken lips making her look hard and resentful. Wearing his shorts, he would sprawl on the living-room sofa with his bare feet up, resting his head on a mound of cushions. Sometimes Avigail would join them, though she was observing the period of mourning, to watch the news magazine, with her strong Slavic peasant's face radiating brisk, uncompromising good nature. The old ladies took care to set out cold and hot drinks and a dish brimming with grapes, pears, plums, and apples on the low table in the living room. It was the end of the summer. In the course of the evening Yoel would pour himself two or three glasses of imported brandy, a present from Le Patron. Sometimes Netta would emerge from her room and stand for a minute or two in the doorway of the living room before leaving. But if it was a nature program or a British drama she would occasionally decide to come in. And sit down, angular, gaunt, her head held high in a kind of unnatural extension, not in an armchair but always on one of the dark high-backed dining chairs. She would sit stiffly until the end of the broadcast, away from the others. At times it appeared as though her gaze were fixed on the ceiling rather than the screen. But this was just the peculiar tilt of her neck. She generally wore a plain dress with large buttons down the front. It emphasized her slight build, her flat chest, and her frail shoulders. Sometimes she seemed to Yoel to be as old as her two grandmothers, if not older. She spoke little: "They showed that one last year." "Could you turn it down, it's blaring." Or: "There's some ice cream in the freezer." When the plot thickened, Netta would say: "The cashier is the killer." Or: "He'll go back to her at the end." "That's stupid. How can she know that he already knows?" In the summer they watched a lot of films about terrorist gangs, espionage, secret-service exploits. Yoel generally fell asleep halfway through and woke up only for the news just before midnight, by which time the two old women had quietly gone off to their bedrooms. He had never taken an interest in such films; he had no time for them. He saw no point in reading spy stories or thrillers. When the whole office was talking about a new book by le Carré, say, and his colleagues made him promise to read it, then he would deign to give it a try. The complications struck him as ridiculously implausible, or, conversely, transparently simple. After a few dozen pages he would put the book down and not pick it up again. In a short story by Chekhov or a novel by Balzac he found mysteries which, so far as he was aware, did not exist in any spy thriller. Once, years before, he had toyed with the idea of writing a little spy story himself when he retired, describing things as he had known them during his own years in the service. But he had dropped the idea because he could not find anything remarkable or exciting in his own doings. Two birds on a fence on a rainy day, an old man talking to himself at the bus stop on the Gaza Road, these and similar events seemed to him more fascinating than anything that had happened to him in his work. In fact he saw himself as a kind of valuator and purchaser of abstract merchandise. He would go abroad to meet a stranger in a café in Paris, for example, or Montreal, or Glasgow, have a conversation or two, and then come to a conclusion. The important things were sensitivity to impressions, intuitive judgment, character assessment, and patient bargaining skills. It had never so much as occurred to him to jump over walls or leap from roof to roof. He saw himself as a long-established merchant with many years' experience in bargaining, arranging deals, building mutual confidence, outlining guarantees and securities, but over and above all, forming an accurate impression of the people he talked with. True, his own dealings were always conducted with a certain secrecy, but Yoel imagined that so it was in the business world, and that if there was a difference it was mainly one of setting and background.

He had never raided a safe house, tailed anyone through a maze of alleyways, wrestled with tough guys, or planted listening devices. Others did that. His business was to establish contact, to arrange and prepare meetings, to allay fears and lull suspicions, without dropping his own guard, to convey to his interlocutor a relaxed, good-humored intimacy, like an optimistic marriage counselor, and in the meantime to penetrate sharply and coolly under the stranger's skin: was he a fraud? an amateur fraud? Or an experienced, cunning deceiver? Or perhaps merely a petty crank? A German overwhelmed by historic guilt? A world-reforming idealist? A deranged person, sick with ambition? A trapped woman bent on a desperate act? An overenthusiastic diaspora Jew? A bored French intellectual hungry for excitement? Or simply bait cast at him by a hidden adversary chuckling somewhere in the dark? Or an Arab driven to the other side by lust for revenge against some private enemy? Or a frustrated inventor with no one to appreciate his genius? These were the crude headings. Behind them lay the really complex and delicate work of classification.

Always and without exception Yoel insisted on deciphering the person opposite him before he would take so much as a single step. The most important thing for him was to know who was talking to him and why. What was the weak point that his interlocutor was trying to conceal from him? What sort of satisfaction or recompense was he after? What sort of impression was the man or woman seeking to make on him? And why that impression in particular? What was the person ashamed of, and what, precisely, was he proud of? Over the years Yoel had formed the conviction that shame and pride were generally stronger than other famous urges that figured more prominently in literature. People were eager to fascinate or charm others so as to fill some void in themselves. A widespread void that Yoel termed love. He had never revealed this to anyone, except once to Ivria. Who had replied, unimpressed, "But that's a well-worn cliché." Yoel had agreed with her at once. Perhaps that was why he had dropped the idea of the book. The wisdom that he had accumulated during his years at work did indeed seem trite to him. People want such and such. They want what they do not have and what they will never be given. And what is attainable, they take for granted.

What about me? he had thought one night traveling in an almost empty train between Frankfurt and Munich; what is it I'm after? What is it that drives me from hotel to hotel across these expanses of darkness? It's duty, he had answered himself, in Hebrew and almost aloud. But why me? And if I suddenly drop dead in this empty train, will I know a little more, or will everything just go blank? It would seem that I have been here for forty-some years and I still haven't so much as begun to work out what's going on. If anything at all. Perhaps something is. At times you can almost sense here and there some hints of a pattern. The sad thing is that I'm not managing to figure it out and it looks as though I never will. Like last night in the hotel in Frankfurt, when the stylized petals printed apparently at random on the wallpaper opposite my bed almost hinted at some shape or form. But if you moved your head slightly or squinted or your attention wandered for a second the impression dissolved; it took an immense effort to make out some islands of set pattern, and you couldn't be entirely certain if it was the same pattern as was hinted at before. Perhaps there was something there, but you were not destined to decode it; or maybe it was only an illusion. Even that you will never know, because your eyes are burning, so that if you try with all your strength to look through the train window perhaps at the very most you can guess that we are traveling through a forest though what you can see is little more than the reflection of the familiar face that looks pale and tired and actually rather stupid too. Best close your eyes and try to snatch some sleep: whatever will be will be.

All the people he had ever confronted had lied to him. Except in the Bangkok case. Yoel found himself fascinated by the quality of lies: how does each person build his own lies? By a flight of fancy and imagination? Negligently, offhandedly? With a systematic, calculated logic or, on the contrary, casually and with a studied lack of system? The way a lie is woven he saw as an unguarded peephole that sometimes allows a glimpse inside the liar.

In the office he was known as the Walking Lie-Detector. Occasionally they tried lying to him deliberately about some trivial matter such as a pay slip or a new telephone operator. Again and again they were astonished to witness the working of the inner mechanism that made Yoel receive the lie in silence, sink his head on his chest mournfully, and eventually remark wistfully: "But Rami, that's not true." Or: "Drop it, Cockney, it's no use." They were trying to be funny but he could never see the funny side of a lie. Or of an innocent practical joke. Not even the usual April Fools' Day pranks in the office. Lies seemed to him like viruses of an incurable disease that even between the four walls of a secure laboratory must be treated with extreme care. Handled only with rubber gloves.

He himself lied only when he had no alternative. And only when lying seemed to him to be the last and only way out, or an escape from danger. In such cases he always chose the simplest, most uncomplicated lie, never more, so to speak, than two steps away from the facts.

Once, he had traveled on a Canadian passport to sort out some business in Budapest. On arrival the uniformed passport officer asked him what the purpose of his visit was, and he answered her in French, with a mischievous smile: "*Espionnage, madame.*" She burst out laughing and stamped his passport.

Occasionally he had to meet strangers with someone covering him. His guardian angels always kept their distance, remaining

38

invisible. Only on one single occasion, one wet night in Athens, was he compelled to draw a gun. Without, however, pressing the trigger. Just to frighten a fool who tried to pull a knife on him in the crowded bus terminal.

It was not that Yoel maintained principles of nonviolence. His confirmed opinion was that there was only one thing worse than the use of violence, and that was submission to violence. He had heard this notion once in his youth from Prime Minister Eshkol, and he had held it dear ever since. He had been careful all these years not to be drawn into violent situations, because he had reached a decision that an agent who uses a gun has failed in his job. Chases, shoot-outs, reckless driving, all forms of running and jumping, belonged in his view to gangsters and their like, but definitely not to his own work.

The essence of his work, as he saw it, was to obtain a necessary item of information at a reasonable price. Financial or otherwise. On this matter there were disagreements and at times even confrontations with his superiors, whenever one or another of them tried to wriggle out of paying the price that Yoel had committed himself to. In such cases he would go so far as threatening to resign. This stubbornness earned him a reputation in the office as an eccentric: "Are you out of your mind? We're never going to need that little shit, and he can't hurt anyone now except himself, so why should we throw away good money on him?" "Because I gave him my word," Yoel would reply, grimly, "and I had authorization to do so."

According to a calculation he had once made in his head, he had spent approximately ninety-five percent of all the hours of his professional life, the hours that made up twenty-three years in all, in airports, on board aircraft, in trains and stations, in taxis, in waiting rooms, in hotel rooms, in hotel lobbies, in casinos, on street corners, in restaurants, in darkened cinemas, in cafés, in gambling clubs, in public libraries, in post offices. Apart from Hebrew, he could speak French and English and a little Romanian and Yiddish. When pressed, he could also get by in German and Arabic. He almost always wore a conventional gray suit. He had got into the habit of traveling the world with a light suitcase and a bag that never contained so much as a tube of toothpaste, a shoelace, or a scrap of paper made in Israel. He had got into the habit of killing whole days alone with his own thoughts. He had learned to maintain his body with the help of some easy morning exercises, careful eating habits, and regular doses of minerals and vitamins. He destroyed receipts, but kept a mental record of every penny of the office's money that he spent. Very occasionally, not more than twenty times in all his years of service, it had happened that desire for a woman's body got the better of him to the point of endangering his powers of concentration, and he had made a cool-headed decision to take a strange or almost strange woman into his bed. Like making an emergency visit to the dentist. But he had refrained from any emotional involvement. Even when circumstances dictated that he should spend a few days traveling with a young operational partner from the office, and the two of them had to check in as man and wife. Ivria Lublin had been his only love. Even when love had gone and given way, in the course of the years, successively or by turns, to mutual pity, friendship, pain, bursts of sensual flowering, bitterness and jealousy and rage, and again Indian summers flickering with sparks of sexual abandon, then vindictiveness and hatred and compassion again, a tissue of interwoven, alternating, ever-changing emotions, swallowed up in strange compounds and unexpected combinations, like cocktails mixed by a lunatic barman. Whatever the mix, there was never a single drop of indifference in the brew. On the contrary: with the passing years Ivria and he had become ever more dependent on each other. Even in their fights. Even in days of loathing and humiliation and fury. A few years earlier, during a night flight to Cape Town, Yoel had read a popular article in *Newsweek* about genetic telepathic links between identical twins. One twin telephones the other at three o'clock in the morning, knowing that neither of them can get to sleep. One twin winces with pain when the other gets a burn, even in another country.

It was almost the same between himself and Ivria. And that

was also how he interpreted the words of the Book of Genesis, "And the man knew his woman." The bond between them was knowledge. Except when Netta had come between them with her condition, with her oddness, or perhaps—Yoel fought off the suspicion with all his might—with her schemes. Even the decision to sleep apart in separate rooms when he was at home had been a joint one. Taken out of understanding and consideration. Out of mutual concession. Out of secret pity. Occasionally they had met at three or four o'clock in the morning at Netta's bedside, having come out of their respective rooms at almost the same moment to check how the girl was sleeping. In a whisper, and always in English, they had asked each other: Your place or mine?

Once, in Bangkok, he had had the job of meeting a Filipino woman, a graduate of American University in Beirut. She was the ex-wife of a notorious terrorist who had been responsible for many killings. She had made the first contact with the office, on her own initiative, by a unique ruse. Yoel, who had been sent to meet her, had pondered before the meeting the details of this ruse, which had been mischievous and daring but carefully thought out and not in the least impulsive. He prepared himself to encounter an intelligent person. He always preferred to do business with rational, well-prepared partners, although he knew that most of his colleagues preferred the other party to be startled and confused.

They had met by prearranged signs in a famous Buddhist temple thronged with tourists. They sat side by side on a carved stone bench, with carved stone monsters looking down on them. She placed her graceful straw basket like a barrier on the seat between them. And began with a question about his children, if he had any, and his relationship with them. Yoel, caught off guard, thought for a moment, and decided to give her a truthful reply. Although he did not go into details. She also asked him where he was born, and he hesitated for a second before replying: in Romania. Thereupon, without further preliminaries, she began to talk to him about the things he really wanted to hear. She spoke

41

clearly, as though painting pictures with words, describing places and people, employing language like a fine pencil. Yet she avoided passing judgment, refraining from condemnation or praise, at most remarking that so-and-so was particularly touchy where his pride was involved, that so-and-so was quick to lose his temper but also quick to make up his mind. Then she made him a present of some good photographs, for which Yoel would gladly have paid her generously had she requested payment.

This young woman, young enough to be his daughter, had left Yoel in a state of deep perplexity. She had almost disoriented him. For the first and only time in his whole professional career. His fine instincts, those sensitive feelers that had always served him so faultlessly, had gone suddenly dead. Like a delicate piece of equipment that encounters a magnetic field, and all its needles go wild.

It was not a case of erotic confusion; even though the young woman was pretty and attractive, his desire was hardly stirred. It happened because to the best of his judgment she had not uttered a single falsehood. Not even one of those petty lies that are needed to avoid uneasiness in a conversation between strangers. Not even when Yoel cunningly inserted a question that invited a lie: "Were you ever unfaithful to your husband in the two years you were married to him?" Yoel knew the answer from the file he had studied at home, and he also knew for certain that the woman had no grounds for imagining that he was aware of what had happened to her in Cyprus. Nevertheless she told him the truth. Although when he went on to put a similar question she replied: "That's irrelevant to the matter in hand." She was quite right.

At the moment when he had to acknowledge that the woman had successfully passed the test to which he had subjected her, for some reason he felt—and it hurt him to admit it—that he himself had been tested. And failed. For forty minutes he tried in vain to catch her in some distortion, exaggeration, or embellishment. When he had finished putting to her all the questions that occurred to him, she went on to volunteer several more pieces of information, as though replying to questions he had forgotten to

42

ask. Moreover, she adamantly refused any reward, financial or other, for the information she had been so lavish with. When he expressed surprise, she declined to explain her motives. So far as Yoel could judge, she had told him everything she knew. It was of great value. Finally she said simply that she had given him everything, and that she would never have any further information, because she had severed her links with those people and she would never have anything more to do with them at any price. And now she wanted to break off all contact forever with Yoel and those who had sent him. That was her only request: that they never get in touch with her again. Having said this, she rose and took her leave without so much as giving him an opportunity to thank her. She turned her back and walked on her high heels toward the lush tropical vegetation of the park attached to the temple. A voluptuous, captivating Asian woman, in a white summer dress with a blue scarf around her delicate neck. Yoel watched her back. And suddenly he said:

My wife.

Not because there was any resemblance. There was none. But in some way that Yoel could not decipher, even after weeks and months of trying, that short meeting had made it clear to him, with the transparent clarity of a dream, how much his wife, Ivria, was essential to his life. Despite the suffering, or because of it.

Then he had pulled himself together and gone back to his hotel, where he had sat in his room to write down everything he had heard from the young woman at the temple while it was still fresh in his memory. But the freshness did not fade. At times he remembered her unexpectedly and his heart ached: why had he not suggested to her there and then that she go with him at once to his room to make love? Why had he not fallen in love with her on the spot and dropped everything to go away with her forever? But the moment had passed and now it was too late.

9

ard himself
Who
So far
. It was
n June
a forma-
and she
purpose.
Yea!
ish that

Meanwhile he kept putting off the promised visit to his American neighbors. Although he occasionally spoke to them, the two of them together or the brother alone, over the hedge that he had not finished clipping. He found it strange to see the brother and sister hugging on the lawn, grappling noisily, like children, as they tried to wrest the ball they were playing with from each other's grasp. At times there flitted through his mind an image of Annemarie or Rosemarie, her breasts, her whispering to him in English, "Tough life, huh?"

Tomorrow is another day, he thought.

In the mornings he would lie almost naked in the hammock in the garden, sunbathing, reading, devouring bunches of grapes. He even replaced *Mrs. Dalloway*, lost in Helsinki. But he could not finish it. Netta started taking the bus by herself into town almost every day, to see a film, borrow books from the public library, perhaps wander the streets window-shopping. She particularly enjoyed watching old films at the Cinémathèque. Sometimes she watched two films in a single evening. Between films she sat in the corner of a small café, always choosing places that were cheap and cheerful. She would sip cider or grape juice. If a stranger tried to start a conversation with her, she would shrug her shoulders and utter some acerbic phrase that restored her solitude.

In August, Lisa and Avigail started doing voluntary work three hours a morning, five mornings a week, in an institution for deaf-mutes on the edge of the suburb, within walking distance of the house. Sometimes they spent the evening sitting at the garden table communicating with each other in sign language, for practice. Yoel watched them curiously. He soon picked up the main signs. Early in the morning, in the bathroom mirror, he would say something to himself in the same language. Yoel arranged for a cleaner to come in on Fridays, a smiling, silent, almost pretty Georgian woman. With her help, his mother-in-law and his mother prepared the house for the weekend. The two old women took his car, with Avigail at the wheel and Lisa raising the alarm every time another car came toward them, and did all the shopping for the week. They cooked for several days ahead, and froze the cooked food. Yoel bought them a microwave oven, and sometimes amused himself by playing with it a little. From professional habit he read the manufacturer's instructions four times, before he remembered that there was no need to destroy the leaflet after memorizing it. With the cleaner, his mother-in-law and his mother kept the house clean and neat. It gleamed. Sometimes the two of them went off together to spend the weekend in Metulla. Or Jerusalem. Then Yoel and his daughter would cook for each other. Sometimes the two of them sat down and played a game of checkers on Friday evening, or watched television. Netta got in the habit of making him an herbal infusion in the evening to help him sleep.

Twice, in the middle of July and again at the beginning of August, Le Patron had come to visit. The first time, he had appeared after lunch without prior warning, had trouble deciding if he had locked his Renault properly, and walked around it two or three times checking all the doors before approaching Yoel's front door and ringing the bell.

He sat with Yoel in the garden talking about office news until Avigail joined them, when they changed the subject and discussed the problem of religious coercion. He brought Netta a present of a new book of poems by Dalia Ravikovich entitled *True Love*, and advised Yoel to read at least the poem that began on page 7 and finished on page 8. He also brought Yoel a bottle of excellent French brandy. The second time, alone with Yoel in the garden, he had told him in broad outline about a certain failure they had experienced in Marseilles. And with no clear connection he had mentioned a different case, which Yoel had been responsible for eighteen months before: he seemed to be trying to hint that this case had not been closed properly, or, let's say, it had been closed but had had to be reopened in a certain sense. There might be a need for a little clarification, in which case they might have to steal an hour or so of Yoel's time one of these days. Of course, only with his consent and at a time that suited him.

Yoel seemed to sense between the words or behind them a faint whiff of irony, almost a veiled warning, and as always he had trouble deciphering Le Patron's tone. Sometimes he would touch on a crucial and very delicate matter as though he were joking about the weather. Whereas when he was joking his face occasionally took on an almost tragic expression. Sometimes he would mix up the tones, his face as expressionless as if he were adding columns of figures. Yoel requested an explanation, but Le Patron was already talking about something else: smiling like a drowsy cat, he mentioned Netta's problem. A few days before, and this was the reason for his visit, he had happened by chance on a magazine article, which he had brought with him, about a new form of treatment that was being developed in Switzerland. Only a popular article, actually. He had brought the magazine along to give to Yoel. His fine, musical fingers never stopped weaving chains from the pine needles that had fallen on the garden furniture. Yoel asked himself if Le Patron were still suffering withdrawal symptoms, even though it was two years now since he had suddenly given up chain-smoking Gitanes. Incidentally, wasn't Yoel sick of gardening? After all, he had only rented this place. Wouldn't he like to go back to work? Even part-time? He was referring, naturally, to a job that would not involve traveling. In the Planning Department, for example. Or in Operations Analysis.

Yoel said: "Not really." And at once the visitor changed the subject, to an affair that was exercising the media at the time. He brought Yoel up to date on the details, though not all of them.

As was his wont, he described the subject as it appeared to each of the sides involved and to various outside observers. Each of the conflicting versions was presented with understanding and with a measure of empathy. He refrained from expressing his own view, even though Yoel asked him for it. At the office he was known as Teacher. Without the definite article, as though it were his name. Perhaps because for many years he had taught history at a secondary school in Tel Aviv. Even when he had attained a senior rank in the service, he had continued to teach one or two days a week. He was a stocky, well-groomed, active man, with thinning hair and a face that inspired confidence: the image of a financial adviser with artistic inclinations. Yoel imagined that he had been good at teaching history. Just as in his work in the office he had always been wonderfully good at reducing the most complex situations to a simple dilemma: yes or no. Conversely, he was also able to foresee complicated ramifications in situations that seemed ostensibly simple. In fact, Yoel did not like this modest, pleasant-mannered widower, with his manicured hands and his woolen suits and quiet, conservative ties. Once or twice the man had dealt him a crushing professional blow. Which he had taken no trouble to soften, not even outwardly. Yoel thought he saw in him a kind of gentle, drowsy cruelty, the cruelty of an overfed cat. It was not clear to him why the man took the trouble to come on these visits. Or what was behind his cryptic remark about the case that was closed but had been reopened. To form a bond of friendship with Le Patron seemed to him as absurd as to make a declaration of love to an optician while she is at work. But he did feel an intellectual respect for him, and even a kind of gratitude which he could not explain. Now it was not even important to him.

Then the visitor apologized, got up from the glider, and went to Netta's room, looking tubby and smelling effeminately of after-shave. The door closed behind him. Yoel, who followed him, heard his soft voice through the door. And Netta's voice too, almost in a whisper. He could not catch any words. What were they talking about? A vague anger stirred within him. And at once he was angry with himself for this anger. He muttered, with his hands over his ears, "Fool."

Was it possible that behind the closed door Teacher and Netta were sitting and discussing his condition? Plotting about him behind his back? At once he pulled himself together and realized that this was impossible and again he felt angry with himself for his momentary upsurge of rage, because of the illogicality of his envy, because of the fleeting temptation he had felt to burst in without knocking. Eventually he went to the kitchen and three minutes later came back, knocked on the door and waited a moment before entering bearing a bottle of chilled cider and two tall glasses containing ice cubes. He found them sitting on the wide double bed absorbed in a game of checkers. Neither of them laughed when he came in. For an instant he had a feeling that Netta flashed a faint wink at him. Then he decided that she had only blinked.

10

He had nothing to do all day long. The days were all alike. Here and there he made various improvements in the house. He fitted a soap dish in the bathroom. A new hat-and-coat rack. A lid with a spring on the garbage can. He hoed the soil around the four fruit trees in the back garden. He lopped off some redundant branches and painted the cuts with black paste. He prowled around the bedrooms, the kitchen, the carport, the terrace, clutching the electric drill with its extension cord always plugged in, like a diver attached to his oxygen tank, with his finger on the trigger, looking for a spot to thrust the tip in. Sometimes he sat in front of the TV in the morning, staring at the children's programs. He finally finished clipping the hedge, on both sides. At times he would shift a piece of furniture, and sometimes the next day he would shift it back again. He rewashered all the faucets in the house. He repainted the carport because he detected some tiny enclaves of rust on one of its supports. He mended the latch on the garden gate and fixed a note to the mailbox in large letters requesting the newspaper delivery boy kindly to place the newspaper in the box and not to throw it down on the path. He oiled the hinges of the doors to stop their squeaking. He took Ivria's dip-pen to be cleaned and to have the nib changed. He also changed the light bulb in Netta's bedside lamp for a stronger one. He ran an extension line from the telephone on the stool in the entrance hall to Avigail's bedroom, so that she and his mother could have their own telephone.

His mother said:

"Soon you'll start catching flies. You should go instead and hear some lectures in the university. You should go to the swimming pool. You should see some people."

Avigail said:

"Assuming he can swim, that is."

And Netta:

"There's a cat that's had four kittens outside in the shed."

Yoel said:

"That's enough. What's going on here? Any more of this and we'll have to elect a committee."

"And what's more, you don't slep enough," said his mother.

At night, after the end of the programs on television, he would stay sprawled on the living-room sofa for a while, listening to the monotonous whistle, and watching the snowflakes on the flickering screen. Then he would go out to the garden to turn off the sprinkler, check the light on the porch, take a saucer of milk or some leftovers of chicken to the cat in the shed. Then he would stand in a corner of the lawn to watch the darkened road and look at the stars, sniffing the air, trying to picture himself without limbs in a wheelchair, and sometimes his feet took him down the street to the fence around the grove to listen to the frogs. Once he thought he heard a solitary jackal in the distance, although he allowed the possibility that it was probably nothing but a stray dog baying at the moon. Then he would return and get into his car and start the engine and drive as if he were in a dream along empty night roads as far as the monastery at Latrun, to the edge of the hills at Kafr Kassem, to the beginning of the Carmel range. He was always careful not to exceed the legal speed limit. He would sometimes pull into a gas station to fill his tank and have a short conversation with the Arab on night duty. He would crawl slowly past the highway whores and study them from a distance, the little wrinkles contracting on his face, those wrinkles that converged at the corners of his eyes and fixed a slightly mocking smile on his face even when his lips gave no hint of a smile. Tomorrow is another day, he thought as he sank at last onto his bed and decided to sleep, then suddenly leaped up to pour himself a glass of milk cold from the refrigerator. If he happened to come across his daughter sitting in the kitchen reading at four o'clock in the morning he would say to her, Good morning, young lady. And what might her ladyship be reading now? And she, after finishing the paragraph, would raise her close-cropped head and say quietly: A book. Yoel would ask: May I join you? Shall I fix us something to drink? And Netta would answer softly, almost warmly: Suit yourself. And then she would continue reading. Until a faint thud sounded outside: whereupon Yoel leaped up and tried in vain to catch the newspaper delivery boy. Who once again had thrown the paper onto the path instead of putting it in the mailbox. He did not touch the figurine in the living room again. He did not even approach the shelf of ornaments above the fireplace. As though fighting temptation. At most he would shoot it a fleeting glance from the corner of his eye, as a man sitting with a woman in a restaurant may steal a hasty glance at another woman, sitting at another table. Even though he imagined that his new reading glasses might enable him him to make something out now. Instead, he began to inspect through his black-framed glasses and also through Ivria's doctor's glasses, systematically, precisely, from very close up, the photographs of Romanesque ruins. Netta had brought these abbeys from her mother's study in Jerusalem and asked his permission to hang them here in the living room above the sofa. He had begun to suspect that there was some foreign object, perhaps an abandoned bag, perhaps the photographer's own equipment box, next to the doorway of one of the abbeys. But the object was too small for him to come to any definite conclusion. The effort made his eyes ache again. Yoel decided to study the photograph through a powerful magnifying glass someday, or perhaps have it enlarged. They could do that for him at the lab at the office; they would do it with pleasure and make a professional job of it. But he put off the decision because he could not see himself explaining to anybody what it was all about. He did not know himself.

11

Then in the middle of August, a fortnight before Netta started her final year at the local high school, there was a little surprise: Arik Krantz, the real-estate agent, dropped in one Saturday morning. He was just looking in to make sure everything was in order. He lived only five minutes away. And in fact his acquaintances, the Kramers, the owners, had asked him to stop by and take a look.

He looked around, chuckled, and said: "I can see you've had a soft landing. Looks as though everything's shipshape here already." Yoel, economical as usual, said only: "Yes. Fine." The agent wanted to know if all the systems in the house were functioning properly. "After all, you fell in love with this property at first sight, so to speak, and love like that often cools down the next morning."

"Everything's fine," said Yoel, who was dressed in an undershirt and running shorts and sandals. Looking like this, he fascinated the agent even more than on their first meeting, in June, when he had rented the house. Yoel struck him as secretive and strong. His face suggested salt, winds, strange women, loneliness, and sun. The prematurely graying hair was cut military fashion, short and well trimmed, without sideburns, with a metallic gray forelock curling up on his forehead, not flopping forward over it. Like a coil of steel wool. The wrinkles at the corners of the eyes suggested a mocking sneer that the lips did not share in. The eyes themselves were sunk, reddened, slightly closed, as though the light were too strong or because of dust and wind. In the jawline an inner power was concentrated, as though the man kept his teeth clenched. Apart from the ironic wrinkles around his eyes, the face was young and smooth, in contrast with the graying hair. The expression hardly varied whether he was speaking or silent.

The agent inquired:

"I'm not disturbing you? Can I sit down for a minute?"

And Yoel, who was holding the electric drill with its extension lead plugged into the socket in the kitchen, on the other side of the wall, said:

"Please. Sit down."

"This isn't a business call," the agent stressed. "I just dropped in to see if I could be of any help. To contribute to establishing the settlement, as they say. Call me Arik, by the way. It's like this: the landlord asked me to tell you that you can link the two air conditioners together and run them to all the bedrooms. Feel free to fix it at his expense. He was planning to do it anyway this summer and didn't manage to get it done. He also asked me to tell you that the lawn needs a lot of watering—the topsoil is thin here—but that the shrubs at the front need to be watered sparingly."

The agent's efforts to please and to establish contact with him, and perhaps the word "sparingly," brought a faint smile to Yoel's lips. He was not aware of it himself, but Krantz received it enthusiastically, exposing his gums, and reassuring Yoel emphatically:

"I truly didn't come here to bother you, Mr. Ravid. I was just passing on my way to the sea. That is, I wasn't exactly passing; the truth is I made a little detour to come and see you. It's a fantastic day today for sailing and I happen to be on my way to the sea. Well, I'm off now."

"Would you like a cup of coffee," Yoel said without a question mark. He put the drill down, as if it were a tray of refreshments, on the coffee table in front of his visitor. Who sat down gingerly in a corner of the sofa. The agent was wearing a sports shirt with the emblem of the Brazilian soccer team above his swimming trunks and gleaming white tennis shoes. Keeping his hairy legs pressed firmly together like a coy girl, he chuckled again and asked:

"How's the family? Do they feel comfortable here? Settled in OK?"

"The grannies have gone to Metullah. Milk and sugar?"

"Don't bother," said the agent. After a moment he added, daringly: "Well, all right then. Just one spoonful and a tiny drop of milk. Just enough to change the color. Call me Arik."

Yoel went to the kitchen. The agent, from where he was sitting, rapidly checked out the living room with his eyes as though searching for a vital clue. It seemed to him that nothing had changed except for three cardboard boxes standing one on top of the other in a corner near the giant philodendron. And the three photographs of ruins over the sofa, which Krantz guessed must be souvenirs from Africa or somewhere. Interesting to know how he makes his living, this government employee who, according to what they say in the neighborhood, doesn't work at all. He gives the impression of being pretty senior. Perhaps he's been suspended from his duties pending an investigation. He looks like a section head in the Ministry of Agriculture or Development, probably with an impressive history in the regular army. Something like a brigadier in the Armored Corps.

"What did you do in the army, if you don't mind my asking? You look, um, sort of familiar. Have you been in the papers ever? Or on television by any chance?" He turned toward Yoel, who entered the room at that moment, carrying a tray with two cups of coffee, sugar bowl and milk pitcher, and a plate of crackers. He placed the cups on the table. All the other things remained on the tray, which he set down between them. And he sat down in an armchair.

"Lieutenant with the army advocate general," he said.

"And afterward?"

"I left the army in '63."

Almost at the last minute Krantz swallowed an additional question that was on the tip of his tongue. Instead he said, as he put milk and sugar in his coffee:

"I was just asking. Hope you don't mind. Personally I hate busybodies. No problems with the oven?"

Yoel shrugged. A shadow crossed the doorway and vanished.

"Your wife?" asked Krantz, and immediately remembered and, apologizing profusely, cautiously expressed the assumption that it must surely have been the daughter. Cute but shy? And once again he saw fit to mention his two boys, both of them soldiers in combat units, both of them were in Lebanon, barely eighteen months between them. Quite a problem. Maybe we should arrange for them to meet your daughter sometime, and see if anything develops? Suddenly he sensed that the person sitting opposite him was eying him with cold, amused curiosity, so he dropped the subject quickly and chose instead to tell Yoel that he had worked for two years when he was young as a qualified TV technician, so if the television gives you any trouble just give me a ring even in the middle of the night and I'll hurry over and put it right for you for nothing; no problem. And if you feel like joining me for a couple of hours' sailing on my boat that's moored in the fishing port in Jaffa, just let me know. Have you got my phone number? Give me a ring whenever the fancy takes you. Well, I'm off.

"Thank you," Yoel said. "I'll be less than five minutes, if you can wait."

It took the agent a few seconds to realize that Yoel was accepting his invitation. At once he was seized with enthusiasm and began to talk about the delights of sailing on a fantastic day like this. Maybe you feel like making a serious expedition? We could go and take a look at Abie Nathan's heap of junk.

Yoel attracted him and aroused a powerful desire to get closer, to make friends, to serve him devotedly, to prove to Yoel how much he could do for him, to demonstrate loyalty, and even to touch him. But the agent contained himself, stopped the pat on the shoulder that was making his fingertips itch, and said:

"Take your time. There's no hurry. The sea won't run away." And he jumped up, agile and happy, to anticipate Yoel and take the tray with the coffee things back to the kitchen himself. If Yoel had not stopped him he would have washed them.

From then on Yoel started going to sea with Arik Krantz on Saturdays. He had known how to row from his childhood; now he learned to hoist a sail and to tack. But only rarely did he break his silence. This did not cause the agent disappointment or offense but, on the contrary, provoked an emotion resembling the infatuation that sometimes takes hold of an adolescent who falls under the spell of an older boy and longs to serve him. Unconsciously he began to imitate Yoel's habit of putting a finger between his neck and his shirt collar, and his way of taking a deep breath of sea air and holding it in his lungs before releasing it slowly through a thin crack between his lips. When they were out at sea Arik Krantz of his own accord told Yoel everything. Even about being slightly unfaithful to his wife and his methods of cheating on his income tax and postponing his reserve army service. If he sensed he was tiring Yoel, he would stop talking and play him some classical music: he had taken to bringing with him, on those days when his new friend joined him, a sophisticated battery cassette player. After a quarter of an hour or so, finding it difficult to put up with their silence and Mozart, he would set about explaining to Yoel how he could maintain the value of his money in times like these or about the classified methods by which the navy was able now to seal the coast hermetically against terrorists infiltrating by boat. The unexpected friendship excited the agent to the point that sometimes, unable to contain himself, he telephoned Yoel during the week to talk about the coming weekend.

Yoel for his part thought about the words "the sea won't run away." He found no error in them. As was his wont, he kept his side of the bargain: he enjoyed giving the agent what he wanted precisely by giving him nothing. Except his silent presence. Once as a surprise, he taught Krantz how to say to a girl "I want you" in Burmese. They would return to Jaffa harbor at three or four in the afternoon, even though Krantz secretly prayed that time would stand still or that the dry land would disappear. Then they would go home in the agent's car, and have coffee together. Yoel would say "Thanks a lot. See you." But once he said as they were parting, "Take care, Arik, on the way." Krantz treasured these words joyfully in his heart because he saw them as a small step forward. Meanwhile, of the thousand questions that aroused his curiosity he had managed to put only two or three. And he had received simple answers. He was terrified of spoiling things, of going too far, of being a nuisance, of breaking the magic spell. In this way several weeks passed, Netta started her last year at school, and the pat on the back that Krantz swore to himself every time that he would finally give his friend as they parted did not happen. It was postponed to the next meeting.

12

A few days before the start of the school year Netta's problem
reappeared. Ever since the disaster in Jerusalem in February there
had been no sign of it, and Yoel had almost begun to believe that
Ivria might have been right after all. It happened on a Wednesday
at three o'clock in the afternoon. Lisa had gone to Jerusalem that
day to inspect her apartment, and Avigail was also out, having
gone to listen to a guest lecture at the university.

He was standing barefoot in the front garden, which was
flooded with scorching late-summer light, watering the shrubs.
The neighbor across the street, a Romanian whose broad posterior put Yoel in mind of an overripe avocado, had climbed up on
the roof of his house with two Arab boys who looked like students on vacation. The boys had dismantled the old television
aerial and were replacing it with a new and apparently more sophisticated one. The Romanian was aiming a continuous stream
of criticisms, rebukes, and suggestions at them in broken Arabic.
Though Yoel imagined that they could speak better Hebrew than
he could. The neighbor, an importer of wines and spirits, occasionally conversed with Yoel's mother in Romanian. Once, he
had offered her a flower, and bowed to her exaggeratedly, as
though in jest. At the foot of the ladder stood the Alsatian whose
name Yoel knew, Ironside, stretching his neck upward and uttering suspicious broken barks that sounded almost bored. Doing
his duty. A heavy truck entered the little street, reached the fence
around the citrus grove that marked its end, and started to shudder backward with much panting and screeching of brakes. The

exhaust fumes hung in the air, and Yoel asked himself what had become of the refrigerated truck that had belonged to Mr. Vitkin, Eviatar, Itamar. And where was the guitar that he had played Russian tunes on.

Then the summer-afternoon silence returned and enfolded the street. On the lawn, extraordinarily close to him, Yoel suddenly noticed a little bird that had buried its beak under its wing and was standing there, frozen and silent. He moved the stream of water to the next bush and the bird-statue flew away. A child ran past along the street, shouting in shrill outrage, "We said I was the cops!" Who he was shouting to Yoel could not see from where he was standing. Soon the child too disappeared, and Yoel, with one hand holding the hose, bent down and with his other hand repaired a worn wall of the irrigation basin around the bush. He remembered how his wife's father, the veteran policeman Shealtiel Lublin, used to give him a broad wink and say: "When it comes to it, we all have the same secrets." This sentence always filled him with rage, almost with loathing, directed not at Shealtiel but at Ivria.

It was Lublin who had taught him how to construct irrigation basins and how to move the hose with a slight circular movement so as not to wear down the mounds of earth. He was always wreathed in gray cigar smoke. Anything connected with digestion, sex, disease, or other bodily functions always made him tell a joke. Lublin was a compulsive joke-teller. It was as though the body itself excited in him a malicious glee. And at the end of each joke he would burst into a strangled smoker's laugh that sounded like gargling.

Once, he had dragged Yoel into the bedroom in Metullah and lectured him in a low, smoke-wrecked voice: "Listen. A man spends three-quarters of his life running wherever the tip of his prick happens to be pointing. As though you're a new recruit and he's the sergeant. Attention! Run! Jump! Attack! If only our pricks would release us from this compulsory service at the end of two, three, five years, then each of us would have enough time left to write the poems of Pushkin or to invent electricity. However hard you try for him, he's never satisfied. He'll never leave you in peace. Give him steak, he'll want schnitzel. Give him schnitzel, he'll want caviar. It's lucky for us that God took pity on us and only gave us one of them. Imagine what it would be like if you had to spend fifty years of your life feeding and clothing and heating and entertaining five of them." Having spoken, he began to gurgle and choke, and at once swathed himself in the smoke of a new cigar. Until he finally died at half past four one summer's morning sitting on the toilet, with his trousers down and a lighted cigar between his fingers. Yoel almost knew the joke that Lublin would have remembered and then burst out coughing if the same thing had happened to somebody else—to Yoel, for instance. Perhaps he *had* managed to see the funny side of his death and gone off laughing. His son Nakdimon was a clumsy, taciturn youth who had always had a talent for catching venomous snakes. He could milk their venom, which he sold for making serum. Though he apparently held extreme political views, most of his acquaintances were Arabs. When sitting among Arabs he would be seized suddenly by a frenetic urge to speak, which vanished as soon as he changed back to Hebrew. His relations with Yoel and even with his sister, Ivria, were those of a tightfisted, suspicious peasant. On the rare occasions when he came to Jerusalem, he used to bring them a present of a can of his own olive oil or a dried Galilee thistle for Netta's collection. It was almost impossible to make him say anything beyond his fixed two- or three-word answers such as "Yes, sort of" or "Never mind" or "Yes, thank God," and even these came out of his mouth with a sort of truculent whine, as though he instantly regretted having let himself be lured into replying at all. He addressed his mother, sister, and niece, if at all, as "girls." Yoel, for his part, was in the habit of addressing Nakdimon the same way he had addressed his late father: he called them both Lublin, because he found their forenames ridiculous. Ever since Ivria's funeral, Nakdimon had not been to see them once. Although Avigail and Netta sometimes used to visit him and his sons in Metullah, and come back in a state of faint infatuation. On Passover Eve, Lisa also joined them, and she said on her return: "One has to know how to live." Yoel was secretly glad he had refused to succumb and had chosen to spend the holiday alone at home. He had watched television and gone to sleep at half past eight and slept deeply until nine o'clock the next morning, as he had not slept for ages.

He had still not entirely accepted the view that when it comes to it, we all have the same secrets. But it no longer made him feel angry. Now, as he stood in his garden with the empty street bathed in white summer sunlight, he sensed, like a pang of longing, the following thought: Maybe we do, maybe we don't, but either way we'll never know. When she used to whisper compassionately to him at night "I understand you," what had she meant by it? What had she understood? He had never asked her. Now it was too late. Perhaps the time had really come to sit down and write the poems of Pushkin or invent electricity? Unconsciously, as he moved the hose in gentle circular motions from plant to plant, he suddenly let out of his chest a strange low sound, not unlike the gurgling of Lublin senior. He was remembering the deceptive patterns that had appeared, disappeared, and transformed themselves as though playing hide-and-seek with him on the wallpaper that night in the hotel room in Frankfurt.

A girl passed along the street in front of him carrying a heavy shopping basket and clutching two large bags to her breast with her other hand. An Asian girl, a maid who had been imported by some wealthy neighbors to live in a small self-contained apartment and look after their home. She was petite and slightly built, yet she carried the shopping basket and the bulging bags without visible effort. She glided past as though the laws of gravity had given her a discount. Why not turn off the water, catch up, and offer to help her carry her shopping? Or else behave like a father with his daughter: bar her way, take the bags out of her hands, and walk her home while striking up a light conversation on the way? For a moment Yoel could feel on his chest the pain of the bags pressed against her breast. But she would be startled, she wouldn't understand, she might think he was a thief, or a pervert; the neighbors would get to hear and tongues would wag.

Not that he cared: in any case, the other residents of the little street had probably already started gossiping about him and his ways. But with his sharp, well-honed senses, and thanks to his professional training, he accurately estimated the distance and time and realized that before he could catch her she would already have slipped indoors. Unless he were to run. And he had always disliked running.

She was very young, beautifully shaped, with a wasp waist, her profuse black hair almost concealing her face, her torso squeezed into a flowery cotton dress with a long zipper down the back. By the time he had finished inspecting the curve of her legs and her thighs she had disappeared from view. His eyes suddenly burned. Yoel closed them and imagined an Asian shantytown, in Rangoon or Seoul or Manila, masses of little homes built of corrugated iron and plywood and cardboard, stacked and huddled one against the other, half-sinking in the thick tropical mud. A filthy, stifling alley with an open drain running down the middle. Mangy dogs and cats being chased by sickly, barefoot, dark-skinned toddlers dressed in rags, paddling in the stagnant sewage. A broad, docile old ox standing harnessed with rough ropes to a miserable cart, its wooden wheels sinking into the sludge. And everything drenched in pungent, suffocating odors, with a sort of warm tropical rain pouring down ceaselessly over everything. Drumming on the carcass of a rusting jeep like a muffled salvo of gunfire. And there, propped up on the slashed driver's seat of the jeep, is the limbless cripple from Helsinki, as white as an angel and smiling as if he knows.

13

Just then a vague banging noise came from the direction of Netta's window, along with coughing sounds. Yoel opened his eyes.
He played the hose on his bare feet, washed off the mud, turned
off the water, and took large strides. By the time he was indoors
the gurglings and spasms had stopped, and he knew that the
problem was a minor one. The girl was lying on the rug in the
fetal position. The fainting fit had softened her features, so that
for a moment she looked almost pretty. He placed two pillows
under her head and shoulders to ensure that she could breathe
freely. He went out and came back and put a glass of water on
the table with two pills that he would give her when she came
around. Then, unnecessarily, he spread a white sheet over her
body and sat by her head, on the floor, clasping his knees with
his arms. He had not touched her.

The girl's eyes were shut but not tightly, her lips were half-
open, her body was frail and calm under the sheet. He realized
now how she had sprouted up over these past months. He noticed the long eyelashes that she had inherited from her mother
and the high smooth brow that she had inherited from his own
mother. For an instant he felt like taking advantage of her sleep
and the solitude to kiss her earlobes as he used to do when she
was little. As he had done to her mother. Because she looked now
like that child with the knowing eyes who had sprawled quietly
on a mat in a corner of the room fixing grown-ups with an almost ironic look, as though she understood everything, including
things that could not be expressed in words, and as though it

was only her tact and sensitivity that prevented her from speaking. The baby he had always taken with him on all his travels in a little picture-wallet in his inside jacket pocket.

For six months now Yoel had been hoping that the trouble had vanished. That the disaster had brought about a change. That Ivria had been right and he had been wrong. He vaguely recalled that such a possibility was indeed mentioned here and there in the medical literature he had read. One of the doctors had talked to him once, not in the presence of Ivria, and with many reservations, about a certain possibility that adolescence would bring about a recovery. Or at least a considerable improvement. And indeed, since Ivria's death there had been no incident.

Incident? At that moment he was overwhelmed with bitterness. She wasn't here any more. From now on we can stop saying "problem" and "incident." From now on we can say "attack." He almost spoke the word aloud. The censorship was lifted. Finished. The sea doesn't run away. From now on we'll use the proper word. And at once, with mounting rage, with a violent, angry gesture, he bent over to dislodge a fly that was traveling over the pallid cheek.

The first time it had happened was when Netta was four. One day she had been standing at the washbasin in the bathroom bathing a plastic doll when she had suddenly fallen backward. Yoel remembered the horror of the open, upturned eyes, showing only the blood-flecked whites. The bubbling foam at the corners of the mouth. The paralysis that had taken hold of him even though he realized that he ought to run and call for help. Despite everything he had been taught in his years of training and work, he had not managed to uproot his feet or remove his eyes from the little girl, because he had the impression that a shadow of a smile appeared and reappeared on her face, as though she were straining not to laugh. It was Ivria, not he, who had managed to pull herself together first and rush to the telephone. He had unfrozen only when he heard the ambulance siren. Then he had snatched his daughter from Ivria's arms and run down the steps and stumbled and bumped his head on the railing and everything had gone misty. By the time he had waked up in the emergency ward Netta had recovered consciousness.

Ivria had said to him quietly: "I'm surprised at you." And left it at that.

The next day he had had to go to Milan for five days. By the time he returned the doctors had already reached a provisional diagnosis and the girl had been sent home. Ivria had refused to accept the diagnosis, had refused to administer the drugs that had been prescribed, had clung stubbornly to what seemed to her a hint of a certain disagreement between the doctors, or an impression that one of them had doubts about his colleagues' opinion. She threw the medicines he bought straight into the trash. Yoel said: You're out of your mind. And she, with a calm smile, had replied: Look who's talking.

When he was away she had dragged Netta from one private specialist to the next, had consulted famous professors, then psychologists of various schools, therapists, and finally, despite his opposition, all kinds of witch doctors who advised various diets, exercises, cold showers, vitamins, mineral baths, mantras, and herbal infusions.

Every time he came back from one of his trips he used to go and buy the medicines all over again, and administer them to the child. But whenever he was away Ivria would get rid of them all. One day, in a fit of tearful rage, she forbade him ever to use the words "illness" and "attack." You're stigmatizing her. You're shutting her off from the world. You're signaling to her that you approve of the performance. You'll destroy her. There is a problem, so Ivria used to formulate it, but in fact it's not Netta's problem; it's our problem. In the end he yielded to her and got into the habit of using the word "problem" himself. He saw no sense in quarreling with his wife over a word. And as a matter of fact, Ivria would say, the problem isn't with her or even with us, but with you, Yoel. Because the moment you go away, it disappears. No audience—no performance. It's a fact.

Was it really a fact? Yoel was filled with doubts. For some reason that was unclear to him he refrained from clarifying it.

Was he afraid that it would become clear that Ivria was right? Or, on the contrary, that she was wrong?

The arguments initiated by Ivria arose every time the problem occurred. And also between occurrences. When she finally despaired, after a few months, of her witch doctors and quacks, she nonetheless proceeded with a sort of lunatic logic to blame him and him alone. She demanded that he stop his traveling, or, on the contrary, that he go away forever. Make up your mind, she said, what really matters to you. Such a hero against women and children, sticking the knife in and running away.

Once, in his presence, during a fit, she started to beat the motionless child on her face, her back, her head. He was shocked. He begged, he pleaded, he asked her to stop. Finally he was compelled for the only time in his life to use force to stop her. He grabbed her arms, bent them up behind her back, and dragged her into the kitchen. When she stopped resisting and dropped onto a stool as limp as a rag doll, he raised his hand unnecessarily and hit her hard across the face. It was only then that he noticed that the child was awake and was leaning against the kitchen doorjamb, watching the two of them with a sort of cool scientific curiosity. Ivria, panting, pointed to the girl and spat at him: "There. Now look." He hissed through his teeth: "Tell me, are you totally insane?" And Ivria replied: "No. I'm clean off my rocker—for agreeing to live with a murderer. You ought to know that, Netta. A murderer, that's his profession."

14

Next winter, in his absence, she made up her mind, packed a
couple of suitcases, took Netta, and went to live with her mother,
Avigail, and her brother, Nakdimon, in the house where she was
born in Metullah. When he got back from Bucharest on the last
day of Hanukkah he found the apartment empty. On the clean
kitchen table there were two notes waiting for him, side by side,
one under the salt and the other under the matching pepper shaker.
One was an opinion from some Russian immigrant, according to
his letterhead a world expert in bioenergetic therapy and a tele-
kinetic counselor, who certified in broken Hebrew that "Miss Niuta
Raviv is free from illness epilepsia and suffers only deprivation,
signed Dr. Nikodim Shaliapin." The other note was from Ivria,
and declared, in firm round writing: "We are in Metullah. You
can call but don't come."

He obediently stayed away all that winter. Perhaps he was
hoping that when the problem reared its head there, in Metullah,
without his presence, Ivria would be forced to come to her senses.
Or perhaps, on the contrary, he was hoping that the problem
would not appear, and that Ivria, as usual, would turn out to be
right after all.

Then at the beginning of the spring they both came back to
Jerusalem, laden with flowers in pots and other presents from
Galilee. A good period ensued. His wife and daughter almost
competed with each other to pamper him each time he came home
from a trip. The little one used to leap on him as soon as he sat
down, pull off his shoes, and put his slippers on his feet. Ivria

revealed hidden culinary skills, and amazed him with inspired dinners. He, not to be outdone, insisted on doing things around the house between trips, just as he had done through the winter while they were away. He made sure the refrigerator was stocked. He combed the delicatessens of Jerusalem in search of peppery salami and unusual ewes' milk cheeses. Once or twice he broke his own rules and brought a cheese or a sausage home from Paris. One day, without saying a word to Ivria, he replaced their black-and-white television with a color set. Ivria retorted by changing the curtains. For their wedding anniversary she bought him a stereo player of his own, in addition to the one in the living room. And they often took his car and went away for the weekend.

The girl had grown in Metullah. And filled out a little. In the set of her jaw he thought he identified a Lublin family trait that had skipped Ivria and reappeared in Netta. Her hair was longer. He brought her a magnificent cashmere sweater from London, and for Ivria he brought a knitted suit. His discerning eye and good taste in selecting women's clothes had caused Ivria to say, more than once, You could have gone a long way as a fashion designer. Or as a set designer.

What had happened in Metullah that winter he neither knew nor attempted to discover. His wife seemed to be undergoing a late flowering. Had she found a lover? Or had the fruit of Lublin's land refreshed her inner juices, made her sap rise? She had changed her hairstyle: she had a fetching ponytail now. She had learned to make up her face for the first time, and did it tastefully and with restraint. She had bought a spring dress with a daringly low neckline, and underneath it she sometimes wore a style of underwear that had not suited her before. Sometimes, as they sat at the kitchen table late in the evening and she peeled a peach and put each slice to her mouth and seemed to test it carefully with her lips before starting to chew, Yoel could not take his eyes off her. She had also started using a new perfume. So began their Indian summer.

Several times he entertained a suspicion that she was passing on to him what she had learned from another man. To atone for this suspicion, he took her for a four-day holiday to a hotel on the Ashkelon coast. All the years so far they had always made love earnestly, in a concentrated silence; from now on they sometimes did it convulsed with laughter.

But Netta's problem did not go away, although it may have decreased.

Nevertheless, the arguments ceased.

Yoel was not certain if he should believe what his wife told him—that throughout that winter in Metullah there had been no sign of the problem. He could easily have found out, without Ivria or the Lublins knowing that he was looking into the matter; his profession had taught him to crack more complicated cases than this one without leaving a trace. But he preferred not to investigate. To himself he merely said: Why shouldn't I believe her?

Nevertheless he did ask her, on one of those good nights, in a whisper: Who did you learn this from? Your lover? Ivria laughed in the dark and said: What would you do if you knew? Go and murder him without leaving a trace? Yoel said: On the contrary, he deserves a bottle of brandy and a bunch of flowers for teaching you so well. Who's the lucky winner? Ivria let out one of her crystal laughs before answering: With your sharp eyes you'll go far. He hesitated for a moment before getting the point and joining guardedly in the laughter.

And so, without explanations or heart-to-heart talks, as though of their own accord, the new rules were fixed. A new consideration prevailed. Neither of them broke it, not even by mistake, not even in a moment of abstraction. No more witch doctors, et cetera. No more complaints and recriminations. On condition that the problem must not be mentioned. Not even obliquely. If it happened—it happened. And that's that. Not a word must be said.

Netta also kept these rules. Although no one had told her. As though she had made up her mind to compensate her father because she felt that the new arrangement was based mainly on his renunciation and tolerance, she often climbed into his arms that

69

summer and snuggled up to him, purring contentedly. She sharpened the pencils on his desk. She folded his newspaper neatly and left it beside his bed when he was away. She would give him a glass of fruit squash from the refrigerator even if he forgot to ask for one. She arranged her drawings from school and her work from the pottery class like a display on his desk, to wait for him on his return. Wherever he went in the apartment, even in the bathroom, even among his shaving things, she left delicate drawings of cyclamens, which were his favorite flowers. He might even have named his daughter Rakefet, meaning "cyclamen," if Ivria had not put her foot down.

Ivria, for her part, showered him in bed with surprises he could not have imagined, even in the early days of their marriage. He was sometimes alarmed by the force of her hunger mingled with tenderness, generosity, a kind of musical preparedness to guess his every wish. What have I done? he asked in a whisper once. How have I earned all this from you? It's simple, whispered Ivria. My lovers don't satisfy me. Only you do.

And he really did excel himself. He gave her a scorching pleasure and when her body was seized with shuddering spasms and her teeth chattered as though with cold he got much more of a thrill out of her pleasure than he got from his own. Sometimes Yoel had the feeling that it was not his sexual organ but his whole being that was penetrating and luxuriating inside her womb. That he was entirely wrapped up and quivering inside her. Until with each caress the difference between caresser and caressed vanished, as though they had ceased being a man and a woman making love and had become one flesh.

15

One of his friends at work, a rough, sharp man who was known as Cockney or sometimes as the Acrobat, told Yoel one of those days to watch out, it stuck out a mile that he was having a bit on the side. When Yoel protested his innocence, the Acrobat, bewildered by the conflict between the evidence of his own eyes and his confidence in Yoel's habitual veracity, hissed mockingly: "Forget it. After all, you're supposed to be our resident righteous man. So enjoy yourself. As the Good Book says, I have not seen the righteous man forsaken, nor his seed begging for . . . bed."

Sometimes in hotel bedrooms, by the fluorescent light that he always left on in the bathroom, he would wake up in the middle of the night aching with desire for his wife and say to himself, Come here. Until once, for the first time in all his years of traveling and in flat contradiction to the rules, he could not stop himself from phoning her at four o'clock in the morning from Nairobi, and there she was, waiting for him. She picked up the receiver at the first ring, and before he could make a sound said: Yoel. Where are you? And he said things to her that by morning he had forgotten and that four days later, when he was home and she tried to remind him, he adamantly refused to listen to.

If he got home while it was still light, they used to deposit the child in front of the new television and lock themselves in the bedroom. When they emerged after an hour Netta would nestle in his arms like a kitten and he would tell her stories about bears, in which there was always one stupid but endearing bear called Zambi.

Three times, during the school holidays, they left the child with the Lublins in Metullah or with Lisa in Rehavia and went off for a week by themselves, to the Red Sea, to Greece, and to Paris. They had not done this since the problem first appeared. But Yoel knew that everything hung by a thread, and indeed at the beginning of the following autumn, when she was in the third grade, she passed out on the kitchen floor one Saturday morning and only came around the following afternoon in the hospital after extensive treatment. Ivria broke the rules ten days or so later by remarking with a smile that that girl could make a successful career as an actress. Yoel decided to let it pass.

After this long fit, Ivria forbade Yoel to touch Netta even casually. When he ignored the prohibition, she fetched the sleeping bag from the trunk of the car, which was parked in the open basement of the block of apartments, and took to sleeping in the child's bedroom. Until he took the hint and suggested that they swap: she and Netta could sleep in the double bed in the main bedroom and he would move into the nursery. That way they would all be more comfortable.

That winter Ivria went on a strict diet and lost a lot of weight. A tough, bitter line was blended into her beauty. Her hair started to go gray. Then she decided to resume studying in the English Literature Department, and to get a second degree. To write an MA thesis. Meanwhile Yoel several times saw himself going away and not coming back. Settling down under an assumed name somewhere far away like Vancouver or Brisbane and starting a new life. Opening a driving school, an investment business, or purchasing a log cabin cheaply and living alone by hunting or fishing. These were the kind of dreams he had dreamed as a child, and now here he was dreaming them again. Sometimes in his imagination he would introduce into the log cabin an Eskimo slave-woman, silent and submissive, like a dog. He imagined nights of wild lovemaking in front of the fire in the cabin. But very soon he began to betray this Eskimo mistress with his own wife.

Whenever Netta regained consciousness after a fit Yoel managed to be there before Ivria. The special training he had received years before had given him sharp reflexes and a number of stratagems. He would dash like a runner at the sound of the starter's pistol, pick the child up, shut himself with her in her room that was his room now, and lock the door. He would tell her stories about Zambi the bear. Play hunter-and-rabbit with her. Cut funny shapes out of paper for her, and volunteer to be a father to all her dolls. Or build towers out of dominoes. Until after an hour or so Ivria would give in and knock at the door. Then he would immediately stop, open the door, and invite her to join them on a tour of the palace of bricks or a cruise in the chest where the bedclothes were normally kept. But something changed the moment Ivria came in. As though the palace were abandoned. As though the river they were sailing on had suddenly frozen.

16

When she was older, Yoel started to take his daughter with him on long journeys over the detailed world map he had bought in London and hung on the wall above her former bed. When they reached Amsterdam, for example, he had an excellent street plan that he opened out on the bed so as to take Netta to the museums, to sail down the canals, and to visit the other attractions. From there they went on to Brussels or Zurich or sometimes as far afield as Latin America.

So it was until one day, after a short attack in the hall on the evening of Independence Day, Ivria managed to beat him to it; she darted up to the girl almost before she opened her eyes. For an instant Yoel was terrified that she would hit her again. But Ivria, calmly and solemnly, merely picked the girl up in her arms and carried her to the bath. Which she filled with water. And the two of them locked themselves in and had a bath together for nearly an hour. Maybe Ivria had read something of the sort in the medical literature. Throughout those long years of silence Ivria and Yoel had never stopped reading medical material on subjects related to Netta's problem. Without talking about it. They would silently deposit clippings from the medical pages of the newspapers, articles that Ivria had photocopied in the university library, medical journals that Yoel bought on his trips, on each other's bedside tables. They always left these documents in sealed brown envelopes.

From then on, after each attack Ivria and Netta shut themselves away in the bathroom. The bath became a sort of heated swimming pool for them. Through the locked door Yoel could hear giggles and sounds of splashing. That was the end of the cruises in the bed-linen chest and the flights over the world map. Yoel did not want any quarrels. All he wanted in his home was peace and quiet. He began to buy her dolls of all the nations in traditional costume in airport souvenir shops. For some time he and his daughter were partners in this collection, and Ivria was forbidden to so much as dust the shelves. So the years went by. From about the fourth grade Netta began to read a lot. Dolls and towers of dominoes no longer interested her. She excelled in her schoolwork, especially in arithmetic and Hebrew, and later in literature and mathematics. And she collected sheet music, which her father bought for her on his trips abroad and her mother at shops in Jerusalem. She also collected dried thistles as she wandered in the wadis in summer, and she arranged them in vases in the double bedroom, which continued to be her room even after Ivria left it and migrated to the living-room sofa. Netta had hardly any girlfriends, either because she did not want any or because of rumors about her condition. Even though the problem never occurred at school, or in the street, or in other people's homes, but only within their own four walls.

Every day, after doing her homework, she would lie down on her bed and read until supper, which she was in the habit of eating alone whenever she felt like it. Then she would return to her room and lie down and read on the double bed. For a time Ivria tried to wage a campaign about the time she turned her lights out. Eventually she gave up. Sometimes Yoel would wake up at some indeterminate hour of the night, grope his way to the refrigerator or the bathroom, and be drawn half-asleep toward the strip of light that filtered under Netta's door, but he chose not to approach. He would patter to the living room and sit for a few minutes in an armchair facing the sofa where Ivria was sleeping.

When Netta reached the age of puberty her doctor asked them to send her to a therapist. Who after a while requested to see both parents together and then each of them separately. Under her guidance both Ivria and Yoel were compelled to give up spoiling the girl after her attacks. That was the end of the ceremony of cocoa-without-the-skin and there were no more joint mother-daughter bathing sessions. Netta started to help sometimes, unenthusiastically, with the housework. She no longer welcomed Yoel with his slippers in her hand, and she stopped making her mother up before they went out to the cinema. Instead they began to have weekly staff meetings in the kitchen. At the same period Netta began spending long hours at her grandmother's apartment in Rehavia. For some time she persuaded Lisa to dictate her memories to her: she bought a special notebook and used a little tape recorder that Yoel had brought back from New York for her. Then she lost interest and dropped the project. Life calmed down. In the meantime Avigail too moved to Jerusalem. For forty-four years, ever since she left her birthplace, Safed, to marry Shealtiel Lublin, Avigail had lived in Metullah. There she had brought up her children and taught arithmetic in the primary school, lending a hand with the chickens and the fruit and vegetables, and reading nineteenth-century travel books in the evenings. After she was widowed she had volunteered to look after the four sons of her elder child, Nakdimon, who was widowed himself a year after she was.

Now her grandsons had grown up and Avigail had decided to start a new life. She rented a small apartment in Jerusalem, not far from her daughter, and enrolled for a BA in Jewish Studies at the university. It was the same month that Ivria resumed her studies and began her MA thesis on the *Shame in the Attic*. Sometimes they would meet for a light lunch at the cafeteria in the Kaplan Building. Sometimes the three of them, Ivria, Avigail, and Netta, would go out together to a literary evening. If they went to the theater, Lisa joined them too. Eventually Avigail decided to leave her rented studio and move in with Lisa in her two-room apartment in Rehavia, about a quarter of an hour's walk from their children's home in Talbiyeh.

17

And between Ivria and Yoel hibernation reigned once more. Ivria found a part-time job as an editor with the Ministry of Tourism. Most of her time she devoted to her thesis on the novels of the Brontë sisters. Yoel was promoted again. Le Patron hinted to him in a tête-à-tête that this was not the last word and that he ought to start thinking of higher things. In a casual conversation on the stairs one weekend the truck-driver neighbor, Itamar Vitkin, explained that, now that his sons were grown up and his wife had left him and Jerusalem, his apartment was too big for him. He offered to sell Mr. Raviv a room. A building contractor appeared early in the summer, a pious Jew accompanied by a single workman, a middle-aged man so gaunt he looked consumptive. A hole was knocked through the wall and a new door was fitted. The old door was sealed up and plastered over with several layers, but one could still make out its outline on the wall. The work took some four months because the workman fell ill. Then Ivria moved into her new study. The living room was evacuated. Yoel remained in the nursery, and Netta in the double bedroom. Yoel put up some extra shelves for her there, to contain her library and her collection of sheet music. On the walls she hung pictures of her favorite Hebrew poets: Steinberg, Alterman, Lea Goldberg, and Amir Gilboa. Gradually the problems decreased. The incidents became rarer, not more than three or four a year. And they were generally light. One of the doctors even saw fit to offer them limited grounds for hope: The whole saga of your young lady is not exactly unambiguous. It is a slightly unclear case. There is scope for different interpretations. Perhaps in time she will manage to grow out of it completely. Provided that she really wants to. And that you do too. It can happen. He was personally aware of two precedents at least. It was naturally a matter of a prospect, not a prognosis, and in the meantime it was very important to encourage the girl to cultivate a little more of a social life. Staying shut up at home never helped anybody's health. In a word: expeditions, fresh air, boys, Mother Nature, kibbutz, work, dancing, swimming, healthy pleasures.

From Netta, and also from Ivria, Yoel learned of the new friendship with the middle-aged neighbor, the refrigerated-truck driver, who had begun to visit them at times for a glass of tea in the kitchen at the end of the day when Yoel was away. Or to invite them to his apartment. Sometimes he played tunes for them on his guitar. Netta commented that they would have sounded better on a balalaika. And Ivria said that they reminded her of her childhood, when Russianness was widespread in the country, especially in Upper Galilee. Sometimes Ivria called on him alone in the late afternoon. Even Yoel was invited once, twice, a third time, but he found no opportunity to accept, because during that last winter he had to travel more than usual. In Madrid he had managed to pick up a lead that excited him, and his instinct told him that there might be a specially valuable prize waiting at the end of the line. But he would have to deploy various stratagems that demanded patience, cunning, and feigned indifference. Consequently he adopted an indifferent manner that winter. He saw no harm in the friendship between his wife and the older neighbor. He too had a certain weakness for Russian tunes. And he even detected the first signs of a thaw in Ivria: something in the way she let her graying blond hair fall down over her shoulders now. Something in the way she made fruit compote. The style of shoes she had taken to wearing.

Ivria said to him: You look lovely. So brown. Is something nice happening to you?

Yoel said: Sure. I've got an Eskimo mistress.

Ivria said: When Netta goes to Metullah, bring your mistress here. We'll have a ball.

And Yoel: Seriously, though, isn't it time we had a holiday, just the two of us?

He didn't mind what the reason was for the change that was visibly taking place, whether it was her success in the ministry (she also had been promoted), her enthusiasm for her thesis, her friendship with the neighbor, or maybe her pleasure at having her new room that she liked to lock herself into when she was working and also at night when she was asleep. He started to plan a little summer holiday for the two of them, after a period of six years when they had not traveled together. Except for one time when they went to Metullah for a week, but on the third night the phone rang and Yoel was summoned back to Tel Aviv at once. Netta could stay with the grannies in Rehavia. Or else the grannies could come and stay in Talbiyeh while they were away. This time they could go to London. His plan was to surprise her with a British holiday, including a special tour of her own territory, Yorkshire. She had a map of the county hanging on her study wall, and from professional habit Yoel had memorized the layout of the road system and various points of interest.

Sometimes he used to stare hard at his daughter. He found her neither pretty nor feminine. She almost seemed to take pride in it. Clothes that he bought her in Europe for her birthday she occasionally deigned to put on, as though to please him, but she managed to wear them with a sloppy air. Yoel made a note to himself: sloppy, not careless. She dressed in gray and black, or black and brown. Most of the time she went around in a pair of baggy pants that seemed to Yoel as unfeminine as a circus clown's.

One day a young man called, and in a diffident, polite, almost embarrassed voice asked to speak to Netta. Ivria and Yoel exchanged glances and ceremonially left the living room and shut themselves in the kitchen until Netta had put the receiver down, and even then they did not hurry back. Ivria suddenly chose to invite Yoel to her study for a cup of coffee. But when they finally emerged, it transpired that after all the boy had only called to ask Netta for the telephone number of another girl in her class.

Yoel preferred to attribute it all to a somewhat delayed puberty. Once her breasts grow, he thought, the telephone will never stop ringing. Ivria said to him: That's the fourth time you've thrown that stupid joke at me, just to spare yourself the trouble of looking in the mirror for once to see who the girl's jailer is. Yoel said: Don't start all that again, Ivria. And she replied: All right. Anyway it's hopeless.

Yoel could not see what was hopeless. In his heart he was confident that Netta would soon find herself a boyfriend, and stop accompanying her mother when she visited the guitar-playing neighbor or her grandmothers when they went out to concerts and plays. For some reason he imagined this boyfriend as a large, hairy kibbutznik with thick arms, the loins of a bull, heavy legs in shorts, and sun-bleached eyelashes. He would take her away to his kibbutz, and Ivria and he would be left by themselves.

When he was not away on a trip he used to get up sometimes at one o'clock in the morning or so, avoiding the strip of light filtering underneath Netta's door, knock gently on the study door, and bring his wife a tray of sandwiches and iced fruit squash. Because Ivria had taken to working late. Occasionally he was invited to lock the study door. Sometimes she would ask his advice on some technical matter such as how to divide the work into chapters or different ways of typing the footnotes. Just you wait, he said to himself; on our wedding anniversary, the first of March, you'll have a little surprise. He had decided to buy her a word processor.

On his recent trips he had been reading books by the Brontë sisters. He never got around to telling Ivria. Charlotte's writing struck him as facile, and in *Wuthering Heights* he found a puzzle, not in Catherine or Heathcliff, but in the downtrodden Edgar Linton, who even appeared on one occasion in his dream in a hotel in Marseilles, a short time before the disaster, with a pair of spectacles pushed up on his high, pale brow that looked like

Ivria's reading glasses: square, frameless, giving her the appearance of a gentle family doctor of an earlier generation.

Whenever he had to leave for the airport in the early hours of the morning, he would silently enter his daughter's room. Tiptoeing among the vases sprouting forests of thistles he would kiss her eyes without letting his lips touch her and smooth the pillow near her hair with his hand. Then he would go to the study, wake Ivria, and take his leave. All these years he had always awakened his wife in the early morning to say good-bye when he was leaving on a trip. It was Ivria who insisted on it. Even when they were fighting. Even when they were not on speaking terms. Perhaps their common hatred of the hairy kibbutznik with the thick arms forged a bond between them. As though beyond despair. Or perhaps it was a remembrance of the kindness of youth. A short time before the disaster he could almost smile when he remembered the favorite saying of policeman Lublin, that when it comes to it, we all have the same secrets.

18

When Netta regained consciousness he took her to the kitchen. He made her some strong percolated coffee, and decided to help himself to an early brandy. The electric clock on the wall over the refrigerator said ten to five. Outside, the summer-afternoon sunlight was still strong. With her cropped hair, her baggy pants, and her large yellow shirt draped over her angular body, his daughter reminded him of a consumptive young nobleman from an earlier century putting in an appearance at a ball he found boring. Her fingers were clasped around the coffee cup as though they were warming themselves on a winter's night. Yoel noticed a slight redness of her knuckles that contrasted with the whiteness of her flat fingernails. Was she feeling better now? She looked up at him sideways, her chin fixed to her chest, with a faint smile, as though disappointed by his question: No, she was not feeling better, because she hadn't felt bad. What had she felt? Nothing special. Didn't she remember fainting? Only the beginning. What was the beginning like? Nothing special. But look at yourself. So gray. And tough. As if you were ready to kill. What's the matter with you? Drink your brandy; it'll make you feel a bit better, and stop staring at me as though you've never seen anybody drinking a cup of coffee in a kitchen before. Have your headaches come back? Do you feel ill? Shall I massage your neck for you?

He shook his head. Obeyed her. He stretched his neck backward and swallowed his brandy in one long gulp. Then, hesitantly, suggested that she shouldn't go out this evening. Had he only imagined that she was planning to go into town? To the Cinemathèque? To a concert?

"Do you want me at home?"

"Me? I wasn't thinking about myself. I was thinking that perhaps for your own good you ought to stay in this evening."

"Are you frightened of staying alone?"

He almost said, Why on earth. But he changed his mind. He picked up the saltcellar, stopped its hole with his finger, turned it over, and examined its underside. Then he suggested sheepishly:

"There's a wildlife film on TV tonight. Tropical life in the Amazon. Something like that."

"So what's your problem?"

Again he stopped himself. Shrugged. And said nothing.

"If you don't feel like staying by yourself, why don't you go next door tonight? That knockout and her funny brother. They're always asking you. Or call your buddy Krantz. He'll be here in ten minutes. Like a shot."

"Netta."

"What?"

"Stay in tonight."

He had the impression that his daughter was concealing a sneer behind her raised coffee cup, over which he could see only her green eyes flashing at him, indifferently or slyly, and the outline of her ruthlessly cropped hair. Her shoulders were hunched, her head sunk between them, as though she were preparing herself for him to get up and beat her.

"Listen. The fact is I wasn't even thinking of going out this evening. But now that you've started your routine, I've remembered that I really do have to go out. I've got a date."

"A date?"

"You'll probably insist on a full report."

"Not at all. Just tell me who with."

"Your boss."

"What on earth for? Has he been converted to modern poetry?"

"Why don't you ask him? Why don't you two cross-examine each other? All right. I'll spare you the trouble. He called two days ago, and when I said I'd call you, he said not to bother. It was me he was calling. He wanted to make a date with me."

"What for, the national checkers championship?"

"Why are you so tense? What's got into you? Maybe it's just that he also has problems with spending the evening at home alone."

"Netta. Look here. I haven't got a problem with being alone. Why should I? It's just that I'd be happier if you didn't go out after your . . . after not feeling very well."

"It's all right; you can say the word 'attack.' Don't be scared. The censorship's been lifted. Maybe that's why you're trying to pick a quarrel with me."

"What does he want from you?"

"There's the phone. Call him. Ask him."

"Netta."

"How should I know? Perhaps they've started to recruit flat-chested girls. Mata Hari style."

"Let's get this straight. I'm not interfering in your affairs, and I'm not trying to pick a quarrel with you, but—"

"But if you weren't always such a coward, you'd simply say that you forbid me to go out, and if I don't do as you say, you'll beat the daylights out of me. Full stop. And that you especially forbid me to meet Le Patron. The trouble with you is that you're a coward."

"Look here," said Yoel. But he did not continue. Absently he put the empty brandy glass to his lips. Then put it gently on the table, as though taking care not to make a sound or hurt the table. The grayish evening light was in the kitchen but neither of them got up to turn the light on. Every movement of the breeze in the branches of the plum tree at the window sent complex shadows trembling on the ceiling and the walls. Netta reached out, shook the bottle, and refilled Yoel's glass. The small hand of the clock over the refrigerator hopped rhythmically from second to second. Yoel suddenly saw in his mind's eye a little pharmacy in Copenhagen where he had finally identified a well-known Irish terrorist and photographed him with a miniature camera concealed in a cigarette pack. For a moment the motor of the refrigerator found new strength, gave out a dull rumble, making the glasses tremble on the shelf, then changed its mind and fell silent.

"The sea won't run away," he said.

"What?"

"Nothing. I just remembered something."

"If you weren't such a coward, you'd simply say to me, Please don't leave me alone at home tonight. You'd say you find it hard. And I'd say, All right, with pleasure, why not. Tell me something: what are you afraid of?"

"Where are you supposed to meet him?"

"In the forest. In the Seven Dwarfs' house."

"Seriously."

"Café Oslo. Top of Ibn Gabirol Street."

"I'll give you a lift."

"Suit yourself."

"On one condition: that we eat something first. You've eaten nothing all day. And how will you get home?"

"In a carriage drawn by white horses. Why?"

"I'll come and get you. Just tell me what time. Or give me a call from there. But I want you to know that I'd rather you stayed in tonight. Tomorrow is another day."

"Are you forbidding me to go out this evening?"

"I didn't say that."

"Are you asking me nicely not to leave you alone in the dark?"

"I didn't say that either."

"So what are you saying? Could you try to make your mind up?"

"Nothing. Let's have something to eat, you get dressed, and we'll be off. I need to get some gas on the way. You go and get dressed and I'll make an omelette."

"Like she used to beg you not to go away? Not to leave her alone with me?"

"That's not true. It wasn't like that."

"Do you know what he wants from me? You must have some idea. Or some suspicion."

"No."

"Do you want to know?"

"Not especially."

"Are you sure?"

"Not especially. Actually, yes: what does he want from you?"

"He wants to talk to me about you. He thinks you're in a bad way. He has a hunch. That's what he said to me on the phone. Seems he's looking for some way to get you back to work. He says that we're living on a desert island here, and he and I have got to try to work out some solution together. Why are you against my seeing him?"

"I'm not against it. Get dressed and we'll go. While you get dressed I'll make an omelette. A salad. Something quick but good. Just a quarter of an hour, and we're off. Go and get dressed."

"Have you noticed that you've said 'get dressed' ten times? Do I look as if I'm not wearing anything? Sit down. What are you jumping around for?"

"So you won't be late for your date."

"Of course I'm not going to be late. You know that very well. You've already won the game. In three easy moves. I don't understand why you're still carrying on with this charade. After all, you're a hundred and twenty percent sure."

"Sure? Of what?"

"That I'm not going out. Shall we make an omelette and a salad? There's some cold meat left over from yesterday, the kind you like. There's some fruit yogurt too."

"Netta. Let's get this straight—"

"Everything's perfectly straight."

"Not to me it isn't. I'm sorry."

"You're not sorry. What's the matter, have you had enough of wildlife films? Were you wanting to run across to the woman next door? Or did you want to ask Krantz over to wag his tail at you? Or go to bed early?"

"No, but—"

"Listen. It's like this. I'm dying for tropical life in the Amazon or something like that. And stop saying you're sorry, when you've got exactly what you wanted. As usual. And you've got it without even using violence or exerting authority. The enemy didn't just give in; the enemy melted away. Now drink that brandy to celebrate the triumph of the Jewish brain. Just do me one favor: I haven't got the phone number. You call Le Patron and tell him yourself."

"Tell him what?"

"That it'll have to be some other time. That tomorrow is another day."

"Netta. Run and get dressed and I'll take you to the Café Oslo."

"Tell him I had an attack. Tell him you're out of gas. Tell him the house burned down."

"An omelette? Some salad? How about some chips? Would you like some yogurt?"

"Suit yourself."

19

Quarter after six in the morning. Blue-gray light and flashes of sunrise among the eastern clouds. A light morning breeze brings a smell of burning thistles from far away. And there are two pear trees and two apple trees whose leaves have started to turn brown with the tiredness of summer's end. Yoel is standing behind the house, in a white undershirt and running shorts, barefoot, holding the newspaper still rolled up in its wrapper. Once again he has failed to catch the delivery boy. His neck is stretched backward, his head toward the sky. He is watching flocks of birds migrating southward in arrowhead formation. Storks? Cranes? They are flying now over the tiled roofs of neat houses, over gardens and woods and citrus groves, absorbed eventually among the feathery clouds brightening in the southeast. After the orchards and fields will come rocky slopes and stone villages, valleys and ravines, and then at last the silence of deserts and the gloom of the eastern mountain ranges veiled in dull mist and, beyond more desert, plains of shifting sands, and beyond them the last mountains. In fact, he was intending to go to the garden shed to feed the cat and her kittens and to find a wrench to mend or change the dripping faucet beside the carport. He was only waiting for a moment for the newspaper boy to finish the street and turn around, and then he'd catch him on his way back. But how do they find their way? And how do they know that the time has come? Suppose that at some remote spot in the heart of the African jungle there is a sort of base, a sort of hidden control tower, which day and night transmits a regular, fine, high-pitched sound, too high for any human ear to catch, too sharp to be intercepted by even the most delicate, sensitive, and sophisticated sensors. The sound extends like an invisible beam from the equator to the far north, and the birds fly along it toward light and warmth. Yoel, like a man who has almost experienced a small illumination, alone in the garden whose branches had begun to turn gold in the glow of sunrise, instantly imagined that he could receive—not receive, sense—between two vertebrae in the base of his spine, the birds' African orientation sound. If only he had wings he would respond and go. The feeling that a woman's warm finger was touching or almost touching him a little above the coccyx was almost like a physical thrill. At that moment, for the space of a breath or two, the choice between living and dying seemed to be an insignificant one. A deep calm surrounded and filled him, as though his skin had ceased to divide the inner calm and the calm of the outside world, as though they had become a single calm. During the twenty-three years he had been in the service, he had perfected the art of small talk with strangers, chatting about the exchange rate or the advantages of Swissair or about French versus Italian women, while simultaneously studying the other party. Figuring out how he could crack the safe where the other kept his secrets. Like starting to solve a crossword puzzle with the easiest clues so as to get a purchase here and there on the harder parts. Now, at half past six in the morning in his own garden, a widower, unattached in almost every sense of the word, he felt the stirrings of a suspicion that nothing at all could be understood. That the obvious, simple, everyday things—the chill of dawn, the smell of burned thistles, a small bird among the apple leaves rusting from the touch of autumn, the feverish touch of the breeze on his bare shoulders, the scent of watered soil, and the taste of the light, the yellowing of the lawn, the tiredness of his eyes, the thrill he had briefly felt in the small of his back, the shame in the attic, the kittens and their mother in the shed, the guitar that had started to sound like a cello at night, a new pile of round pebbles on the other side of the hedge at the end of the Vermonts' porch, the yellow sprayer he had borrowed and ought to return to Krantz, his mother's and daughter's underwear hanging on the clothesline at the other end of the garden and billowing in the morning breeze, the sky that was clear now of migrating birds—everything held a secret.

And everything you have deciphered you have only deciphered for an instant. As though you were forcing your way through thick ferns in a tropical forest that closes in behind you as soon as you have passed, leaving no trace of your passage. As soon as you have managed to define something in words, it has already slipped—crawled—away into blurred shadowy twilight. Yoel recalled what his neighbor Itamar Vitkin had said to him once on the stairs that the Hebrew word *shebeshiflenu* in Psalm 136 could easily be a Polish word, whereas the word *namogu* at the end of chapter 2 of the Book of Joshua has an indubitably Russian sound to it. Yoel compared in his memory the neighbor's voice as he had pronounced *namogu* with a Russian accent and *shebeshiflenu* in mock-Polish. Was he really trying to be funny? Perhaps he was trying to say something to me, something that existed only in the space between the two words he was using? And I missed it because I wasn't paying attention? Yoel pondered for a moment the word "indubitably" that, to his surprise, he had suddenly whispered to himself.

In the meantime he had yet again missed the paper boy, who had apparently turned around at the end of the street and passed the house on his way back. To Yoel's astonishment and contrary to what he had imagined, it transpired that the boy, or the man, did not ride a bicycle but drove a shabby old Susita car, and threw the papers through the window into the garden paths as he went past. Perhaps he never even saw the note that Yoel had attached to the mailbox, and now it was too late to chase after him. A faint anger stirred within him at the thought that everything held a secret. But in fact secret was not the right word. It was not like a sealed book, but, rather, like an open book in which one could freely read clear, everyday things, indubitable things, morning, garden, bird, newspaper, but where one could also read in other ways. Combining, for example, every seventh word in reverse order. Or the fourth word of every other sentence. Or substituting certain letters. Or circling every letter that is preceded by a c. There is no limit to the number of possibilities, and each of them may indicate a different interpretation. An alternative meaning. Not necessarily a deeper, or more fascinating, or more obscure interpretation: just a totally different one. Without any resemblance to the obvious explanation. Or perhaps not? Yoel felt angry at the faint rage that stirred within him at these thoughts, because he always wanted to see himself as a calm, self-controlled man. How can you know which is the right access code? How can you discover, among the infinite combinations, the correct prefix? The key to the inner order of things? Moreover, how could you tell whether the code was universal, or whether it was personal, like a credit card, or unique, like a lottery ticket? How could you be sure that it didn't change every seven years, for example? Or every morning? Or every time somebody died? Especially when your eyes are tired and almost weeping from the effort, especially when the sky has cleared: the storks have flown away. Unless they were cranes.

And what if you never do decipher it? Surely you are being treated to special grace. You have been permitted to sense for an instant, in the moments before the dawn, that there really is a code. Through a half-felt touch on your spine. Now you know two things that you didn't know when you strained to make out the design of the elusive shapes on the wallpaper in the hotel room in Frankfurt: that there is an order, and that you will not decipher it. And what if there is not one code, but many? Suppose each person has his own code? You, who amazed the entire service when you managed to discover what it was that really made the blind millionaire coffee tycoon from Colombia seek out the Jewish secret service on his own initiative and volunteer an up-to-date mailing list of Nazis in hiding, from Acapulco to Valparaiso, how is it you are unable to distinguish between a guitar and a cello? Between a short circuit and a power outage. Between illness and longing. Between a panther and a Byzantine icon. Between Bangkok and Manila. And where the hell is that confounded wrench hiding? Let's go and fix the faucet, and then we'll turn the sprinklers on. Soon there'll be coffee too. That's it. Off you go. Forward march.

20

Then he put the wrench away. He filled a saucer with milk for
the cat and her kittens in the shed. He turned on the sprinklers
for the lawn and watched them for a while, then entered the
kitchen through the back door. Remembering that the newspaper
was still outside on the windowsill, he went back and picked it
up, then put on the percolator. While the coffee was brewing, he
made some toast. And took the jam and cheese and honey out of
the refrigerator, set the table for breakfast, and stood at the window. Still standing he glanced at the headlines of his newspaper,
but he could not take in what was written. He did take in that it
was time and switched on the transistor radio to listen to the
seven o'clock news, but by the time he remembered to listen to
what the newscaster was saying the news was over and the out-
look was fair to partially overcast with moderate temperatures
for the time of year. Avigail came in and said: "You've got it all
ready by yourself again. Just like a big boy. But how many times
have I told you not to take the milk out of the refrigerator till
it's needed. It's summer, and milk that's left out soon turns sour."
Yoel thought about this for a moment; he found no error in her
words. Although the word "sour" struck him as rather too strong.
He said: "Yes. That's right." Just after the beginning of Alex
Anski's chat show, Netta and Lisa joined them. Lisa was wearing
a brown housecoat with huge buttons down the front, and Netta
was in her light-blue school uniform. For a moment she struck
Yoel as not plain, almost pretty, and after a moment there came
into his mind the suntanned, mustached, thick-armed kibbutznik,

and he was almost glad that her hair, for all that she washed it in all kinds of shampoos, always looked greasy.

Lisa said: "All the night I didn't close my eyes. Again I have all kinds of pains. Whole nights I don't slep."

Avigail said: "If we took you seriously, Lisa, we should have to believe that you haven't slept a wink for the past thirty years. The last time you slept, according to you, was before the Eichmann trial. Since then you haven't slept."

Netta said: "You slep like logs, the pair of you. What's all this nonsense?"

"Sleep," said Avigail, "One says sleep, not slep."

"Tell that to my other granny."

"She only says slep to make fun from me," Lisa said ruefully. "I am sick with pains and this child is making fun from me."

"Of me," said Avigail. "One does not say 'make fun from me,' one says 'make fun of me.' "

"That's enough," said Yoel. "What is all this? That'll do now. If it goes on like this, they'll have to send the peacekeeping troops in."

"You don't slep at night neither," declared his mother sadly, and nodded her head several times as though she were mourning for him or agreeing with herself at last after a hard inner dispute. "You got no friends, you got no work, you got nothing to do with yourself, you'll end up making yourself ill or else religious or something. Better you should go swimming every day in the swimming pool."

"Lisa," said Avigail, "what a way to speak to him. What do you think he is, a baby? He's almost fifty years old. Leave him alone. Why do you get on his nerves all the time? He'll find his way in his own good time. Let him be. Let him live his own life."

"The one who really ruined his life," Lisa hissed in a whisper. And stopped in mid-sentence.

Netta said: "Tell me, why do you always jump up before we've finished our coffee and start clearing the table and washing up? Is it because you want us to finish and piss off? Or is it a protest against the oppression of men? Or do you want to make everyone feel guilty?"

"It's because it's already quarter to eight," Yoel said, "and you should have been off to school ten minutes ago. You'll be late again."

"And if you clear away and wash up, will that stop my being late?"

"All right. Come on, I'll give you a lift."

"I have pains," Lisa said softly, to herself this time, as though mourning, repeating the words twice, as though she knew no one would listen, "pains in the belly, pains in the side: all night I didn't slep, and then in the morning they make fun."

"All right," Yoel said. "All right, all right. One at a time, please. I'll deal with you in a minute." And he drove Netta to school without saying a word on the way about their meeting in the kitchen in the early hours of the morning, with the Safed cheese and the spicy black olives and the fragrant mint tea and the tender silence that went on for about half an hour, until Yoel went back to his room, without either of them violating it.

On the way back he stopped at the shopping center and bought his mother-in-law some lemon shampoo and a literary magazine she had asked him to get. When he got home he called and made an appointment for his mother with her gynecologist. Then, carrying a sheet, a book, a newspaper, a pair of glasses, a transistor radio, suntan lotion, two screwdrivers, and a glass of iced cider, he went outside to lie in the hammock. Out of professional habit he noticed from the corner of his eye that the Asiatic beauty who worked for the neighbors was carrying her shopping not in a heavy basket and bags but in a wire cart. Why hadn't they thought of it before? he asked himself. Why is everything always solved too late? Better late than never, he replied, in the words his mother always used. Yoel checked this sentence as he lay in the hammock, and found no error in it. But his rest was disturbed. He left everything behind and went to look for his mother in her room. The room was empty and flooded with morning light and tidy and pleasant and clean. He found her in the kitchen, still sitting shoulder to shoulder with Avigail; they were whispering animatedly while they chopped vegetables for a soup for lunch. The moment he entered they stopped talking. Again they looked to him as alike as two sisters even though he knew that really there was no resemblance. Avigail looked at him with the strong, bright face of a Slav peasant, with high, almost Mongolian cheekbones, her young blue eyes expressing resolute good nature and crushing kindness. His mother, on the other hand, looked like a bedraggled bird, with her elderly brown dress, her brown face, her pursed or sunken lips, and her bitter, offended expression.

"Well? So how are you feeling now?"

Silence.

"Are you feeling better? I've made an urgent appointment for you to see Dr. Litwin. Make a note. It's at two o'clock on Thursday."

Silence.

"And Netta got there just as the bell went. I jumped two traffic lights to get her there in time."

Avigail said:

"You've upset your mother and now you're trying to make amends, but it's too little and too late. Your mother is a sensitive person and she's not well. It would seem that one catastrophe was not enough for you. Think carefully, Yoel, before it's too late. Think carefully and maybe you'll decide to try a little harder."

"Of course," Yoel said.

Avigail said:

"There you are. You see. That's just what I mean. With that same coolness. That irony of yours. That self-control. That's how you finished her off. And that's how you'll bury all of us one by one."

"Avigail," said Yoel.

"All right. Off you go," said his mother-in-law. "I can see you're in a hurry. Your hand's already on the door handle. Don't let us keep you. And she loved you. Maybe you didn't notice, or

96

no one remembered to tell you, but she loved you all those years. Right to the end. She even forgave you for Netta's trouble. She forgave you for everything. But you were too busy. It's not your fault. You simply didn't have time, and that's why you didn't take any notice of her or her love for you until it was too late. Even now you're in a hurry. So go. What are you standing there for? Go. What is there for you to do in this old people's home? Off you go. Will you be back for lunch?"

"Maybe," said Yoel. "I don't know. We'll see."

His mother suddenly broke her silence. She addressed not him but Avigail, and her voice was soft and logical:

"Don't you start with all that again. Enough of that we heard from you already. All the time you just try to make us feel badly. What's the matter? What did he do to her? Who shut herself away like in a golden palace? Who didn't let the other one come in? So just you leave Yoel alone. And after everything that he did for you all. Stop making us all feel badly. As if you're the only one that's all right. What's the matter? We don't keep up the mourning properly? So do you keep up the mourning? Who was it went straight off to have her hair done and a manicure and a facial even before the stone-setting? So you can't talk. In the whole country there's no other man does half as much in the home as what Yoel does. All the time trying. Worrying. He doesn't even slep at night."

"Sleep," said Avigail. "One says sleep, not slep. I'm going to give you two Valium tablets, Lisa. They'll do you good. Help you calm down."

"See you later," said Yoel.

And Avigail said:

"Wait a minute. Come over here. Let me just arrange your collar for you if you have a rendezvous. And comb your hair, otherwise no young lady will even look at you. Are you coming home for lunch? At two o'clock, when Netta comes back? Why don't you simply bring her home from school?"

"I'll see," said Yoel.

"And if you get detained by some beauty, at least give us a

call to let us know. So we don't wait lunch for you till all hours. At least try to remember your mother's mental and physical condition, and don't add to her worries."

"Let him be, already," said Lisa. "He can come home whenever he likes."

"Listen how she speaks to her fifty-year-old child." Avigail chuckled, her face radiating forgiveness and overwhelming good nature.

"See you later," said Yoel.

As he was leaving Avigail said:

"What a pity. I could have just done with the car this morning, so I could take your electric pad in to be mended, Lisa. It helps you so much with your pains. But never mind, I'll walk. Why don't we both go for a nice stroll? Or shall I just call Mr. Krantz and ask him for a lift? Such a lovely man. I'm sure he'll come and get me and bring me back. Don't be late. Good-bye. What are you standing there in the doorway for?"

21

Later that afternoon, when Yoel was roaming around the house in his bare feet, with Yitzhak Rabin being interviewed on the transistor radio in his one hand, the other hand carrying the electric drill on its extension cord, looking to see where else he could ram its tip in and improve something, the telephone in the entrance hall rang. It was Le Patron again: How are you all, what's new, do you need anything? Yoel said, Everything's fine, we don't need anything, thanks, and added: Netta's not here. She's gone out. Didn't say when she'd be back. Why Netta, said the man on the other end of the line, laughing; what, haven't you and I got anything to talk about?

And with a smooth gear change he began to talk to Yoel about a new political scandal that had captured the headlines and was threatening to bring the government down. He refrained from expressing his own opinion, but gave an excellent sketch of the various differences. Warmly and sympathetically, as was his wont, he described conflicting standpoints as though each of them were the embodiment of a higher type of justice. Finally, with acute logic, he reduced what might happen to two scenarios, one of which, A or B, was inevitable. Until Yoel despaired of understanding what was required of him. Then the man altered his tone again and inquired with special affection whether Yoel felt like dropping into the office for a cup of coffee tomorrow morning: There are some good friends here who are dying to see you, longing for the benefit of your wisdom, and perhaps—who knows?—the Acrobat might feel like taking the opportunity to put one or two questions to you about some ancient case that you handled with your habitual expertise but that was perhaps not carried through to its ultimate conclusion, and one way or another the Acrobat still has a question or two sitting in his soft belly and only your assistance can finally bring him peace of mind. In a nutshell—it'll be fun and not in the least boring. Around ten tomorrow, then. Tsippy has brought one of her delicious homemade cakes in, and I fought like a tiger to make sure they didn't finish it so there'll be a few pieces left over for you tomorrow. And the coffee is on the house. Will you come? We'll have a good old chin-wag. Maybe we'll even turn over a new leaf.

Yoel asked whether he was supposed to infer that he was being called in for questioning. At once he realized that he had blundered badly. At the sound of the word "questioning" Le Patron let out a cry of pained alarm, like an elderly rabbi's wife who has just heard a shocking obscenity. Pish, the man exclaimed. Shame on you. We're just inviting you for a—how should I put it?—for a family reunion. There, there. We were offended but we've forgiven. We won't breathe a word to anybody about your little slip of the tongue. 'Questioning' indeed! I've forgotten all about it. Even electric shock wouldn't make me remember. Don't worry. It's finished. You never said it. We'll contain ourselves. We'll wait patiently for you to begin to miss us. We won't wake or rouse you. And of course we won't bear grudges. In general, Yoel, life's too short for taking offense or feeling insulted. Drop it. Let it rest in peace. In a nutshell, if you feel like it, look in for coffee tomorrow morning at ten, a bit earlier, a bit later, it doesn't matter. Whenever suits you. Tsippy knows you're coming. Come straight up to my room and she'll show you right in without asking any questions. I said to her, Yoel has the right of free access here for life. Without prior arrangement. Day or night. No? You prefer not to come? Then just forget all about this call. Just give Netta a pat from me. Never mind. Incidentally, we wanted to see you especially tomorrow so we could pass on some greetings for you from Bangkok. But we won't mess around with the message. Suit yourself. All the best.

100

Yoel said: "What!" But the man had decided, apparently, that the conversation had already gone on far too long. He apologized for taking up precious time. Once again he asked him to give his love to Netta and his best respects to the two ladies. He promised to arrive someday like a thunderbolt out of a clear sky, begged Yoel to get better and get plenty of rest, and took his leave with the words: "The only thing that matters is to take good care of yourself."

For several minutes Yoel sat almost motionless on the stool by the phone in the hall, with the electric drill on his lap. He dissected Le Patron's words into small units, which he then rearranged in various combinations. As he had been accustomed to do in his work. "Two scenarios, one of which is inevitable." Also "soft belly," "greetings from Bangkok," "fifty-year-old child," "loved right to the end," "electric shock," "right of free access," "rest in peace," "such a lovely man." These combinations seemed to him to point toward a small minefield. Whereas in the advice "take good care of yourself" he could not manage to find any error. For a moment he thought of using the drill to remove the tiny black thing from the entrance of the ruined Romanesque abbey. But he immediately came to his senses and realized that he would only spoil it. All he had wanted to do was to see what else he could fix, as best he could.

He went off again on his tour of the empty house, checking each room in turn. He picked up and folded a blanket lying in a heap at the foot of Netta's bed and laid it beside her pillow. He glanced at a novel by Jacob Wassermann on his mother's bedside table, and instead of putting it back as it was, open and upside down, he slipped a bookmark inside it and placed it at right angles next to her radio. He put her heap of medicine bottles and pillboxes in order. Then he sniffed Avigail Lublin's perfumes, attempting in vain to recall the odors to which he was trying to compare them. In his own room he stood for a few moments inspecting through his French priest's glasses the expression on the face of his landlord, Mr. Kramer, the section manager for El Al, in his old photograph in Armored Corps uniform, clasping

101

the hand of the Chief of Staff, General Elazar. The Chief of Staff looked gloomy and tired, his eyes half closed, like a man who can see his own death not far off and is not particularly moved. Whereas Mr. Kramer glowed in the picture with the radiance of someone who is turning a new page in his life and is certain that from now on nothing will be as it was, everything will be different, more festive, more exciting, more important. Finding a fly-speck on the landlord's chest in the photo, he immediately removed it with the nib of the pen that Ivria had had to dip in the inkwell every ten words. Yoel remembered coming home sometimes toward the end of a summer's day, when they were still living in Jerusalem, and sensing, rather than hearing, when he was still on the stairs the sound of the lonely neighbor's guitar coming from his own apartment. Taking care to enter like a thief, without making a sound as he turned the key in the lock, walking with silent steps, as he had been trained to do, he found his wife and daughter, one sitting in an armchair and the other standing with her back to the room and her face to the open window, through which could be seen, between a wall and the branches of a dusty pine tree, a small section of the barren Mountains of Moab beyond the Dead Sea. The two of them carried away by the music, and the man sitting and pouring his soul into his strings, with his eyes closed. On his face Yoel could sometimes see an unbelievable expression, a strange blend of melancholy longing and sober bitterness, which was concentrated perhaps in the left corner of his mouth. Unawares, Yoel tried to arrange his own face into such an expression. They were so alike, the mother and daughter, engulfed by the music, with the evening twilight spreading among the furniture, and the electric light not switched on, that on one occasion Yoel, tiptoeing in silently, kissed the back of Netta's neck, mistaking her for Ivria. Though he and his daughter were generally careful not to touch.

Yoel turned the photograph over, examined the date, and tried to calculate how much time had passed between the day it was taken and the sudden death of Chief of Staff Elazar. He imagined himself at that moment a limbless cripple, a sack of flesh topped by a head that was neither a man's nor a woman's but of some more delicate creature, more delicate than a child even, bright and wide-eyed, as though knowing the answer and secretly delighted at its almost unbelievable simplicity. Almost unbelievable; yet here it was almost in front of your eyes.

Then he went to the bathroom and took two new rolls of toilet paper out of the cabinet; he fitted one of them beside the seat and left the second as a spare in the other bathroom. He collected all the towels and threw them in the laundry basket, except for one, which he used to clean the washbasins before throwing it in as well. Then he hung up fresh towels in place of the old ones. Here and there he noticed a long woman's hair, held it up to the light to identify it, threw it in the toilet, and flushed it away. In the medicine cabinet he discovered a small oilcan which belonged outside in the shed, so he went to put it away there. On the way it occurred to him to oil the hinges of the bathroom window, and then those of the kitchen door, then those of the wardrobes, and while he was holding the oilcan he went around the house looking for other things he could oil. Finally, after oiling the electric drill itself and the hinges of the glider in the garden, he noticed that the can was empty and now there was no need to put it away in the shed. As he went past the living-room door he had a slight shock, because for an instant he thought he noticed a faint, almost imperceptible movement among the furniture in the dark. Apparently it was merely a rustling of the leaves of the giant philodendron. Or the curtain? Or something behind it? The movement ceased the moment he switched on the light in the room and peered in every corner, but seemed to stir again slowly behind his back when he switched it off and turned to leave the room. So he crept barefoot to the kitchen, without putting the light on, almost without breathing, and stared into the sitting room for a moment or two beyond the passthrough. There was nothing there but darkness and silence. Perhaps just a faint smell of overripe fruit. But as he turned to open the door of the refrigerator he sensed a sort of rustling again behind his back. He spun around very quickly and switched all the lights on. Nothing there. So he switched them off and went outside, as stealthily as a robber, crept around the house, peeped cautiously through the window, and almost managed to catch something stirring in the darkness in a corner of the room. Which ceased the moment he looked, or the moment he thought he had seen something. Was there a bird trapped in the room, fluttering and struggling to get out? Had the cat from the shed got into the house? Perhaps it was a lizard. Or a snake. Or just a draft stirring the leaves of the potted plant. Yoel stood there among the bushes patiently peering into the darkened house. The sea won't run away. It suddenly occurred to him that it was reasonable to suppose that instead of a screw there might be a long thin sliver sticking into the left hind paw which was an extension of the stainless-steel base. And that was why from above there was no sign of any nail or screw. The same cunning with which the artist had captured such a magnificent, tragic leap had made him decide in advance to make a base with a protruding lug all of a piece with it. This solution seemed logical and pleasing to Yoel, but its disadvantage was that there was no way of checking whether it was right or wrong without splitting the paw in question open.

The question therefore presented itself whether the constant agony of a blocked leap, an arrested takeoff, which never ceased for a moment yet was never achieved, or never ceased because it was never achieved, was harder or easier to bear than the smashing of the paw once and for all. To this question he could find no answer. What he did find was that meanwhile he had missed most of the television news. So he abandoned the rest of his ambush, went back indoors, and switched on the television. While the set was warming up there was only the voice of the newscaster describing mounting difficulties in the fishing industry, migrations of fish, defections among the fishermen, the indifference of the government, and when the picture finally appeared the report on this subject was more or less finished. There was nothing on the screen but a twilight sea, green-gray, empty of ships, looking almost congealed, with just a few gentle foam-flecked waves

104

flickering and disappearing in one corner of the picture as the man read the weather forecast, and the temperatures expected for the next day appeared over the sea. Yoel waited for two additional news items to conclude the magazine, watched a commercial, and when he saw that there was another to follow he got up, switched it off, put Bach's "Musical Offering" on the record player, and poured himself a brandy. For some reason he visualized the simile Le Patron had used at the end of his phone call: a thunderbolt out of a clear sky. He sat down on the telephone stool with the glass of brandy in his hand and dialed Arik Krantz's home number. His idea was to borrow Krantz's second car, the small one, for half a day or so, in order to leave his own car for Avigail when he went to the office at ten the next morning. Odelia Krantz told him in a voice seething with stifled animosity that Arye wasn't in and she had no idea when he would be back. If ever. Nor did she particularly care whether he came back or not. Yoel deduced that they had had another fight, and tried to recall what Krantz had told him while they were sailing the previous weekend, something about the redheaded bombshell he had fired into outer space in a hotel by the Dead Sea, totally oblivious of the fact that her sister was his wife's sister-in-law or something of the sort, more or less, and as a result he had been put on red alert. Odelia Krantz asked if she could give Arye some message, anyway, or leave him a note. Yoel hesitated, apologized, finally said: "No. Nothing special. Actually, why not, you could tell him I called and ask him to call me back if he gets in before midnight." And saw fit to add: "If it's not too much trouble. Thank you." Odelia Krantz said: "Nothing's too much trouble for me. But perhaps I could know with whom I have the pleasure?" Yoel knew how ridiculous was his unwillingness to pronounce his own name on the telephone, but nevertheless could not overcome a slight hesitation before he gave her his first name, thanked her again, and said good-bye.

Odelia Krantz said: "I'll be right over. I need to talk to you. Please. We don't know each other, but you'll understand. Just for ten minutes?"

Yoel said nothing. He hoped he would not have to use a lie. Noticing his silence, Odelia Krantz said: "You're busy. I understand. I'm sorry. I didn't mean to invade you. Perhaps we can meet some other time. If possible." And Yoel said warmly: "I'm very sorry. Just at the moment it's rather difficult for me." "Never mind," she said. "It's difficult for all of us."

Tomorrow is another day, he thought. And he stood up and took the record off, then went outside and walked in the dark as far as the end of the street to the fence around the citrus grove and stood there watching a rhythmic red flashing above the outline of the roofs and the trees, perhaps from warning lights on top of some tall mast. Just then between the blinks a line of milky-blue light flickered, moving slowly across the sky, as in a dream, a satellite, or perhaps a meteor. He turned and went back. That's enough, he muttered to the dog Ironside, who barked lazily at him on the other side of his fence. He intended to go home, to see if the house was still empty, if he had remembered to switch the record player off, and he also thought of pouring himself another glass of brandy. But to his utter amazement he found himself standing not at his own house but, by mistake, at the Vermonts' front door, and it gradually dawned on him that he must have absentmindedly rung the bell, because as he turned to beat a retreat the door opened and the man who looked like a large pink healthy Dutchman in an advertisement for choice cigars roared three times in English, "Come in." Yoel, having no alternative, obediently went in.

22

He went inside and blinked on account of the green aquariumlike light that suffused the living room: a light that seemed to be filtered through jungle foliage or rising from the ocean depths. The beautiful Annemarie, with her back toward him, was leaning over the coffee table arranging photographs in a heavy album. As she leaned over, her fine shoulder blades stretched the skin, and she struck Yoel as less seductive than childishly touching. Clutching her gold-colored kimono to her chest with a thin hand, she turned toward him and exclaimed happily in English: "Wow, look who's here!" adding in Hebrew: "We were beginning to be afraid that you found us repulsive." At that moment Vermont thundered from the kitchen: "I bet you'd care for a drink!" and began to reel off the options.

"Sit down over here," Annemarie said gently. "Relax. Breathe deeply. You look so tired."

Yoel asked for a Dubonnet, not so much because he was drawn to the taste of the drink as because of the sound of the name. Which in Hebrew made him think of bears. Or perhaps because a tropical forest dripping with mist and water was growing on three of the room's walls. It was a series of outsize posters, or else wallpaper or painting. The forest was a dense one, with a muddy track winding among the tree trunks under the leafy canopy. On either side of the track grew dark bushes, and among the bushes there were mushrooms. Yoel associated the word "mushrooms" with truffles, even though he had no idea what truffles looked like, had never set eyes on one; all he knew about them was that the word "truffle" sounded to him like "tearful." The greenish watery light in the room was filtered through the forest foliage. It was a trick of lighting, intended to give the room a sense of softness and depth. Yoel said to himself that everything, the wallpaper covering three of the walls, and the effect of the light combining with it, was indicative of poor taste. Nevertheless, for some childish reason, he could not contain the emotion aroused in him by the sight of the wetness sparkling at the base of the conifers and oak trees, as though the forest were full of fireflies. And a hint of still waters, a stream, a brook, a rivulet, meandering with flashes of brilliance through the lush dense greenery, among shadowy plants that might have been blackberries or red currants, although what red currants and blackberries might be Yoel had not the faintest idea; even their names he knew only from books. But he found that the light in the room helped his tired eyes. It was here, this evening, that it finally became clear to him that the white-hot summer light might be one of the reasons for his aching eyes. In addition to his new reading glasses, he should buy some sunglasses too.

Vermont, freckled, ebullient, brimming with assertive hospitality, poured Yoel a Dubonnet, and Camparis for himself and his sister, muttering all the while something about the secret beauty of life and how brainless bastards waste and destroy the secret. In the background, Annemarie put on a record of Leonard Cohen songs. And they talked about the political situation, the future, the approaching winter, the difficulties of the Hebrew language, and the advantages and disadvantages of the supermarket in Ramat Lotan as against the rival establishment in the neighboring residential development. The brother declared in English that for some time now his sister had been saying that Yoel ought to be photographed and blown up into a poster to show the whole world the image of the sensual Israeli male. Then he asked Yoel if he didn't find Annemarie an attractive girl. Everybody found her attractive, and even he himself was enchanted by Annemarie; he guessed that Yoel was not indifferent to her charms either. Annemarie asked, What's all this, the beginning of a blue evening? Preparing the ground for an orgy? And she angered her brother by saying, as though revealing the most secret cards to Yoel, that Ralph was actually dying to marry her off. At least, one part of him was, while another part—but that's enough, we mustn't bore you. Yoel said:

"You're not boring me. Go on."

And, as though to please a little girl, he added:

"You really are very pretty." For some reason these words were easy to say in English, and impossible in Hebrew. In company, in the presence of friends and acquaintances, his wife had sometimes said to him in English, casually, with a laugh, "I love you." But it had been only rarely and always when they were alone and always in utter seriousness that the same words left her mouth in Hebrew. Yoel had shuddered to hear them.

Annemarie indicated the photographs that were still scattered all over the coffee table and that she had been busy arranging in an album when Yoel arrived on his surprise visit. These were her two daughters, Aglaia and Thalia, now aged nine and six respectively; she had had them by different husbands, and she had lost them both in Detroit, at an interval of seven years, in two divorce suits in which she had also lost all her possessions, "down to my last nightie." Then they had turned the two little girls against her, so that they could be made to come and see her only by force, and the last time, in Boston, the older girl had not let her so much as touch her, while the younger one had spat at her. Her two ex-husbands had ganged up against her; they had jointly hired a lawyer and plotted her ruin down to the last detail. Their scheme was to drive her to suicide or out of her mind. If it hadn't been for Ralph, who had literally saved her—but she must apologize for talking so much.

So saying, she stopped. Her chin was dropped at an angle on her chest and she wept without making a sound, looking like a bird with a broken neck. Ralph Vermont put his arm around her shoulders, and after a moment's hesitation Yoel, sitting to her left, made up his mind and took her little hand in his; he sat looking at her fingers without saying anything until her sobs began to subside. He, who for several years had not so much as touched his own daughter. And the boy in this picture here, the brother explained in English, taken on the beach in San Diego, that's Julian Aeneas Robert, my only son; I lost him too in a complicated divorce suit ten years ago in California. So my sister and I were left alone, and here we are. What would you like to tell us about your own life, Mr. Ravid? Yoel, if you don't object? Has your family also split up? I've heard tell that in Urdu there's a word that if you write it from right to left it means adoration, and if you write it from left to right it means loathing. Same letters, same syllables, just depends which way. For God's sake, don't feel you've got to repay one personal story with another. It's not a business deal, just an invitation to get it off your chest, as they say. There's a story about some old rabbi from Europe who said the soundest thing in the whole world is a broken heart. But you mustn't feel obligated to trade one story for another. Did you eat already? If not, there's some excellent veal pie left over that Annemarie can warm up in two shakes. Don't be shy. Eat. Then we'll have coffee and watch a good film on the VCR, just as we always promised you."

But what could he tell them about? His neighbor's guitar, that started playing like a cello at night after he died? So he said:

"Thank you both. I've already eaten." And he added: "I didn't mean to disturb you. Please forgive me for intruding like this without warning."

Ralph Vermont roared in English: "Nonsense! No trouble at all!" And Yoel asked himself why it is that other people's disasters always seem a little exaggerated or ridiculous, too complete to be taken seriously. Nevertheless he was sorry for Annemarie and her pink, overfed brother. As though replying belatedly to the previous question but one, he smiled and said: "I had a relative—he's dead now—he used to say that everybody has the same secrets. Whether it's really true or not I don't know, and I believe there's even a small logical fallacy there. Once you compare secrets, they stop being secrets, so they're ruled out by definition.

But if you don't compare them, how can you know if they're the same or different? Never mind. Let's drop it."

Ralph Vermont said in English:

"It's goddam nonsense, with all due respect to your relative or whoever."

Yoel settled more comfortably in the armchair and stretched his legs out on the footrest. As though preparing himself for a deep and prolonged rest. The slim, childlike body of the woman sitting opposite him in a gold-colored kimono, with both hands repeatedly clutching its folds to her bosom, aroused in him images he preferred to thrust away. Her nipples squinted this way and that under the enfolding silk, and with every movement of her hand they trembled as though they were burrowing underneath the kimono, as though they were kittens wriggling and struggling to get out. He imagined his own broad, ugly hands roughly clasping those breasts and putting an end to their convulsions, like catching warm chicks. The stiffening of his member troubled him and even hurt him, since Annemarie did not take her eyes off him and he was unable to reach down unobtrusively and ease the pressure of his tight jeans on his erection, which was trapped at an angle. He imagined he noticed the shadow of a smile between brother and sister when he attempted to raise his knees. And he almost joined them in smiling, except that he was not certain if he had really noticed or only imagined what had passed between them. For a moment he felt rising within him the old complaint that Shealtiel Lublin used to voice against the tyranny of the sexual organ, which pushes you around and complicates your whole life, and doesn't let you concentrate and write the poems of Pushkin or invent electricity. His desire spread upward and downward from his loins, up his back toward his neck, and down his thighs to his knees and right down to his feet. The thought of the breasts of the beautiful woman sitting opposite him stirred a slight shiver around his own nipples. His imagination showed him her childlike fingers giving him rapid little pinches on his back and on the back of his neck, as Ivria used to do when she wanted to speed up his beat, and because he was thinking about Ivria's hands he opened his eyes and saw Annemarie's hands slicing triangles of quivering cheesecake for him and her brother. Suddenly he noticed a number of brown blotches on the back of her hand, from the pigment that was inescapably concentrating because of the aging of the skin. At once his desire went limp and instead there came gentleness and compassion and sorrow and also memories of her weeping a few minutes earlier and the faces of the girls and the boy that the brother and sister had lost in their divorce suits. He stood up and said he was sorry.

"Sorry for what?"

"It's time for me to go," he said.

"Out of the question," Vermont erupted, as though offended beyond his powers of forbearance. "You're not walking through that door. The night is still young. Sit down. Let's watch something on the VCR. What do you like? Comedy? A thriller? Maybe something a little racy."

Now he remembered that it was Netta who several times had urged him to call on these neighbors, and almost forbidden him to stay in by himself. And to his own surprise he said: "All right. Why not." He sat down again in the armchair and stretched his legs out comfortably on the footrest, and added: "I don't mind. Whatever you choose will be fine for me." Through the webs of tiredness he noticed a hurried whispering between brother and sister, who stretched her arms so that the sleeves of her kimono opened out like the wings of a bird in flight. She left the room and came back wearing a different kimono, a red one, and affectionately rested her hands on her brother's shoulders as he bent over and tinkered for a moment with the VCR. When he finished he straightened up heavily and tickled her under her ears the way one pets a cat to make it purr. They poured Yoel another Dubonnet, the lighting in the room changed, and the television screen began to flicker. Even if there is some simple way of liberating the predator in the figurine from the torment of its trapped paw without breaking it or hurting it, there is still no answer to the question how and where a creature will leap if it has no eyes.

112

The source of the torment, after all, is not in the point of fusion between the base and the paw, but somewhere else. Exactly as the nails in the Byzantine crucifixion scene were delicately fashioned and there was not a drop of blood exuding from the wounds, so that it was clear to the observing heart that it was not a matter of liberating the body from its attachment to the cross but liberating the youth with the feminine features from the prison of the body. Without breaking or causing further pain and torment. With a slight effort Yoel managed to concentrate and to reconstruct in his thoughts:

Boyfriends.

Crises.

The sea.

And the city at your fingertips.

And they shall be one flesh.

And rest in peace.

Shaking off his thoughts he saw that Ralph Vermont had softly left the room. Perhaps at this moment by secret agreement with his sister he was peeping through a crack in the wall, perhaps through a tiny pinhole in the boughs of one of the conifers in the sylvan backcloth. Silent, childlike, flushed, Annemarie sprawled on her back on the rug at his side, ready for a little love. Which Yoel was not ready for at that moment, because of the tiredness or because of the sadness that was inside him, but he was ashamed of his limpness and decided to lean forward and stroke her head. She took his ugly palm between her own hands and placed it on her breast. Pulling at a copper chain with her toes, she dimmed the forest lights still further. As she did so her thighs were exposed. Now he had no doubt that her brother was watching them and taking part, but he did not care, and in his heart he repeated the words "Itamar or Eviatar, what difference does it make now?" The leanness of her flesh, her hunger, her sobbing, the projection of her fine shoulder blades under the thin skin, unexpected nuances of little modesties within her eager yielding—there flickered through his head the shame in the attic, the thistles that surrounded his daughter, and Edgar Linton—Annemarie whispered in his ear: You're so considerate, so compassionate. And indeed from moment to moment he no longer considered the thrill of his own flesh, as though he had taken leave of his flesh and clothed himself in the flesh of the woman he was attending to, as though he were bandaging a tortured body, soothing a tormented soul, healing a little girl's suffering, attentive and precise to his fingertips, until she whispered to him: Now. And he, flooded with mercy and generosity, for some reason whispered back: Suit yourself.

When the comedy on the VCR was finished, Ralph Vermont returned and served coffee with special little mint chocolates wrapped in green foil. Annemarie left the room and returned this time wearing a burgundy blouse and baggy corduroy pants. Yoel looked at his watch and said, Well, comrades, it's the middle of the night, time for bed. At the door the Vermonts urged him to come and visit them again whenever he had a free evening. The ladies were all invited too.

Feeling limp and drowsy he walked across from their house to his, humming an emotional old Yaffa Yarkoni song. He stopped for a moment to say "Shut your trap, Ironside" to the dog, then went on humming and remembered Ivria asking him what had happened, why was he suddenly so happy, and answering her that he had found an Eskimo mistress, and her laughter and almost at that very moment his own discovery of how eager he was to deceive the Eskimo mistress with his own wife.

That night Yoel collapsed on his bed fully dressed and fell asleep almost as soon as his head touched the pillow. He only managed to remind himself that he had to return the yellow sprayer to Krantz and that it might after all be a kindness to make a date to see Odelia and listen to her troubles and complaints, because it's pleasant to be a good man.

23

At half past two in the morning Yoel was awakened by a hand on his forehead. For a few moments he did not stir, but went on pretending to be asleep, enjoying the gentle touch of the fingers that smoothed the pillow under his head and stroked his hair. But suddenly panic hit him and he sat up abruptly. Hurriedly switching on the light he asked his mother what the matter was and clasped her hand in his.

"I had a horrible dream. They were getting rid of you and the Arabs came and took you."

"It's all because of your quarrel with Avigail. What's the matter with the two of you? Just you make your peace with her tomorrow, and put an end to it all."

"Inside a sort of carton they put you. Like a puppy."

Yoel got out of bed. Gently but firmly he maneuvered his mother to the armchair, sat her down in it, and wrapped her in a blanket from his bed.

"Sit here for a while. Calm down. Then go back to sleep."

"I never slep. I got pains. I got bad thoughts."

"So don't sleep. Just sit here quietly. There's nothing for you to be frightened of. Do you want to read a book?"

And he got back into his bed and switched the light out. But he was quite unable to get back to sleep with his mother in the room, even though he could not even hear her breathing in the darkness. He imagined she was walking around the room without making a sound, peering into his books and notes in the dark, reaching into the unlocked safe. He turned the light on again quickly and saw his mother asleep in the armchair. Reaching out for the book by his bedside he remembered that *Mrs. Dalloway* had been left behind in the hotel in Helsinki and the woolen scarf that Ivria bought him had got lost in Vienna on the way back and his reading glasses were on the table in the sitting room. So he put on the square frameless glasses and began to study the biography of the late Chief of Staff Elazar that he had found here in the study among Mr. Kramer's books. In the index he found Teacher, his superior, who appeared neither under his real name nor under one of his nicknames, but under this assumed name. Yoel leafed through the book until he came to the praises that were heaped on Le Patron because he was one of the few who gave warning in time of the attack of Yom Kippur 1973. For purposes of emergency contact from abroad, Le Patron had been his brother. But Yoel found no brotherly affection in his heart toward the cold, needle-sharp man who was at this moment attempting, so Yoel suddenly deduced close to three in the morning, to set a cunning trap for him in the guise of an old family friend. A strange, piercing instinct like an alarm bell inside him started to warn that he must change his plans for tomorrow and not go to the office at ten o'clock. What were they going to use to catch or trip him? The promise he had made to the Tunisian engineer but not kept? The woman he had met in Bangkok? His negligence in the matter of the pale cripple? And because it was obvious to him that he would not get back to sleep tonight, he decided to devote the coming hours to preparing a line of defense for the next morning. When he began to think calmly, point by point, as was his habit, the room was suddenly filled with the sound of his mother's snoring. He turned the light off, pulled the bedclothes over his head, and tried vainly to block his ears and to concentrate on his brother, on Bangkok, on Helsinki. Finally he realized that unless he woke her up, he could not stay here. As he got up he felt that it was getting colder, so he covered his mother with a second blanket from his bed, stroked her brow, and went out into the hall carrying his mattress on his back. He stood there wondering where to go, except to the feline predator in the living room. He decided to go to his daughter's room, and there, on the floor, he laid out his mattress, covered himself in the single light blanket he had withheld from his mother, and promptly fell asleep till morning. The moment he woke up he glanced at his watch and knew at once that he was too late: the paper had already come and been thrown onto the concrete path from the window of the Susita despite the request outside to put it in the mailbox. When he got up he heard Netta muttering in her sleep in a provocative, challenging tone of voice, "And who isn't?" Then she fell silent. Yoel went out into the garden with no shoes on to feed the cat and her kittens in the shed, to see how the fruit trees were doing, and to watch the migrating birds for a while. Shortly before seven he went in and called Krantz to ask him to lend him his little Fiat for the morning. Then he went from room to room and woke the ladies. He returned to the kitchen just in time for the seven o'clock news and prepared breakfast while his eyes were ranging over the headlines in the newspaper. Because of the newspaper he did not concentrate on what the newscaster was saying, and because of the radio he did not manage to take in what was in the headlines. As he was pouring his coffee he was joined by Avigail, as fresh and fragrant as a Russian peasant who had spent the night in a haystack. She was followed by his mother, with a grumpy expression and sunken lips. Netta arrived at half past seven. She said: Today I'm really late. Yoel said: Have something to drink and let's go. I'm free today till nine-thirty. Krantz and his wife are coming in convoy and bringing their Fiat, so that our car can be here for you, Avigail.

Then he started to clear away the breakfast things and wash them up in the sink. Netta shrugged and said quietly:

"Suit yourself."

117

24

"We've tried offering her someone else," said the Acrobat, "but it doesn't work. She won't bestow her favors on anyone but you."

"You fly out in the early hours of Wednesday morning," Teacher recapitulated, his after-shave lotion smelling like ladies' perfume; "you meet on Friday, and by Sunday night you'll be home again."

"Just a moment," said Yoel. "You're going a little too fast for me." He stood up and walked over to the only window, at one end of the long, narrow room. The sea showed green-gray between two tall buildings, with a motionless bundle of clouds pressing down on it. That's how autumn begins here. Six months or so had passed since he left this room for the last time intending never to return. He had come to hand over his job to the Acrobat, to say good-bye, and to return the things he had kept all those years in his safe. Le Patron had said, "with a final appeal to your head and heart," that he could still withdraw his resignation, and that, insofar as it was possible to glimpse into the future, one could see that Yoel, if he agreed to continue, was marked out as one of three or four favorite candidates, the best of whom would be sitting in a couple of years' time on the southern side of this desk, when he himself went off to settle in a vegetarian village in Galilee, to devote himself to observation and longings. Yoel had smiled at this and said, Sorry, but it seems I'm not cut out for your southern side.

Now, as he stood at the window, he noticed the shabbiness of the curtains and a certain sadness, almost an elusive air of neglect, that hung over the Spartan office. So contrary to Le Patron's scent and manicured nails. The room was neither large nor well lit, and in front of the black desk flanked by two file cabinets there was a coffee table with three wicker armchairs. On the walls there was a reproduction of a landscape of Safed by the painter Rubin and another of the walls of Jerusalem by Litvinowsky. At the end of a bookshelf laden with legal tomes and books about the Third Reich in five languages there was a pale-blue Jewish National Fund collection box with a map of Palestine from Dan to Beersheba more or less, not including the triangle of the Negev, and like flyspecks scattered here and there on the map were the blotches that the Jews had managed to purchase from the Arabs up to 1947. The inscription on the box said: "Bring Redemption to the Land." Yoel asked himself if there had really been years when he had ached to inherit this gloomy office, to bring Ivria here on the pretext of asking her advice about changing the furniture or the curtains, to seat her facing him across the desk, and, like a child showing off to his mother who had misjudged him and underestimated him all these years, let her digest the surprise in her usual way: Look, from this unpretentious office he, Yoel, now controlled a secret service said by some to be the most sophisticated in the world. It might occur to her to ask him, with her delicate, forgiving smile playing around her long-lashed eyes, what the essence of his work was. To which he would reply modestly, Well, when all's said and done, I'm just a sort of night watchman.

The Acrobat said:

"Either we arrange a meeting for her with you, she said to our contact man, or else she won't speak to us at all. Obviously you managed to win her heart at your previous meeting. And she also insists that it should be in Bangkok again."

"It's been more than three years," said Yoel.

"A thousand years in your sight are as a day," declared Le Patron. He was stocky, podgy, cultivated, his thinning hair neatly groomed, his fingernails impeccably rounded, his face that of an honest man who inspires confidence. And yet there glimmered at

119

times in those placid, slightly clouded eyes a certain courteous cruelty, as of an overfed cat.

"I should like to know," Yoel said quietly, as though from the depth of his thoughts, "precisely what she said to you. What words she used."

"Well it's like this," replied the Acrobat, ostensibly with no connection to the question. "It turns out that the lady knows your first name. Would you happen to have some explanation for that?"

"Explanation," said Yoel. "What is there to explain? Evidently I must have told her."

Le Patron, who had hardly spoken so far, now put on his reading glasses, picked up from his desk, as though handling a sharp splinter, a rectangular note, a piece of a card, and read in English infected with a slight French accent:

"Tell them I have a lovely present that I'm prepared to hand over in a personal meeting with their man Yoel, the one with the tragic eyes."

"How did it come?"

"Curiosity," said the Acrobat, "killed the cat."

But Le Patron ruled:

"You're entitled to know how it came. Why not? She passed the message via the Singapore representative of an Israeli construction company. A clever chap. Plessner. The Czech. You may have heard of him. He was in Venezuela for a few years."

"And how did she identify herself?"

"That's precisely the nasty side of the story," said the Acrobat. "It's the reason you're sitting here now. She identified herself to this guy Plessner as 'a friend of Yoel.' How do you account for that?"

"Evidently I must have told her. I don't remember. Of course I realize it's against the rules."

"Of course," the Acrobat hissed, "some people are above the rules."

He shook his head several times, uttering four times, with long pauses between, the word "tsk."

120

Finally he snorted viciously:

"I just can't believe it."

Le Patron said:

"Yoel. Do me a personal favor. Eat Tsippy's cake. Don't leave it on the plate. I fought like a tiger yesterday to make sure they left you a piece. She's been in love with you for the past twenty years, and if you don't eat it she'll murder the lot of us. You haven't touched your coffee either."

"All right," said Yoel, "I get it. What's the bottom line?"

"Just a minute," said the Acrobat. "Before business I've got another little question. If you don't mind. Apart from your name, what else—how shall I put it?—slipped out of you in Bangkok?"

"Hey," said Yoel, "Ostashinsky. Don't overdo it."

"I only ask it," said the Acrobat, "because it turns out, lover-boy, that this chick knows that you're Romanian, that you're fond of birds, and even that your little girl's called Netta. So maybe it would be better if you took a deep breath, thought hard, and then explained to us nice and sensibly who's overdoing what here precisely, and why, and what else the lady knows about you and about us."

Le Patron said:

"Children. Please. Behave yourselves."

He fixed his eyes on Yoel. Who did not speak. He remembered the games of checkers between the man and Netta. And remembering Netta, he tried to understand the point of reading sheet music if you can't play an instrument and don't want to or intend to learn. And he saw in his thoughts the poster that used to hang in her old room in Jerusalem, which had become his room, showing a cute little kitten snuggling in its sleep against an Alsatian dog with the responsible look of a middle-aged banker. Yoel shrugged, because the sleeping kitten gave no hint of curiosity. Le Patron addressed him gently:

"Yoel?"

He concentrated and directed his tired eyes at Le Patron.

"So I am being accused of something?"

The Acrobat, rather formally, declared:

"Yoel Rabinovich wants to know if he's being accused."

And Le Patron:

"Ostashinsky. That will do. You may stay, but strictly in the background, if you please." Turning to Yoel he continued: "After all, you and I are—how should I put it?—more or less brothers. And quick on the uptake too. As a rule. So the answer is definitely negative. We're not accusing. Not investigating. Not muckraking. Not poking our noses in. Pouf. At most we're a little surprised and saddened that such a thing should have happened to you of all people, and we trust that in future, et cetera. In a word: we are asking a very great kindness of you, and if, heaven forbid, you refuse—but surely you couldn't refuse us a tiny little favor."

Yoel therefore picked up the plate with Tsippy's cake on it from the coffee table, inspected it closely, seeing mountains, valleys, and craters, hesitated, and suddenly visualized the temple garden in Bangkok three years before. Her straw bag like a barrier on the stone seat between his body and hers. The cornices covered with brightly colored ceramic mosaics with twisted golden horns, the gigantic wall mosaics that went on for several meters displaying scenes from the life of the Buddha in childish hues that were at variance with the melancholy, calm features, the carved stone monsters contorting before his eyes in the scorching equatorial light, lions with dragons' bodies, dragons with tigers' heads, tigers with serpents' tails, something that looked like flying jellyfish, wild combinations of monstrous deities, gods with four identical faces looking to the four winds and with many limbs, columns standing on six elephants each, pagodas twirling heavenward like thirsty fingers, apes and gold, ivory, and peacocks, and at that instant he knew that he must not err this time, because he had made enough errors in the past and others had paid for them. That the heavy, shrewd man with cloudy eyes, who was sometimes code-named his brother, and the other man in the room, a man who had once frustrated the massacre of the Israel Philharmonic Orchestra by a gang of terrorists, were both his mortal enemies and that he must not let himself be taken in by their smooth talk or fall into their traps. It was they who had taken Ivria from him, it was because of them that Netta— And now it was his turn. This Spartan room, this whole modest building surrounded by a high stone wall and hidden by a dense row of cypresses, penned in behind much taller new buildings, and even the National Fund collection box with the flyspecks on it, and the giant Larousse-Gallimard globe, and the single ancient telephone, a square black telephone from the 1950s made, perhaps, of Bakelite, its numbers yellowed and half-erased in their holes, and outside waited the corridor whose walls had at long last been lined with cheap sheeting made to look like wood over a layer of acoustic insulation, and even the cheap noisy air-conditioning in Tsippy's office and the promise of her undying love— everything was against him and everything here was set to trap him cunningly, with honeyed lips and perhaps also with veiled threats, and if he was not careful he would be left with nothing or there would be nothing left of him; until then they would not let him be; or perhaps it would be so anyhow, even if he was as careful as he possibly could be. Rest in peace, Yoel said to himself, moving his lips.

"Pardon?"

"Nothing. Just thinking."

Facing him, in the other wicker armchair, the middle-aged youth with the tight, drumlike paunch also sat saying nothing. They called him the Acrobat here, although his appearance did not in the least suggest the circus or the Olympic Games; he looked more like a Labor Party veteran, a former pioneer and road builder who had risen over the years to become manager of a cooperative store or a regional boss in a dairy collective.

Meanwhile Le Patron saw fit to allow the silence to continue up to the precise moment that he sensed to be the right one. Then he leaned forward and asked softly, almost without disturbing the silence:

"What do you say, Yoel?"

123

"If the tiny favor is that I come back to work, the answer's negative. That's final."

Again the Acrobat began to shake his head slowly from side to side, as though refusing to believe his own ears, and while he did so, with long pauses, he once again uttered four times the word "tsk."

Teacher said:

"*Bon*. We'll let it go for the time being. We'll come back to it later. We'll drop it on condition you go and meet your lady friend this week. If it turns out that she can offer, this time, even a quarter of what she granted you last time, then I can afford to send you for a romantic reunion with her even in a gold carriage drawn by white horses."

"Buffalo," said Yoel.

"Pardon?"

"Buffalo. I believe that's the correct plural. You don't see horses in Bangkok, white or otherwise. Everything that's drawn is drawn by buffalo. Or oxen. Or a similar beast called a banteng."

"And I have no particular objection, if you see a reasonable need, you can feel free to reveal to her even the maiden name of your step-great-grandmother on your in-laws' cousin's side. Silence, Ostashinsky. Don't interrupt."

"Just a minute," said Yoel, unconsciously running his finger, as he often did, between his shirt collar and his neck. "You haven't drawn me into anything, yet. I'll need to think it over."

"My dear Yoel," Le Patron began, as though embarking on a eulogy, "you are most mistaken if you have formed the impression that freedom of choice exists here. We do uphold such freedom, with certain reservations, but not in this particular instance. Because of the excitement that you apparently aroused last time in this lovely lady, the ex-wife of you-know-who, the goodies she heaped on you and indeed on us, there are a fair number of people who are alive today, and not merely alive but living it up, without suspecting even in their wildest dreams that were it not for those goodies they would be defunct. So we're not talking about a choice between a romantic cruise and a holiday in Bermuda. We're talking about a job of a hundred or a hundred and five hours from door to door."

"Just give me a moment," Yoel said wearily. He closed his eyes. For six and a half hours Ivria had waited for him in vain at Ben-Gurion Airport one winter's morning in '72 when they had arranged to meet at the inland terminal to catch a flight to Sharm-esh-Sheikh for a holiday together and he hadn't been able to find a safe way to let her know that he would be late coming back from Madrid because at the last moment he'd managed to pick up a lead, which had turned out after a couple of days to be a complete dead end, a waste of time. And after waiting for six and a half hours she had got up and gone home to relieve Lisa, who was looking after Netta, at that time eighteen months old. When Yoel got home at four o'clock the following morning she was waiting for him, sitting at the kitchen table in her white clothes, with a glass of long-cold tea in front of her, and without raising her eyes from the oilcloth she had said, Don't bother to explain; you're so tired and disappointed and I can understand you even without explanations. Many years later when the Asiatic woman had left him in the temple garden in Bangkok he had experienced exactly the same peculiar sensation: someone was waiting for him, but they wouldn't wait forever and if he was late it would be too late. But for the life of him he could not discover where in that miserable, ornamental city the woman had vanished to; she had simply been swallowed up in the crowd after imposing on him a decisive condition, to break off contact forever, which he had accepted and had promised; so how could he chase after her now even if he knew where?

"When do you need to have my answer by?" he asked.

"Now, Yoel," said Teacher with a sort of grimness Yoel had never seen in him before. "Now, there's nothing to soul-search about. We're sparing you all that. We're not giving you any choice."

"I need to think it over," he insisted.

"By all means," the man conceded at once. "Think it over. Why not? Think about it until you've finished Tsippy's cake. After that go along to Operations with the Acrobat, and they'll sit down with the two of you to work out the details. I forgot to mention that the Acrobat is going to be your launcher."

Yoel lowered his aching eyes toward his feet. As though, to his great confusion, they had suddenly started speaking to him in Urdu, that language in which, according to Vermont, the meaning of each word depends on whether it is read from right to left or vice versa. Unenthusiastically he took a single forkful of the cake. The sweetness and creaminess filled him with sudden rage, and without moving in his chair he began to struggle and writhe like a fish that has swallowed the bait, the hook catching in his flesh. He visualized the sticky lukewarm monsoon in a Bangkok swathed in warm mist. The slurping sound of the lush tropical vegetation swollen with poisonous sap. The buffalo sinking in the mud of the narrow street, and the elephant drawing a cart laden with bamboo and the parrots in the treetops and the little long-tailed monkeys leaping around and making faces. The wooden shacks in the slums and the stagnant sewage in the streets, the thick creepers, the flights of bats even before the last light of day dies away, the crocodile raising its snout from the water of the canal, the glow of the air rent by the humming of millions of insects, the giant ficus trees and maples, the magnolias and rhododendrons, the mangroves in the morning mist, the forests of mahogany trees, the undergrowth teeming with ravenous creatures, the plantations of bananas and rice and sugarcane rising from the shallow mud of fields flooded with foul water, and rising over everything dirty, glowing steam. There her cool fingers were waiting for him; if he allowed himself to be beguiled into going, he might never come back, and if he refused to obey, he might be too late. Slowly, with particular gentleness, he put the plate down on the arm of the wicker chair. And standing up he said: "Well. I've thought. The answer's negative."

"Exceptionally"—Le Patron pronounced the word with emphatic, measured politeness, and Yoel felt he noticed the French background lilt growing slightly, almost imperceptibly, stronger— "exceptionally, and against my better judgment"—he nodded his chin up and down as though lamenting over something that was irreparably broken—"I shall wait," and he shot a glance at his watch, "I shall wait another twenty-four hours for a rational answer. By the way, do you happen to have any idea what the problem is with you?"

"Personal," said Yoel, ripping out with a single inner motion the hook embedded in his flesh.

"Get over it. We'll help you. Now you go straight home without stopping on the way and tomorrow morning at eleven o'clock"—again he glanced at his watch—"at ten past eleven o'clock, I'll give you a call. And I'll send someone to fetch you for a meeting with Operations. You'll leave first thing Wednesday morning. The Acrobat will be your launcher. I'm sure you'll work splendidly together. As always. Ostashinsky, will you apologize nicely? And you can also finish the piece of cake that Yoel's left. Good-bye. Take care on the way. And don't forget to give Netta an old man's fondest love."

25

But the man decided not to wait till the following morning. The same day, in the late afternoon, his Renault appeared in the little street in Ramat Lotan. He walked around it twice, tried all the doors twice to make sure they were properly locked, and finally turned toward the garden path. Yoel was there, bare to the waist and perspiring, pushing the rumbling lawnmower. Over its roaring he made a sign to the visitor: Hang on. Nearly finished. The visitor in turn signaled: Switch off, and Yoel, by force of twenty-three years' habit, obediently switched off the mower. A sudden silence fell.

"I've come to solve the personal problem you were hinting at. If the problem is Netta—"

"I'm sorry," said Yoel, realizing at once from his experience that this was the precise moment of crisis and decision. "It's a pity to waste our time, because I'm not going, and that's final. I've told you already. And as for my private affairs, well, they happen to be just that—private. Full stop. On the other hand, if you've just come around for a game of checkers, why not go inside; I believe Netta has just come out of the shower and she's sitting in the living room. Sorry I'm not free."

With these words he tugged on the starter cord and at once the earsplitting roar of the lawnmower broke out again and silenced the visitor's reply. He turned and went into the house, and emerged a quarter of an hour later, by which time Yoel had moved over to the corner of lawn at the side of the house, under Lisa's and Avigail's windows. He mowed this little corner doggedly a second, a third, and a fourth time, until the Renault had disappeared. Only then did he switch off the motor, put the machine away in the garden shed, get out a rake, and start piling the grass cuttings into precisely equal little heaps; and he continued doing this even after Netta came out, barefoot, her eyes flashing, wearing a loose shirt over baggy pants, and asked him without preamble whether his refusal was in some way connected with her. Yoel said, What on earth, and after a moment he corrected himself and said, Well as a matter of fact perhaps yes, a little, but not in the narrow sense of course, that is, not because there's any problem about leaving you. There's no problem at all about that. And after all, you're not alone here.

"So what *is* your problem," Netta said, as a statement, delivered with a touch of scorn. "Isn't this meant to be a fateful journey to save the homeland or something?"

"Well. I've done my share," he said. He smiled at his daughter, although it was rare for a smile to pass between them. She replied with a bright expression that struck him as new and yet not new, including a very faint quiver at the corner of the lips that used to show on her mother's face when she was young, whenever she was straining to conceal emotion. "Look. It's like this. It's very simple. I'm through with that madness. Tell me, do you remember, Netta, what Vitkin used to say to you when he used to drop in to play his guitar of an evening? Do you remember his words? He used to say, I've come in search of signs of life. And that's where I've got to. That's what I'm in search of now. But there's no hurry. Tomorrow is another day. I feel like sitting at home and doing nothing for another few months. Or years. Or forever. Until I manage to discover what's going on. Or what it's all about. Or am convinced, from personal experience, that it's impossible to discover anything. So be it. We'll see."

"You're a funny character," she said earnestly, almost with a kind of suppressed enthusiasm. "But you might just happen to be right about this particular trip. Either way, you'll suffer. So suit yourself. Don't go. Stay here. I quite like it that you're around the house all day, or in the garden, or that sometimes you turn up in the kitchen in the middle of the night. You're rather nice sometimes. Only stop looking at me like that. No, don't go in yet. Just for a change I'll make supper for us all tonight. 'Us all'—that means you and me, because the grannies have walked out on us. They've got a party at the Sharon Hotel for Open Heart for Immigrants; they'll be back late."

26

The simple, open, habitual things—the morning chill, the scent of burned thistles wafted from the nearby citrus grove, the chirping of the swallows before sunrise on the branches of the apple tree now rusting from autumn's touch, the shudder from the chill on his bare shoulders, the scent of watered soil, the savor of the light at dawn, which soothed his aching eyes; the recollection of their overwhelming desire in the night in the orchard on the edge of Metullah and of the shame in the attic, the guitar of the dead Eviatar or Itamar that in the darkness seemingly continued to produce the sound of a cello; the thought that, seemingly, they died together in an accident with their arms around each other, if it really was an accident; the thought of the moment he drew his gun in the crowded bus terminal in Athens; forests of dimly lighted conifers in Annemarie and Ralph's home; miserable Bangkok swathed in thick steaming tropical mist; Krantz's wooing, the eagerness to be friends and to make himself helpful and indispensable—whatever he pondered or remembered seemed at times enigmatic. In everything, as Teacher put it, there could at times be discerned signs of things being beyond repair. "Retarded chick that she was," Shealtiel Lublin used to say about Eve; "where were her brains? She ought to have eaten an apple from the other tree. But the joke is, before she could have the brains to eat from the second tree she had to eat from the first one. And that's how we all got screwed up." Yoel pictured the image conjured up by the word "indubitably." And he also tried to envisage the meaning of the phrase "thunderbolt out of a clear sky." It seemed to him that by these efforts he was somehow fulfilling his allotted task. Yet he knew he lacked the power to find an answer to a question that in fact he had not managed to formulate. Or even to understand. And that was why so far he had not deciphered anything, and apparently never would. On the other hand, he found pleasure in preparing the garden for the approaching winter. At Bardugo's Nurseries at Ramat Lotan junction he bought saplings and seeds and pesticides and some sacks of fertilizer. He was leaving the pruning of the roses till January-February, but he already had a plan. Meanwhile he was turning over the flower beds with a fork he found near the cat and her kittens in the garden shed, and digging in the concentrated fertilizer, deriving a physical thrill from inhaling its sharp, provocative smell. He planted a ring of assorted chrysanthemums. And also carnations, gladiolus, and snapdragons. He pruned the fruit trees. He sprayed the edges of the lawn with weed killer to make them as straight as a ruler. He returned the sprayer to Arik Krantz, who was delighted to come over to collect it and have coffee with Yoel. He trimmed the hedge both on his side and on the Vermonts', who were once again wrestling laughingly on their lawn, panting like a pair of puppies. In the meantime the days grew shorter, the evenings drew in earlier, the night chill intensified, and a sort of strange orange vapor encompassed the glow of lights that hung over Tel Aviv at night beyond the neighboring rooftops. He felt no urge to go into the city, which was, as Krantz had said, at his very fingertips. He had almost entirely given up his nocturnal expeditions too. Instead, he sowed sweet peas in the thin soil along the walls of the house. There was peace and calm again between Avigail and Lisa. In addition to their voluntary work five mornings a week in the institution for deaf-mutes on the edge of the suburb, they had started attending the local yoga class every Monday and Thursday evening. As for Netta, she remained faithful to the Cinemathèque, but she had also signed up for a lecture series on the history of Expressionism at the Tel Aviv Museum. Only her interest in thistles seemed to have disappeared forever. Even though just at the end of their street, in the strip of wasteland between

132

the end of the asphalt and the wire fence around the citrus grove, the late-summer thistles were turning yellow and gray, and some of them as they expired produced a kind of savage death-blossom. Yoel wondered if there was any connection between the end of her passion for thistles and the little surprise she sprang on him one Friday afternoon, when the neighborhood was empty and quiet as the light turned gray and there was no sound to be heard apart from the faint, pleasant sound of recorder music through a closed window in another house. Clouds came down almost to the treetops and from seaward the thunder sounded dully, as though smothered by the clouds' cotton wool. On the concrete path, Yoel had laid out little black plastic bags, each containing a carnation plant, and started planting them one by one in holes he had prepared previously, advancing from the outside inward toward the door of the house, when suddenly there was his daughter planting from the inside outward. That night, around midnight, when Ralph had led him flabbily, joyfully home from Annemarie's bed, he found his daughter waiting for him in the entrance hall bearing a cup of herbal tea on a little tray. How she had known the precise moment of his return and that he would come back thirsty, and for herbal tea of all things, Yoel could not understand and it did not occur to him to ask. They sat down in the kitchen and chatted for a quarter of an hour about her examinations and about the intensification of the debate about the future of the occupied territories. When she went to her bedroom to sleep he accompanied her as far as her door and complained in a whisper, so as not to wake the old ladies, that he had nothing interesting to read. Netta thrust a book of poetry called *Blues and Reds* by Amir Gilboa into his hand, and Yoel, who was not a reader of poetry, leafed through it in bed until close to two o'clock, and among others he found on page 360 a poem that really said something to him, even though he did not entirely understand it. Later that night the first rains began to fall, and continued without interruption for most of Saturday.

27

It sometimes happened on these autumn nights that the smell of the cold sea infiltrating through the closed windows, the sound of the rain drumming on the roof of the garden shed behind the house, the whispering of the wind in the darkness, kindled within him suddenly a sort of quiet, powerful joy that he had not imagined he was still capable of feeling. He was almost ashamed of this strange joy: he found it almost ugly that he should feel that the fact he was alive was a great achievement, whereas Ivria's death indicated her failure. He knew well that people's acts, all people, all acts, acts of passion and ambition, acts of fraud, seduction, accumulation, evasion, acts of malice and defection, competition and flattery and generosity, acts meant to impress, to attract attention, to be engraved on the memory of the family or the gang or the country or the human race, petty acts and grandiose ones, calculated or uncontrollable or vicious acts, almost all of them almost always take you somewhere you had not the slightest intention of ending up. This general and constant deflection or diversion of people's various actions Yoel tried to call in his heart the universal practical joke, or the black humor of the universe. But he changed his mind: the definition struck him as too high-flown. The words "universe," "life," "essence" were too grandiose for him; they seemed ridiculous. So he contented himself in his thoughts with what Arik Krantz had told him about his one-eared regimental commander in the artillery, Jimmy Gal by name, you must have heard of him, he used to say that between any two points there was only one straight line, and that line was always full of imbeciles.

And since he had remembered the one-eared regimental commander, he thought more and more frequently about the order that Netta had received to report to the recruiting center in a few weeks' time. By summer she would have finished school and the exams would be over. What would come to light during her physicals at the recruiting center? Was he hoping that they would take Netta in the army? Or was he apprehensive? What would Ivria have demanded that he do when the order to report arrived? At times he imagined the strong kibbutznik with the thick arms and the hairy chest, and he said to himself in English and almost aloud: Take it easy, buddy.

Avigail said: "If you ask me, that girl is healthier than the lot of us."

Lisa said: "All the doctors, they should be healthy, don't know from their life. A man which lives from other people's illnesses, what good would it do for him if they all got better suddenly?"

Netta said: "I'm not intending to ask for a deferment."

And Arik Krantz: "Listen carefully, Yoel. Just give me the green light, and I'll fix the whole business up for you in a flash."

While outside, between showers, drenched half-frozen birds sometimes appeared at the window, standing immobile at the tip of a dripping branch as though they were a wonderful winter fruit that had grown, despite the fallen leaves and hibernation, on the gray fruit trees.

28

Two more times Teacher tried to change Yoel's mind and persuade him to take on the undercover mission to Bangkok. Once he telephoned at quarter of six in the morning, and so ruined the ambush for the newspaper man again. Without wasting words on apologies for the early hour he began to share with Yoel his thoughts concerning the alternation of prime ministers under the rotation agreement between the coalition parties. As usual he indicated with few words and in sharp, clear lines the advantages, sketched the disadvantages in a few trenchant sentences, depicted simply and precisely three possible scenarios for the immediate future, and skillfully linked each foreseeable development to the consequences that would inevitably flow from it. Although, naturally, he resisted the temptation to prophesy—even by so much as a hint—which of the developments he described would be more likely to materialize. When Teacher used the words "system malfunctioning," Yoel, who was, as always, the passive party in conversation with him, tried to visualize the malfunctioning system as a kind of frenzied electronic device that had gone wrong and started to run amok, chirping and wailing and flashing colored lights and electric sparks shooting from its contacts and a smell of burning rubber. Meanwhile he lost the thread. Until Le Patron addressed him in an imploring, didactic tone, with the hint of a French lilt in his pronunciation of the words: "And if we miss Bangkok and as a result somebody dies someday whose death could have been prevented, you, Yoel, will have to live with that."

Yoel said quietly:

"Look. You may or may not have noticed. I am living with it, even without Bangkok. I mean with exactly what you just said. And now I'm sorry but I've got to hang up, so that I can try to catch the newspaper man; if you like I'll call you back later at the office."

The man said:

"Think, Yoel."

And so saying he hung up and cut the conversation short.

Next day the man invited Netta to meet him at eight o'clock in the evening at the Café Oslo at the top of Ibn Gabirol Street. Yoel gave her a lift and let her out on the other side of the street. "Cross carefully," he said to her. "Not here—use the crossing." Then he drove home and took his mother to Dr. Litwin for an urgent examination, and an hour and a half later he went back to pick Netta up, not at the Café Oslo but, as before, across the street. He waited, sitting at the wheel of the car, for her to come out, because he could not find a parking space and in fact he did not even look for one. There came into his mind his mother's stories about their journey, in the carriage and on foot, from Bucharest to Varna and the dark space in the belly of the ship with rows and rows of beds full of men and women spitting, perhaps throwing up over each other, and the fierce fight that broke out between his mother and his bald, rough, unshaven father, with scratching, shrieking, belly kicks, and bites. And he had to remind himself that the stubbly murderer was not his father but, apparently, more or less a stranger. His father in the Romanian photograph was a thin, sallow man in a brown striped suit, whose face conveyed embarrassment or humiliation. And perhaps even cowardice. He was a Roman Catholic, who had walked out of his mother's life and his own when Yoel was a year old.

"Suit yourself," said Netta after a few traffic lights on their way home, "but as far as I'm concerned you can go. Why not? Maybe you really ought to."

There was a long silence. His driving, between the interchange and the complicated traffic lights, through the stream of lights and crossings and dazzling headlights, in the middle lane between strained nerves on either side, was precise and relaxed.

"Look," he said, "as it stands now—" and he stopped to search for words and she neither interrupted nor helped. Again they were silent. Netta noticed a resemblance between his driving and his way of shaving in the morning, the cool, controlled way he ran the razor over his cheeks and his precision in the cleft of his chin. Ever since she was a child she had always enjoyed sitting near him on the marble edge of the bathroom basin and watching him shaving, even though Ivria used to scold them both for it.

"What was it you were going to say," she said. It was not a question.

"The way it looks now, I wanted to say, I'm just no good at that kind of thing any more. It's like, say, a pianist who has rheumatism in his fingers. Better to give up in time."

"Bullshit," said Netta.

"Just a minute. Let me explain better. These . . . these trips, the jobs, it works, if at all, only if you concentrate a hundred percent. Not ninety-nine. Like a man who juggles with plates in an amusement park. And I can't concentrate any more."

"Suit yourself. Stay or go. It's just a pity you can't see yourself, let's say, shutting off the empty gas tank and opening up a full one by the kitchen door: as concentrated as can be."

"Netta," he said suddenly, swallowing his saliva, hurriedly changing into fourth gear as he was released for a moment from the crush of the traffic. "You still haven't grasped what it's all about. It's either us or them. Never mind. Let's drop it."

"Suit yourself," she said. They had reached the Ramat Lotan junction, Bardugo's Nurseries were closed by now, or maybe they were still open despite the late hour. Half the lights were on. Out of professional habit he made a mental note that the door was closed and there were two cars there with their side lights on.

They exchanged no further words until they were home. When they had arrived Netta said:

"One thing though: I can't stand the way your friend drenches himself with perfume. Like an old ballerina."

And Yoel said;

"Too bad. We've missed the news."

29

And so autumn faded into winter almost without any noticeable change. Even though Yoel was on the alert, watching for any sign, however faint, that would enable him to pinpoint the moment of transition. The sea breezes stripped the last brown leaves off the fruit trees. At night the reflection of the lights of Tel Aviv shimmered on the low winter clouds with an almost radioactive glare. The garden shed was clear of the cat and her kittens, though Yoel occasionally observed one or another of them among the garbage cans. He no longer brought them leftovers of chicken. In the late afternoon the street stood empty and desolate, lashed by wet gusts. In every garden the tables and chairs were folded up and put away. Or covered with plastic sheets, the chairs placed upside down on the tables. At night the even, unexpressive rain beat at the shutters and drummed drearily on the asbestos awning over the kitchen door. In two separate places in the house signs of leaks appeared; Yoel did not attempt to treat them superficially, but chose to climb up to the roof on a ladder and change six roof tiles. Which stopped both the leaks. He took advantage of the opportunity to adjust the angle of the television aerial slightly, and the reception did indeed improve.

At the beginning of November, thanks to Dr. Litwin's contacts, his mother was admitted to Tel Hashomer Hospital for tests. And it was decided that she should have an urgent operation, to remove something small but superfluous. The senior consultant in the department explained to Yoel that there was no immediate danger, although, of course, at her age, who could tell? In fact they did not issue guarantees at any age. Yoel preferred to note the words in his memory without further inquiry. He almost envied his mother a day or two after the operation, seeing her with gleaming white bedclothes, surrounded by boxes of chocolates, books and magazines, and vases of flowers, in a special room with only one other bed. Which was empty.

Avigail barely stirred from Lisa's bedside for the first couple of days, except when Netta came to relieve her after school. Yoel placed the car at Avigail's disposal, and she would deliver all sorts of instructions and warnings to Netta and drive home to shower, change her clothes, sleep for an hour or two, and then return and release Netta and stay by Lisa's side until four o'clock in the morning. Then she drove home again for three hours' rest, and at half past seven she reappeared at the hospital.

For most of the day the room was filled by their fellow volunteers from the Committee for Retarded Children and from Open Heart for Immigrants. Even the Romanian neighbor across the street, the gentleman with the ample posterior who reminded Yoel of an overripe avocado, arrived with a bunch of flowers, bent over and kissed Lisa's hand, and talked to her in their own language.

After the operation his mother's face beamed like that of a village saint in a church mural. Lying on her back with her head on a pile of clean white pillows, draped in a sheet as though in snow she looked compassionate and flowing with human kindness. She interested herself tirelessly in the details of her guests' health, and their children's, and their neighbors', dispensing reassurance and good advice to one and all, behaving toward her visitors like a guru distributing amulets and blessings to pilgrims. Several times Yoel sat facing her on the empty bed, next to his daughter or his mother-in-law or between the two of them. When he asked how she was, if she still had any pain, if she needed anything, she replied with a beaming smile, as though in the grip of a profound inspiration:

"Why do you do nothing? Catching flies all day long. Better you should get into some business. Mr. Krantz wants you so much with him. I give you a little money. So buy something. Sell. See people. If you go on like this, you'll go mad soon or you'll start to get religious."

Yoel said:

"It'll be all right. The important thing is for you to get well soon."

And Lisa:

"All right it won't be. Just look what a sight you are. Sitting and eating your heart out."

For some reason her last words aroused apprehension in him and he forced himself to go back to the doctors' room. What he had learned by experience in his work enabled him to extract from them without any difficulty everything he wanted to know, except for the thing he wanted to know most of all, namely, how long in this business the intervals between one episode and the next were likely to last. The senior consultant and the junior doctors all insisted that there was no way of knowing. He tried to decipher their thoughts in one manner or another but he finally came to believe or almost to believe that they were not conspiring to withhold the truth from him, so that here too there was no way of knowing.

30

As for the pale cripple he might have seen twice in the street in Helsinki on the sixteenth of February, the day of Ivria's death, either he was born without limbs or it was in an accident that he lost his arms at the shoulder and his legs at the groin.

At quarter past eight in the morning, after taking Netta to school and Lisa to the physiotherapy center, and driving home and handing the car over to Avigail, Yoel shut himself in Mr. Kramer's study that served as his bedroom. He examined the question of the cripple again under a magnifying glass, under a focused beam of light; he carefully studied the plan of Helsinki, scrutinized his route from the hotel to his meeting with the Tunisian engineer at the railroad station, and he found no error. It was true that the cripple looked familiar to him. And it was true that during an operation it is your duty to stop everything while you discover the meaning of any familiar face you have seen, even if it is only vaguely familiar. But now, with careful hindsight, Yoel agreed with himself almost beyond any doubt that he saw the invalid in the street that day in Helsinki not twice but once only. His imagination had deluded him. Once again he broke his memory of that day into its smallest details, reconstructing the segments of time on a large sheet of squared paper that he ruled off into units of a quarter of an hour. He concentrated on this work until half past three in the afternoon, internalizing the plan of the city, working calmly and stubbornly, bent over the desk, straining to rescue one crumb after another from oblivion, to piece together the sequence of events and places. The smells of the city almost came back to him. Every couple of hours he made himself a cup of coffee. By midday the tiredness of his eyes had begun to impede his work, and he made use alternately of his Catholic priest's intellectual glasses and the pair that suggested a family doctor. Finally there began to emerge a working hypothesis that he could live with: at five past four, by the electric wall clock over the counter of a branch of the Nordic Investment Bank, he had changed eighty dollars and walked out onto the esplanade. Consequently the crucial time was limited to between fourfifteen and five-thirty. The place was, apparently, the corner of Marikatu and Kapitaninkatu, outside a large ochre building in the Russian style. He could visualize almost with certainty a newsstand nearby. That was where he had seen the poor wretch in the wheelchair. Who seemed familiar because he may have reminded him of a figure he had seen once in a museum; it might have been the one in Madrid, a portrait that had also seemed familiar to him at the time because it reminded him of a face he knew.

Whose face? Here there was a danger of slipping into a vicious circle. Best to concentrate. To return to Helsinki on the sixteenth of February and to hope that the logical conclusion was that it was apparently a case of a reflection of a reflection. Nothing more. Let us suppose a crescent moon is reflected on a patch of water. And let us say that the water projects the reflection of the moon onto a darkened window in a hut on the edge of the village. So it happens that the glass, even though the moon rises in the south and the window faces north, suddenly reflects something that is apparently impossible. But in reality it is reflecting not the moon-in-the-clouds but only the moon-in the-water.

Yoel asked himself whether this hypothesis could also help him in his present investigations; for example, in connection with the African beam guiding the migrating birds? Could a patient, protracted, systematic examination of a reflection of a reflection reveal a hint, a crack through which you could peer at something that was not accessible to us? Or was it, rather, the opposite: do the contours become fainter from reflection to reflection, as in a copy of a copy, the colors fading, the shapes becoming blurred, the whole being darkened and distorted?

One way or another, at least in the matter of the cripple, his mind was at rest for the time being. Only, he observed that most forms of evil are out of the question for somebody with no arms or legs. The invalid in Helsinki really did have the face of a girl. Or, rather, of something gentler still, gentler than a child, shining and wide-eyed as though he knew what the answer was, and quietly rejoiced over its unbelievable simplicity, though here it was, before your very eyes.

31

Yet there was still the question of whether the wheelchair was self-propelled or whether, which seemed more reasonable, there was somebody pushing it. And if so, what did that person look like?

Yoel knew that here he must stop himself. This was a line that must not be crossed.

That evening, sitting in front of the television, he looked at his daughter. With her hair cropped so fiercely that only bristles were left, with her forceful jawline whose undoubted origin was in the Lublin family, but which had skipped Ivria to reappear in Netta, with her clothes that struck him as neglected, his child looked to him like a lean recruit who has been put into trousers that are too big and baggy for him, but who tightens his lips and says nothing. In her eyes there sometimes flickered a sharp, greenish glint, which preceded by a few seconds the utterance "Suit yourself." This evening she had chosen as usual to sit stiffly upright on one of the dark straight-backed chairs in the corner by the dining table. As far away as possible from her father sprawling on the sofa and her grandmothers in their armchairs. When the plot thickened on the television screen, she would make her usual asides, such as "The cashier is the killer," or "Either way she won't be able to forget him," or "He'll end up crawling back to her on all fours." Sometimes she would say: "How stupid. How can she know that he doesn't know yet?"

If one of the grandmothers (it was generally Avigail) asked her to make tea or get something from the refrigerator, Netta would obey without a word. But whenever anyone commented on her clothes, her haircut, her bare feet, her fingernails (generally these comments emanated from Lisa), Netta would silence her with a single acid remark and continue sitting silently on her stiff-backed chair. On one occasion Yoel tried to come to his mother's aid on the question of Netta's social isolation or her unfeminine appearance. Netta said:

"Femininity isn't exactly your subject, is it?"

And so she silenced him.

What was his subject? Avigail implored him to sign up for some courses at the university, both for the pleasure and to broaden his horizons. His mother maintained that he ought to go into business. Several times she hinted to him about a considerable sum of money she had available for a sensible investment. And there was a persistent appeal from a former colleague who kept promising Yoel the moon if he would agree to join him as a partner in a private detective agency. Krantz tried to inveigle him into some sort of nocturnal adventures in a hospital; Yoel did not even bother to grasp what he was talking about. Meanwhile Netta sometimes lent him a book of poetry that he would leaf through to the accompaniment of the rain beating at the windows as he lay in bed at night. Occasionally he would stop and read a few lines, sometimes even a single line over and over again. Among the poems of Y. Sharon in his book *A Period in a City* he discovered the last five lines on page 46 and he read them four times in succession before deciding to agree with the poet, even though he was not entirely certain that he had fully understood his meaning.

Yoel had a blue notebook in which over the years he had been writing down general notes about epilepsy, which was the disease it was generally agreed that Netta had suffered from—albeit in a mild form—since she was four. Some of the doctors, admittedly, were not entirely in agreement with this diagnosis. Ivria had joined them with a poignant fervor that verged at times on hatred. Yoel had dreaded this state, but he was also fascinated by it, and occasionally, indirectly, somewhat inflamed it. He had

147

never shown the notebook to Ivria. He had always kept it locked in the safe. After he left his job and took early retirement, the safe was emptied and transferred from Jerusalem to Ramat Lotan, and Yoel saw no further need to hide it in the floor, nor even to keep it always locked. If he did lock it, it was only because of the notebook. And the drawings of cyclamens that his daughter had made for him when she was at nursery school or starting primary school, because it was his favorite flower. Had it not been for Ivria, he thought, not for the first time, he might have called his daughter Rakefet, "cyclamen." But between Ivria and himself there was a permanent state of mutual awareness and compromise. Hence he had not put his foot down about the name. Both Ivria and Yoel had hoped that their daughter would get better when the time finally came for her to become a woman. And they were both revolted by the thought that one day some thick-limbed youth would take her away from them. They were sometimes aware that Netta came between them, and yet they knew that when she went away they would be left face to face with each other. Yoel was ashamed of the secret joy he sometimes derived from the thought that Ivria's death meant her defeat and that he and Netta had finally been victorious. The word "epilepsy" means "fit" or "seizure." Sometimes it is an idiopathic disease and sometimes it is organic, and there are cases where it is both. In the second case it is a question of a disease of the brain, not a mental illness. The symptoms are attacks of contractions accompanied by loss of consciousness, occurring at irregular intervals. Frequently the attacks are announced by manifestations, known collectively as the aura, such as dizziness, tinnitus, blurred vision, and melancholia, or else its opposite, euphoria. The fit itself takes the form of a stiffening of the muscles, difficulty in breathing, cyanosis, and sometimes also biting the tongue, and the appearance of blood-flecked foam on the lips. This phase, known as the tonic phase, rapidly passes. It is generally followed by the clonic phase, which lasts for a few minutes and is manifested in violent involuntary contractions of various muscles. These contractions too gradually pass. Then the patient may immediately wake up or may lapse into a deep and prolonged slumber. In either case he will have no recollection of the fit on waking. There are some patients who have several attacks a day, and others who have only one in three or even five years. Some experience them during the day and others while they are asleep at night.

And Yoel had also written this in his notebook:

Apart from grand mal, there are those who suffer only from petit mal, the only symptom of which is a momentary loss of consciousness. Approximately half of epileptic children suffer initially only from this minor form of the disease. Some, either in the absence of major or minor fits or in addition to them, experience various kinds of psychologically based attacks, which occur with varying frequency, but always suddenly: vagueness, phobias, paresthesia (disturbance of the sensations), migration urges, fantasies accompanied by hallucinations, outbursts of rage, and states of stupor during which the patient may perform dangerous or even criminal acts that he will entirely forget about on waking.

Over the years the illness in its more severe forms is liable to bring about a change of personality or even a mental breakdown. But in most cases the patient, between attacks, is as sane as anybody else. It is common knowledge that constant insomnia is liable to aggravate the illness, just as the aggravation of the illness is liable to cause constant insomnia in the patient.

Nowadays the illness is diagnosed, except in marginal and ambiguous cases, by psychomotor encephalography, which consists of measuring and recording the electrical waves in the brain. The focus of the problem is in the temporal lobe. Sophisticated tests may sometimes reveal latent epilepsy, an electrical impulse in the brain with no external manifestation, in members of patients' families. These relations are not ill themselves, they do not even suspect that anything is wrong, but they are liable to pass the illness on to their offspring. The illness is almost always hereditary, even if it is usually passed on in quiescent or dormant form from generation to generation, and manifests itself in only a few of the descendants.

And because there have always been a lot of people who pretended to suffer attacks, as long ago as 1760 de Haan discovered in Vienna that a simple inspection of the pupil of the eye generally suffices to detect malingerers. Only in the case of a genuine fit do the pupils not react by contracting when a light is shone into them.

The most widely practiced form of treatment is the avoidance of physical or mental shocks and the controlled use of tranquilizers such as various combinations of bromides and barbiturates.

The saying "Coitus is a kind of epileptic fit" is variously ascribed to the ancient writers Hippocrates and Democritus. Aristotle, on the other hand, in his treatise *On Sleep and Waking*, maintains that epilepsy resembles sleep and that in a certain sense sleep is epilepsy. Here Yoel inserted a question mark in brackets, because at least on the surface he had imagined that coitus and sleep were opposites. A medieval Jewish sage applied to the illness the words of Jeremiah 17:9: "The heart is the most deceitful of all things, desperately sick; who can fathom it?"

Yoel also wrote the following in his notebook, among other things:

Ever since ancient times the falling sickness has trailed a sort of magic train behind it. Many different people have attributed to sufferers either inspiration or possession or prophecy, enslavement to demons or the opposite, a special closeness to the divine. Hence such appellations as *morbus divus* or *morbus sacer* or *morbus unaticus astralis* or *morbus daemoniacus*.

Yoel, who, in spite of Ivria's fury, had accepted that Netta was suffering from a mild form of the illness, refused to be impressed by all these names. There was no sign of lunacy or astral influence in his daughter the day the thing first made its appearance when she was four years old. It was not he, but Ivria who rushed off and called for an ambulance. He, though he had been trained to react quickly, had hesitated because he thought he noticed a faint trembling on the little girl's lips, as though she were teasing them, and holding back her laughter. And then when he pulled himself together and ran toward the ambulance carrying her in his arms, he fell down the steps with her and his head hit the railing; when he came to, he was in the emergency ward and the diagnosis had been virtually agreed on and Ivria only said to him quietly: I'm surprised at you.

Since the end of August there had been no symptoms. Yoel was mainly worried now about the question of her call-up. After weighing various ideas in his head, including Le Patron's influence, he decided to wait and not do anything until the results of the physical examinations she would have to undergo at the recruiting center came.

During these windy, rainy nights he sometimes went to the kitchen at two or three in the morning in his pajamas, his face crumpled from tiredness, and there was his daughter sitting stiffly at the kitchen table, with an empty teacup in front of her and with her ugly glasses on, indifferent to a moth fluttering around the ceiling light, totally absorbed in her reading.

"Good morning, young lady. May I inquire what her ladyship is reading?"

Netta calmly finished the paragraph, or the page, and only then, without raising her eyes, she answered:

"A book."

"Shall I make us some tea? Or a sandwich?"

To which she always replied merely:

"Suit yourself."

So the pair of them sat eating and drinking tea in the kitchen in silence. Though they sometimes put their books down and conversed in low, intimate voices. About the freedom of the press, for example. Or the appointment of a new attorney general. Or the disaster at Chernobyl. And sometimes they sat and drew up a shopping list to replenish the supply of drugs in the bathroom cabinet. Until the newspaper thudded on the garden path, and Yoel dashed out in vain to catch the delivery man. Who had invariably vanished.

32

As the festival of Hanukkah approached, Lisa made doughnuts
and latkes, bought a new Hanukkah menorah and a pack of colored candles, and asked Yoel to find out the order of lighting the
candles. When Yoel protested in astonishment, his mother, in
the grip of a powerful emotion that almost made her shoulders
shake, replied that always, every year, poor dear Ivria had wanted
this, to celebrate the Jewish festivals a little according to the tradition, but you, Yoel, you were never at home, and whenever you
were, you never let her say a word.

Yoel, taken aback, began to remonstrate with her, but for
once his mother interrupted him and rebuked him forgivingly, in
a tone of faint sadness: You always remember only what suits
you.

To his surprise, Netta chose to take Lisa's side for once. She
said:

"So what, if it makes somebody feel good. For all I care, you
can light Hanakkuah candles or even bonfires for Lag B'Omer.
Whichever." Just as Yoel was about to shrug and give in, Avigail
stormed onto the battleground with fresh forces. She put her arm
around Lisa's shoulder and said in her warm, patiently peda-
gogical voice:

"Excuse me, Lisa, but I am a little surprised at you: Ivria
never believed in God, and she had no respect for him either. She
could never tolerate all that religious ceremonial. We cannot understand what you are talking about all of a sudden."

Lisa, stubbornly repeating the expression "poor dear Ivria," fought pugnaciously for her view, with a ferocious expression on her face and a captiously sarcastic tone in her voice:

"You should all be ashamed of yourselves. It's not even a year yet since the poor dear died, and already I can see you want to kill her again."

"Lisa. Stop it. That's enough for today. Go and have a rest."

"All right then. I'll stop it. There's no need. She is not here any more and I'm the weakest one here, so all right. Let it be. I'll give in to you. Just like she always gave in about everything. Only don't you think we've forgotten already, Yoel, who didn't say kaddish for her. Her brother had to say it instead of you. Only from shame I thought I would die on the spot."

Avigail gently expressed an anxiety that since the operation, and of course because of it, Lisa's memory was going. These things did happen and the medical literature was full of examples. Even her specialist, Dr. Litwin, had said that there might be some mental changes. On the one hand, she couldn't remember where she'd just put her duster or where the ironing board was, and on the other hand, she could remember things that never happened. This religiosity must be yet another disturbing symptom.

Lisa said:

"Myself, I'm not religious. On the contrary. It revolts me. But poor dear Ivria always wanted to have a bit of tradition in the house and you always laughed in her face, and now you are spitting on her. Less than a year she's been dead and you're trampling on her grave already."

Netta said:

"I don't remember her as a religious freak. A bit spaced out maybe, but not religious. It could be my memory's gone too."

And Lisa:

"All right then, why not. So let them bring the biggest medical specialist and he can examine everybody one after the other and decide once and for all who is mental and who is normal and who is senile already and who wants to banish the memory of poor dear Ivria out of this house."

Yoel said:

"That's enough. The three of you. We're through now. If it goes on like this they'll have to call in the border patrol."

Avigail remarked sweetly:

"In that case, I give in. There's no need to quarrel. Let it be as Lisa wishes. Let her have her candles and her unleavened bread. In her present condition we must all give in to her."

So the argument was brought to an end and peace reigned until that evening. Then it became clear that Lisa had forgotten her original wish. She dressed up in her black velvet party dress and laid out her homemade doughnuts and latkes. But the menorah, unused, was silently placed on the shelf over the fireplace in the living room. Not far from the figurine of the tormented predator.

Three days later, on the same shelf and without asking anyone, Lisa suddenly placed a small photograph of Ivria that she had fitted in a dark wooden frame.

"So that we should remember her a bit," she said, "so that she should have some memorial in this house."

For ten days the photograph stood at the en of the shelf in the living room and none of them said a word. Through her glasses that suggested a stern family doctor of an earlier generation Ivria looked out of the photograph at her ruined Romanesque abbeys, which hung on the wall opposite. Her face looked even thinner than it had when she was alive, her skin fine and pale; her eyes behind her glasses were bright and long-lashed. In her expression in the photograph, Yoel deciphered, or thought he could decipher, an unlikely mixture of melancholy and slyness. Her hair streaming down over her shoulders had turned half gray. Her fading beauty still had the power to compel Yoel to avoid looking that way. Almost to avoid going into the living room. Several times he even missed the nine o'clock news. More and more he found himself glued to the biography of Chief of Staff Elazar that he had found in Mr. Kramer's bookcase. The details of the judicial inquiry fascinated him. He spent long hours shut in his room, bent over Mr. Kramer's desk, arranging various details on charts he had drawn on graph paper. He used the fine-nibbed pen, and derived a certain satisfaction from the need to dip it in the inkwell every ten words or so. Sometimes he imagined he had sniffed out a certain inconsistency in the findings of the Commission of Inquiry that had found the Chief of Staff guilty, even though he knew well that without access to the primary sources he could produce nothing more than guesses. Nevertheless, he strained to dismantle what was written in the book, down to the finest details, and then to piece them together again, first in one sequence and then in another. Facing him on the desk stood Mr. Kramer in his neatly pressed uniform adorned with badges of rank and decorations, his face radiant with self-satisfaction, clasping the hand of Lieutenant General Elazar, who looked tired and withdrawn, his attention held by something far beyond Kramer's shoulder. There were moments when Yoel imagined he could hear from the living room the strains of ragtime or quiet jazz. He did not hear it with his ears but through the pores of his skin. For some reason, the result was that he went often, almost every other evening, into the forests of Annemarie and Ralph's living room.

After ten days or so, since no one had said anything about the picture of Ivria that she had put up, Lisa placed next to it a photograph of Shealtiel Lublin, with his bushy walrus mustache and British policeman's uniform. It was the picture that had always stood on the desk of Ivria's study in Jerusalem.

Avigail knocked at Yoel's door. She entered and found him hunched over Mr. Kramer's desk. His priest's glasses lent him a scholarly or monkish air. He was copying key passages from the book about the Chief of Staff onto his grid.

"Sorry to intrude, but we must have a little talk about your mother's condition."

"I'm listening," said Yoel, putting his pen down on the sheet of paper and leaning back in his chair.

"We can't brush it aside. It would be quite wrong to pretend that she's entirely normal."

"Go on," he said.

"Haven't you got eyes, Yoel? Can't you see that she's getting more and more scatterbrained by the day? Yesterday she swept the garden path, and then she just went on and started sweeping the street. She was twenty yards from the gate before I stopped her and brought her back. If it hadn't been for me, she would have gone on sweeping all the way to the city center."

"Is it the pictures in the living room that are bothering you, Avigail?"

"It's not the pictures. It's everything. All sorts of things that you, Yoel, insist on not noticing. You insist on pretending that everything's entirely normal. Just remember that you've already made that mistake once before. And we all paid a heavy price for that."

"Go on," he said.

"Have you noticed what's been happening to Netta these last few days, Yoel?"

Yoel replied in the negative.

"I knew you hadn't. Since when have you noticed anybody aside from yourself? It saddens me to have to say that I am not in the least surprised."

"Avigail. What's the matter? Please."

"Ever since Lisa started, Netta hasn't set foot in the living room. I'm telling you that she's starting to go downhill again. And I'm not blaming your mother; she's not responsible for what she does; no, the person who's responsible, apparently, is you. At least that's what the whole world thinks. Only she didn't think so."

"All right," said Yoel, "we'll look into the matter. We'll appoint a commission of inquiry. But the best thing would be if you and Lisa simply patched up your differences and that's that."

"Everything is so simple with you," Avigail said in her headmistress's voice. Yoel interrupted her:

"Can't you see, Avigail, I'm trying to get on with some work."

"I'm so sorry," she said icily. "Don't mind me with my little nonsense." She left, closing the door gently behind her.

Sometimes, after a fierce argument, late at night, Ivria used to whisper to him: "But just remember that I understand you." What had she been trying to communicate to him with those words? What had she understood? Yoel knew very well that there was no way of knowing. Even though right now the question was more important to him than ever, was almost urgent. He was smitten with a sharp longing for the cool touch of her fingers across his naked back and he also yearned to enfold those fingers in his clumsy hands and try to warm them, like reviving a frozen chick. Was it really only an accident? He almost jumped into the car and rushed straight to Jerusalem, to the block of apartments in Talbiyeh to inspect the electric wiring inside and outside, in order to decipher each minute, each second, each movement of that morning. But in his thoughts the block of apartments seemed to be floating among the notes of the melancholy guitar of that Itamar or Eviatar, and Yoel knew that the sadness would be more than he could bear. Instead of driving to Jerusalem he went to the truffle- and mushroom-laden forest next door, to Annemarie and Ralph's, and after supper and a Dubonnet and a country-music tape, Ralph escorted him to his sister's bed and Yoel didn't care whether Ralph stayed or left and he slept with her that evening not for pleasure but for warmth and pity, like a father stroking away his daughter's tears.

When he got back after midnight the house was dark and quiet. For an instant he was alarmed by the silence, as though sensing the closeness of a calamity. All the doors were closed inside except the living room's. He went in and, switching on the light, discovered that the photographs had disappeared and so had the Hanukkah menorah. And he was alarmed, because for an instant he thought that the figurine was gone too. But no, it had merely been moved slightly. It was standing at the end of the shelf. Yoel, fearing its fall, replaced it gently in the middle of the shelf. He knew he ought to find out which of the three had removed the pictures. And he knew that that investigation would not take place. Next morning at breakfast not a word was said about the disappearance of the photographs. Nor during the following days. Lisa and Avigail had made their peace again and went out together to the local keep-fit class and to meetings of the macramé circle. Sometimes they remarked sarcastically and in unison on Yoel's absentmindedness or on his never doing anything from morning to evening. Netta went out in the evenings to the Cinematheque or the Tel Aviv Museum. Sometimes she went window-shopping to pass the time between two films. As for Yoel, he was compelled to drop his little investigation into the affair of the condemnation of Chief of Staff Elazar, even though he now had a strong suspicion that something had gone wrong with the proceedings at the time and that there had been a serious miscarriage of justice. But he recognized that without access to the actual evidence and the classified sources it would be impossible for him to discover how the blunder had occurred.

Meanwhile the winter rains had started up again, and one morning, as he went out to pick up the newspaper from the garden path, he found the cats on the kitchen veranda playing with the stiff corpse of a small bird which had died, apparently, of the cold.

33

One day in the middle of December, at three o'clock in the afternoon, Nakdimon Lublin arrived, wearing an army anorak and with his face red and chafed from the cold winds. He brought a present of a can of olive oil that he had produced himself in his improvised press at the north end of Metullah. He had also brought three or four late-summer thistles in a battered black case that had once housed a violin. He did not know that Netta had lost interest in collecting them.

He strode down the hall, peered suspiciously into each of the bedrooms in turn, located the living room, and entered it with firm steps, as though treading thick clods of earth. His thistles in their violin case and the can of olive oil wrapped in sacking he set down unhesitatingly in the center of the coffee table and discarded his anorak on the floor beside the armchair in which he sat down expansively, with legs outspread. As usual, he addressed the women as "girls" and Yoel as "Captain." He asked the monthly rent that Yoel paid for this "chocolate box." And now that they were on the subject of business, he drew a fat wad of crumpled fifty-shekel notes secured with a rubber band out of the back pocket of his pants and placed it wearily on the table. This was Avigail's and Yoel's semi-yearly share of income from the orchard and the guesthouse in Metullah, in accordance with Shealtiel Lublin's will. On the top note of the pile the sums involved were written out in thick figures, as though in a carpenter's pencil.

"And now," he drawled nasally, *"yallah;* wake up, girls. The man's starving to death."

In an instant the three of them were full of bustling activity, like ants whose entrance to their anthill has been blocked up. They began to rush around, barely managing to avoid bumping into one another in their haste, between the kitchen and the living room. The instant that Nakdimon deigned to remove his legs from the coffee table, a tablecloth was spread, and on it were laid, in a flash, plates, glasses, bottles, napkins, condiments, warm pita and pickles and knives and forks. Though lunch had been cleared away in the kitchen less than an hour earlier. Yoel watched in amazement, dumbstruck at the commanding power of this rough, red-faced, stocky man over these usually unsubmissive women. And he had to stifle his vague anger by saying to himself, Fool, surely you're not jealous.

"Bring out whatever you've got," the guest ordered in his slow, nasal voice, "only don't start confusing me with decisions. 'Muhammad said, Make no mistake: When my belly's empty I'll swallow a snake.' You sit down here, Captain; leave the serving to the girls. You and I have to talk."

Yoel obediently sat down on the sofa facing his brother-in-law. "It's like this," said Nakdimon; then he changed his mind and said, "Hold it a minute." He stopped talking and concentrated for ten minutes with silent expertise on the roast chicken legs, potatoes baked in their jackets, salad and cooked vegetables that were placed before him, washing the whole down with beer, and between beers he downed two glasses of orange seltzer, the pita in his left hand doing duty by turns as spoon, fork, and background chewable, and he let out occasional belches of satisfaction with little sighs of pleasure in an abdominal bass.

Yoel watched him eat with thoughtful concentration, as though seeking in the guest's appearance some hidden detail that would confirm or disprove an old suspicion. There was something in this Lublin's jaws, or in his neck and shoulders, perhaps in his furrowed peasant hands, or in all together, that worked on Yoel like the recollection of an elusive tune that vaguely resembled another, older tune that had faded away. There was no resemblance between this stocky, red-faced man and his dead wife, who had been a slim, pale woman with delicate features and slow, introverted movements. Yoel was almost filled with rage, and at once he felt angry with himself for this rage, because over the years he had trained himself always to be cool. While he waited for Nakdimon to finish his meal, the women sat around the dining table as though in the dress circle, at a slight distance from the two men, who were sitting on opposite sides of the coffee table. Until the visitor had finished munching on his last bone and wiped his plate with pita and turned to demolish the apple compote, hardly a word was spoken in the room. Yoel sat facing his brother-in-law with his knees bent at right angles to the floor and his ugly hands lying open upon them. He looked like a retired fighter from an elite reconnaissance troop, with his strong suntanned face, his curly mop of metallic, prematurely gray hair standing out like a horn over his forehead without falling onto it, those wrinkles around his eyes suggesting a faint irony, the shadow of a smile that his lips did not participate in. In the course of the years he had acquired the ability to sit like that for a considerable length of time, as though in tragic repose, with his knees at right angles and on each of them an open hand lying motionless, with trunk erect but not tense, with shoulders relaxed, and with nothing moving in his face. Until Lublin dried his mouth on his sleeve and his sleeve with a paper napkin, on which he proceeded to blow his nose, then crumpled it up and threw it to drown slowly in a half-full glass of orange seltzer. Feeling sated he let out a sharp fart, like a door slamming, and then opened with almost the same words he had started with before beginning his meal: "OK. You see. It's like this."

It turned out that Avigail Lublin and Lisa Rabinovich, each without the other's knowledge, had written to Metullah at the beginning of the month about the question of erecting a tombstone on Ivria's grave in Jerusalem for the first anniversary of her death, the sixteenth of February. He would never do anything behind Yoel's back, and anyway, if it was up to him, he'd rather

161

leave it to Yoel to deal with the whole business. Though he was willing to pay half. Or even the whole of it. It was all the same to him. She, his sister, when she went away, everything was all the same to her too. Otherwise she might have stayed. But what was the point of trying to get inside her head now. Anyway, with her, even when she was still alive, it was always No Entry from every direction. And because he had some business in Tel Aviv today—selling out his share in a trucking partnership, organizing some mattresses for the guesthouse, getting a permit for a small stone quarry—he had decided to look in on them to have a meal and sort out what needed to be done. That's the picture. So, what do you say, Captain?

"All right. A tombstone. Why not," Yoel replied calmly.

"Will you see to it, or shall I?"

"As you wish."

"Look. I've got a sound slab of stone from Kafr Ajer in my yard. Sort of black with flecks. About so high."

"OK. It'll do."

"Shouldn't we inscribe something on it?"

Avigail interposed:

"And we'd better decide on the wording quickly, before the end of the week; otherwise it won't be ready for the anniversary."

"It's wrong!" Lisa suddenly shouted harshly from her corner.

"What's wrong?"

"It's wrong to speak ill of the dead."

"And who's speaking ill of the dead?"

"The truth of the matter," Lisa replied defiantly, like an obstreperous schoolgirl who has made up her mind to embarrass the grown-ups, "the truth of the matter is that she never liked anybody much. It's not nice to say so, but it's even worse to tell lies. That's how it was. Maybe the only one she loved was her father. And nobody here thought about her a little. It would maybe be nicer for her to lie in a grave in Metullah next to her father than in Jerusalem with all sorts of simple people. But everybody here is only thinking about themselves."

"Girls," Nakdimon drawled drowsily, "would you mind letting us talk it over quietly for a couple of minutes. After that you can jabber away for all you're worth."

"All right," Yoel replied belatedly to an earlier question. "Netta, you're the literary department here, you compose something suitable and I'll have it inscribed on the stone that Lublin will bring. And that's the end of that. Tomorrow is another day."

"Don't touch that, girls," Nakdimon warned the women who were beginning to clear away the remains of the meal. He laid his hand on a small honey pot with a kind of canvas hat on it. "That's full of natural snake juice. I catch them in the winter when they're sleeping among the sacks in the shed, I milk a viper here, a viper there, and then I bring it to town and sell it. By the way, Captain, can you explain to me, why are you all squashed up together here?"

Yoel hesitated. He glanced at his watch and saw the angle between the two main hands, and even followed the little leaps of the second hand, but he didn't grasp what the time was. Then he replied that he didn't understand the question.

"The whole clan in the same hole. What is this? One on top of the other. Like a load of Ay-rabs. The grannies and the kids and the goats and the chickens and the whole darned lot. What's the point of it?"

Lisa interjected stridently:

"Who wants instant coffee and who wants Turkish? Hands up."

And Avigail:

"What's that mole you've got on your cheek, Nakdi. You always had a brown spot there and now it's turned into a mole. You ought to show it to the doctor. Only this week they were talking about moles like that on the radio, saying that they were on no account to be ignored. Go and see Pouchatchewsky, let him examine it for you."

"He died," said Nakdimon. "Way back."

Yoel said:

"OK, Lublin. You bring your black stone and we'll get them

163

to put just the name and dates on it. That'll do. I'll even do without the ceremony on the anniversary. At least that way I won't have to bother with all those cantors and beggars."

"Shame on you!" croaked Lisa.

"Would you like to stay the night, Nakdi?" Avigail asked. "Do stay. Look out the window, see for yourself what a storm is brewing. We've had a little disagreement here lately; dear Lisa has taken it into her head that Ivria was secretly a little pious, and that the rest of us persecuted her like the Spanish Inquisition. Did you ever notice any religious tendencies in her, Nakdi?"

Yoel, who did not catch the question but for some reason thought it was addressed to him, answered pensively:

"She loved peace and quiet. That was what she really loved."

"Listen to this piece I've found," Netta called out, coming back in her baggy pants and a checked shirt as wide as a tent, carrying a large book entitled *Verses on Stone: Epitaphs from the Days of the Pioneers*. "What a gem:

> Here lies a most beloved youth
> A grievous loss to all, in truth:
> JEREMIAH son of AARON, he went to Heaven
> On the New Moon of Iyyar 5661, aged 27.
> Aloft his tragic soul has flown,
> As he could not bear to live alone.
> He was so youthful and so pure,
> And so his memory shall endure."

Avigail rounded on her grandchild in a fury, her eyes sparkling with anger: "That's not funny, Netta. It's disgusting, your mockery. Your cynicism. Your scorn. Your arrogance. As though life were a farce and death were a joke and suffering just an anecdote. Take a good look, Yoel, think about it, apply your mind to it just for once, because she gets it all straight from you. That apathy. That contempt. That shoulder-shrugging. That funereal sneer. Netta gets it all from you. Can't you see that she's a copy of you? You've already caused one disaster with your cold

164

cynicism, and heaven forbid you should cause another one. I'd better close my mouth now so as not to tempt the devil."

"What do you want from him, Avigail?" Lisa exclaimed sadly, with a sort of elegiac tenderness. "Haven't you got eyes? Can't you see that he suffers for all of us?"

And Yoel, as usual replying belatedly to a question that had been put a few minutes earlier, said:

"You can see for yourself, Lublin. We're living together here so that we can always be here to lend each other a hand. Why don't you join us? Bring your sons down from Metullah."

"*Ma'alesh*, never mind," the guest muttered in a catarrhal, hostile tone, pushing back the table, swathing himself in his anorak, and thumping Yoel's shoulder. "It's the other way around, Captain. Better that you should leave all the girls here to amuse each other and you come up to us. First thing in the morning we'll set you to work in the fields, maybe in the beehives, and we'll clean your brains out before you drive each other completely crazy here. How come it doesn't fall over?" he asked, as his glance fell suddenly on the figurine of the predator of the cat family that looked as though it was about to leap off its base at the end of the shelf.

"Aha," said Yoel, "that's what I'd like to know."

Nakdimon Lublin weighed the beast in his hand. He turned it over, base upward, scratched it with his fingernail, turned it this way and that, held the blind eyes close to his nose and sniffed. At that moment the dim-witted, suspicious, tight-clenched peasant look intensified on his face until Yoel could not refrain from uttering to himself the catchphrase: Like a bull in a china shop. Let's hope he doesn't break it.

Finally the visitor said:

"Bullshit. Listen, Captain: there's something screwed up here."

But delicately, in surprising contrast to his words, with what looked like a gesture of deep respect, he replaced the figurine and stroked the tense, curved back gently, slowly with his fingertip. Then he took his leave:

"Well, girls. Be seeing you. Don't nag each other."

And as he stowed the pot of venom in the inside pocket of his anorak he added:

"Come and see me out, Captain."

Yoel accompanied him to his long, wide Chevrolet. As they parted, the stocky man let out, in a tone of voice Yoel was not expecting:

"There's something screwed up with you too, Captain. Don't get me wrong. I don't mind giving you some of the money from Metullah. No problem. And even though it says in the will that you stop getting it if you remarry, as far as I'm concerned you can get married tomorrow and still go on getting the money. No problem. I'm talking about something else. There's an Ay-rab in Kafr Ajer, a good pal of mine; he's a loony, he's a thief, and they do say that he even screws his own daughters, but when his old mum was dying he went off to Haifa and bought her a Frigidaire, a washing machine, a VCR, whatever, everything she'd always wanted to have, so's at least she'd die happy. That's what they call having pity, Captain. You're a very clever man, shrewd even, you're also a decent man. No question about that. Straight as a die. You're a really OK fellow. Trouble is, there's three serious things missing with you: A. desire, B. joy, and C. pity. If you ask me, Captain, those three things come together in a package. If you haven't got number two, then you haven't got numbers one and three either. And so forth. The state you're in, you're in a terrible way. Now you'd better go indoors. Look at this rain. Be seeing you. Whenever I look at you I feel almost like crying."

34

Surprisingly there followed several sunny days, a weekend flooded with brilliant wintry blue. A warm, honey-colored light suddenly strolled among the bare gardens and over lawns bleached by the frost, lightly touching the heaps of dead leaves and raising here and there a molten copper glow. On all the tiled roofs along the street the solar heating panels sparkled with flashes of scorching brilliance. Parked cars, gutters, puddles, broken glass near the edge of the asphalt, mailboxes, and windowpanes, everything shimmered and blazed. A capering spark flew over bushes and lawns, leaping from wall to fence, lighting up the mailbox, darting like lightning across the street and igniting a dazzling bubble on the gate of the house opposite. Yoel suddenly had a suspicion that this restless spark was somehow connected to himself: if he froze and stood without moving, the light too stood still. Eventually he deciphered the connection between the sparkle and the light reflected from his wristwatch.

The air was gradually filled with the hum of insects. A breeze off the sea brought a taste of salt and sounds of people playing farther down the street. Here and there a neighbor came out to weed his muddy flower beds, to make room to plant bulbs of winter flowers. Here and there women brought their bedding outdoors to air it. And a boy was washing his parents' car, no doubt for money. Raising his eyes Yoel saw a bird that had escaped the frost and was now, as though out of its mind at this sudden brilliance, standing on the tip of a bare branch singing with all its might, over and over again, without variation or pause, ecstatically, a single three-note phrase. Which was swallowed up in the flow of light, which was slow and thick like spilled honey. In vain did Yoel try to reach it and touch it with the flash of light from his watch. And far away on the eastern horizon, beyond the tops of the trees in the citrus grove, the mountains were wrapped in a fine vapor, dissolved in it, and turned blue, as though they were casting off their mass and becoming mere shadows of mountains, light pastel strokes on a bright canvas.

And since Avigail and Lisa were away, at the Winter Festival on Mount Carmel, Yoel decided to have a great washday. Briskly, efficiently, methodically, he went from room to room stripping off pillowcases, quilt and cushion covers. He even collected the bedspreads. He gathered all the dirty towels, including the tea towels in the kitchen, and emptied the laundry basket in the bathroom. Then he went around the bedrooms again, looking into closets and on the backs of chairs, picking up blouses, underwear, nightdresses, combinations, skirts, housecoats, undershirts, and stockings. When he had finished he took off all his clothes and, standing naked in the bathroom, piled them on the mound of washing. Then he started sorting the laundry. He devoted some twenty minutes, standing there naked, to a meticulous, precise classification, peering sometimes through his intellectual glasses at the washing instructions printed on the labels, carefully making separate piles for hot wash, warm wash, cold wash, and hand wash, reminding himself what could or could not be wrung, what could go in the tumble dryer, and what would have to be hung out on the revolving clothesline he had put up at the end of the back garden with the help of Krantz and his son Duby. Only after the sorting and planning stages did he get dressed and put the washing machine on, wash after wash, from hot to cold and from resistant to delicate. Half the morning went by, but he was too busy to notice. He was determined to have it all finished before Netta got back from the theater club. He visualized the pure and innocent young man Jeremiah son of Aaron, from the book of epitaphs, confined to a wheelchair. Perhaps that was why he was so pure: there's not much scope for sin in a wheelchair. As for the Agranat Commission of Inquiry and the injustice that might have been done to Lieutenant General Elazar, Yoel took account of what Teacher had always instilled in his subordinates: absolute truth may or may not exist—that is a matter for the philosophers—but any idiot or son of a bitch knows what a lie is.

And what should he do now that all the washing was dried and neatly folded on the shelves in the various closets, apart from those items that were still drying on the line in the garden? He would iron whatever needed to be ironed. And then? He had put the garden shed in order the previous weekend. A fortnight ago he had gone around to all the windows and treated the hinges against rust. He knew he must kick the habit of the electric drill at last. The kitchen was gleaming and there was not so much as a teaspoon visible on the drainboard: everything had been put away. Perhaps he should merge all the half-finished bags of sugar? Or go down to Bardugo's Nurseries at Ramat Lotan junction and buy some bulbs of winter flowers? You'll be ill, he said to himself in his mother's words, you'll be ill if you don't start doing something. He checked this possibility for a moment and found no error in it. He recalled that his mother had hinted to him several times about a considerable sum of money that she was keeping for him to help him get started in business. And he remembered that a former colleague had offered him the moon if he would join him as partner in a private detective agency. And Le Patron's entreaties. Ralph Vermont had also talked to him once about a discreet channel for investments, something linked to a giant Canadian consortium, by means of which Ralph promised to double Yoel's investment within eighteen months. Whereas Arik Krantz never stopped pleading with him to share his latest adventure: twice a week he put on a white coat and worked as a paramedic auxiliary in a hospital, dazzled by the charms of a volunteer nurse named Greta. Arik Krantz had vowed not to give up till he had "cracked her across and down, and diagonally too." He claimed he had already marked out and reserved for Yoel two other volunteers, Christina and Iris: Yoel could take his pick. Or take them both.

Carrying the pile of equipment necessary for setting up his colony—reading glasses, sunglasses, bottle of soda water, glass of brandy, the book about the Chief of Staff, a tube of suntan cream, sun visor, and transistor radio—Yoel went out into the garden to sunbathe on the glider until Netta got back from her Saturday matinee at the theater club, when they could have a late lunch. In fact, why shouldn't he accept his brother-in-law's invitation? He could go up to Metullah alone. Stay there a few days. Perhaps even for a week or two. Why not even several months? He would work half-naked from morn to evening in the fields, the beehives, the orchard, among whose tree trunks he had slept with Ivria for the first time, when she had gone out to turn off the irrigation taps, and he, a soldier who had lost his way on an orienteering exercise during a section commander's training course, was there among the taps filling his water bottle. He noticed her when she was five or six steps away from him and froze with fear; he almost stopped breathing. She would not have noticed him at all if her legs had not collided with his crouched body; just when he was certain she was going to scream, she whispered to him, Don't kill me. They were both stunned, and they hardly spoke more than ten words before their bodies suddenly clung together, clumsily groping, fully dressed, rolling in the mud, panting and burrowing into each other like a pair of blind puppies, and they hurt each other and finished almost before they'd begun and immediately rushed off in opposite directions. And it was there among the fruit trees too that he lay with her the second time, several months later, when he returned to Metullah as though under a spell and waited for her two nights running by the same taps, and on the third night they met and again fell on each other like people dying of thirst and afterward he asked for her hand and she said, Are you out of your mind. And then they started to meet at night; it was only some time later that they first saw each other by daylight, and they promised each other that they were not disappointed by what they saw.

And perhaps in the course of time he could learn a thing or two from Nakdimon. For instance, he could try to master the art of milking venomous snakes. He could study and decipher once and for all the true value of the old man's bequest. He could sort out, very belatedly, what really happened in Metullah that far-away winter when Ivria and Netta ran away from him and Ivria maintained insistently that Netta's problem disappeared because she forbade him to visit them. And between investigations he could toughen and indulge his body in the sunshine, working outdoors, with the birds and the wind, like the time when he was a young trainee on the kibbutz, before he married Ivria and was trans-ferred to the army advocate general's department, from which he was sent on the special-jobs training course.

But thinking about the extent of the property in Metullah and days of physical labor failed to fire him with enthusiasm. Here in Ramat Lotan he did not have heavy outlays. The money Nakdi-mon gave him every six months, the old women's National Se-curity money, his own pension, and the difference between the rent he received from the two apartments in Jerusalem and the rent he paid for the house combined to buy him enough leisure and reflective repose to spend all his time with the birds and the lawn. Even so he was still not near to inventing electricity or writing the poems of Pushkin. Surely if he went to Metullah he would also succumb to an addiction to the electric drill or its equivalent. Suddenly he almost laughed aloud at the memory of Nakdimon Lublin's comically ignorant pronunciation of the Ara-maic memorial prayer at the funeral. The commune or collective that Ralph's ex-wives and Annemarie's ex-husbands had set up in Boston with their children seemed to him logical and almost touching, because in his heart he agreed with the Biblical allusion in the epitaph that Netta had discovered: it is not good for a man to live alone. When all was said and done, it was not a question of shame, of attics, of lunatic-astral illnesses or Byzantine crucifixion scenes that contradict common sense. It was a question more or less like the subject of disagreement between Shamir and Peres: the danger involved in concessions likely to entail more and more concessions as against the need to be realistic and to compromise. There's that cat, a really big boy now, apparently one of the litter born in the garden shed during the summer. And already he's eying the bird on the tree with a hungry look.

Yoel picked up the weekend newspaper, leafed through it, and dropped off to sleep. When Netta got back between three and four she went straight to the kitchen and ate something from the refrigerator, without bothering to sit down; then she took a shower and said to him as he slept: I'm going back into town. It was very nice of you to wash the bedclothes and change the towels, but there was no need. What do we pay a cleaner for? Yoel muttered something, heard her departing footsteps, got up, and moved the white glider toward the center of the lawn, because the sun was beginning to set. Then he lay down again and went back to sleep.

Krantz and his wife, Odelia, approached on tiptoe, sat down at the white garden table and waited, glancing in the meantime at Yoel's newspaper and book. His working years and his travels had accustomed him to wake like a cat, a sort of inner leap straight from sleep to a state of alertness without any transitional stage of drowsiness. While he was still opening his eyes he had dropped his bare feet to the ground and sat up on the glider, taken one look, and come to the conclusion that Krantz and his wife were fighting again, that they had come to ask him to mediate between them, and that it was Krantz again who had violated a previous agreement reached by means of Yoel's mediation.

Odelia Krantz said:

"Admit it: you haven't had any lunch. If you'll let me go into your kitchen for a minute I'll get some plates and things: we've brought you some chicken livers with fried onions and various extra tidbits."

"You see," said Krantz, "the first thing she does is bribe you. So you'll be on her side."

172

"And that," said Odelia, "is the way his mind always works. There's nothing to be done about it."

Yoel put his sunglasses on, because the setting sun hurt his red, aching eyes. And while he devoured the chicken livers with fried onions and steamed rice he asked after the two sons, who, he remembered, were barely a year and a half apart.

"They're both against me," Krantz declared. "They're both lefties, and at home they're always taking their mother's side. And that's after I've just spent in the past two months thirteen hundred dollars on a computer for Duby and eleven hundred on a motorbike for Gilly. And by way of thanks all they do is bash me over the head."

Yoel steered delicately toward the contaminated zone. From Arik he drew only the usual grumbles: she neglects the house, she neglects herself; the fact she bothered to cook those chicken livers today, that was just because it was for you, not for me; she wastes fantastic sums of money but she's a miser in bed, and her sarcasm—first thing in the morning she starts in on me, and last thing at night she makes fun of my paunch or something else. A thousand times I've said to her, Odelia, let's split up, at least for a trial period, and every time she starts threatening me that if I'm not careful she'll burn the house down. Or kill herself. Or talk to the newspapers. Not that I'm afraid of her. On the contrary, she's the one who'd better watch it.

Odelia, in her turn, said with dry eyes that she had nothing to add. You could tell just from listening to him that he was a beast. But she had one request, and nothing would make her drop it: that at least he should mount his cows somewhere else. Not on her living-room carpet. Under the children's noses. Is that too much to ask? Please: let Mr. Ravid—Yoel—judge for himself if she was making unreasonable demands.

Yoel heard them both out very seriously, with a concentrated look on his face, as though a madrigal were being played to him from a long way away, and among all the voices his task was to isolate the one that was singing false. He did not interfere or make any comment, even when Krantz said, All right, if that's

173

the way it is, just let me take my bits and pieces, a couple of bags full, and I'll clear out and not come back. You can keep everything. I don't care. Even when Odelia said, It's true I've got a bottle of acid, but he has a handgun hidden in his car.

Finally, when the sun had set and in an instant the cold set in and the stray bird that had survived the winter, or perhaps another one, suddenly started to sing sweetly, Yoel said:

"Well. I've heard it all. Now let's go inside because it's turned chilly."

The Krantzes helped him carry the plates and glasses and the newspaper and the book and the suntan cream and the visor and the transistor radio into the kitchen. There, barefoot and stripped to the waist for sunbathing, and standing, Yoel delivered his judgment:

"Listen, Arik, since you've given a thousand dollars to Duby and a thousand dollars to Gilly, I suggest you give two thousand to Odelia. Do it first thing tomorrow morning, as soon as the bank opens. If you haven't got it, take out a loan. Ask for an overdraft. Or else I'll lend you the money."

"But why?"

"So that I can take a three-week package tour to Europe," said Odelia. "For three weeks you won't see me."

Arik Krantz chuckled, sighed, muttered something, thought better of it, seemed to redden slightly, and finally said:

"All right. I'll buy it."

Then they had a cup of coffee together, and the Krantzes, as they left, clutching a plastic bag containing the dishes in which they had brought the late lunch, invited him insistently to come and have a meal with them one Friday evening, with his whole harem, "now that Odelia's shown you what a terrific cook she is. And that's nothing. She can do ten times better when she's really in the mood."

"Stop exaggerating, Arye. Come home now," Odelia said. And they vanished gratefully, almost reconciled.

That evening when Netta got back from town and they were drinking herbal tea in the kitchen, Yoel asked his daughter if she

174

thought there was any sense in what her grandfather the policeman used to say, that everybody has more or less the same secrets. Netta asked why he wanted to know that all of a sudden.
And Yoel told her briefly about the task of arbitration that Odelia and Arik Krantz occasionally imposed on him. Instead of answering his question Netta replied in a voice in which Yoel felt
he detected a hint of affection:

"Admit you quite enjoy playing God like that. Look how
burned you are. Shall I rub some cream in, so you won't peel?"

Yoel said:

"Suit yourself."

And after a moment's thought he added:

"In fact, there's no need. Look, I've saved you some of the
chicken livers and onions they brought me, and there's some rice
and vegetables. Eat something, Netta, and then let's watch the
news."

35

On the television news there was a detailed report on a national strike in the hospitals. Old people and chronic invalids were shown lying on urine-soaked beds, and the camera dwelt on signs of filth and neglect all around. One old woman was moaning continuously in a shrill monotonous voice, like a wounded puppy. A feeble, bloated old man, who looked as though he would burst from the pressure of the fluids building up inside him, lay motionless, staring vacantly. There was also a shriveled old person, his skull and face covered with stiff bristles, looking exceedingly filthy, yet constantly grinning and giggling and brandishing at the camera a teddy bear whose belly was ripped open, its floppy innards of grubby cotton wool pouring out. Yoel said:

"Don't you think this country is going to the dogs, Netta?"

"Look who's talking," she said, pouring him a brandy. And went back to folding paper napkins into careful triangles and arranging them in an olivewood holder.

"Tell me," he said after taking a couple of sips, "if it was up to you, would you prefer to be exempted or to do your service?"

"But it *is* up to me. It's a question of telling them my story or not. Nothing will show up in the physical."

"So what will you do? Will you tell them or won't you? And what'll you say if I tell them? Just wait a minute, Netta, before you say 'Suit yourself.' The time has come to find out for once what suits you. You know I could fix the whole business up for you with a couple of phone calls, either way. So let's find out what you want. Though I'm not saying that what you want is necessarily what I'll do."

"You remember what you said to me when Le Patron was putting pressure on you to go away for a few days to save the Homeland?"

"I said something. Yes. I believe I said I'd lost the ability to concentrate. Or something like that. But what's that got to do with it?"

"Tell me something, Yoel. What's biting you? Why are you beating around the bush? What difference does it make to you whether I do my military service or not?"

"Just a moment," he said quietly. "Sorry. But let's hear the weather forecast."

The announcer said that tonight would see the end of the letup in the winter rains. A new trough of low pressure would reach the coastal plain before dawn. The rain and wind would resume. In the inland valleys and on the highlands there was a risk of frost. And now two final news items: An Israeli businessman has lost his life in an accident in Taiwan. His next of kin have been informed. And in Barcelona a young monk has burned himself to death to protest the increasing violence in the world. And that's all for tonight.

Netta said:

"Listen. I can be out of the house by the summer even without going into the army. Or even earlier."

"Why? Are we short of rooms?"

"So long as I'm in the house, could be you've got some problem about bringing the woman next door here? Or her brother?"

"Why should I have a problem?"

"How should I know? Thin walls. It's the same with the wall between us and them—this wall, here—it's as thin as paper. My last exam is on the twentieth of June. After that, if you like, I can rent a room in town. And if you're in a hurry I can do it sooner."

"That's out of the question," said Yoel, in the tone of cool, tender cruelty he had used at times in his work to nip in the bud any spark of malice in his interlocutor. "Full stop." But as he spoke the words he had to struggle to release the sudden grip of rage in his chest, a feeling such as he had not experienced since Ivria went away.

"Why not?"

"No rented room. Forget it. That's that."

"You mean you won't give me the money?"

"Netta. Let's be logical. First, because of your condition. Second, when you start at the university we're just around the corner from the campus here, so why should you drag yourself all the way from the center of town?"

"I can pay for a room myself. You wouldn't have to finance me."

"How?"

"Le Patron is nice to me. He's offered me a job in your office."

"I wouldn't count on it."

"And anyway, Nakdimon is holding lots of money for me until I'm twenty-one, and he's told me he couldn't care less about starting to let me have it right away."

"I wouldn't bank on that either, Netta, if I were you. Anyway, who said you could talk to Lublin about money?"

"Hey, why are you staring at me like that? Take a look at yourself. You look like a killer. After all, I'm only trying to clear out for you. So you can start living."

"Look here, Netta," Yoel said, attempting to inject into his voice a measure of intimacy he was not feeling, "about the woman next door. Annemarie. Let's say—"

"Let's say nothing. The most pathetic thing to do is have it off over there and then come running home to explain. Like your friend Krantz."

"OK. All there is to it really is—"

"All there is to it really is, just let me know when you need the room with the double bed. That's all. Who on earth bought these napkins? Must have been Lisa. Look, how kitsch. Why don't you lie down for a while, take your shoes off; there's a new British series starting in a few minutes. Something about the origins of the universe. Shall we give it a chance? When she moved into that study of hers in Jerusalem and all that, I got the idea it was because of me. But I was too young to move out on my own then. There's a girl in my class, Adva. At the beginning of July she's moving into a two-room apartment she inherited from her grannie. It's on a roof on Karl Netter Street. For a hundred and twenty dollars a month she'll rent me a room with a view of the sea. But if you're anxious for me to push off sooner than that, there's no problem. Just say, and I'll make myself scarce. I've switched on the TV. Don't get up. Two minutes till it starts. I feel like some cheese on toast with tomatoes and black olives. Shall I do some for you? One? Or two? Do you want some hot milk? Or an herbal tea? You got so sunburned today, you ought to drink plenty of liquids."

After the late news, when Netta had taken a bottle of orange juice and a glass and gone to her room, Yoel decided to arm himself with a large flashlight and check what was going on in the shed in the garden. For some reason he had a feeling the cats had moved in there again. But on the way, on second thought, he reasoned that it would be more logical to suppose that the mother had had another litter. The air outside was very cold and dry. In her bedroom, Netta was getting undressed, and Yoel could not banish from his mind the image of her angular body, which always looked hunched, strained, even neglected and unloved. Although there might well be a contradiction there. It was almost certain that no man, no ravenous youth, had ever set eyes on that pitiful body. Perhaps they never would. Even though Yoel reckoned that in another month or two, a year at most, that transmutation into a woman of which the doctors had spoken once to Ivria would take place. And then everything would change, and some broad hairy chest and muscular arms would come and take possession of her and that penthouse in Karl Netter Street, which Yoel that instant decided to go and check out for himself one of these days. Alone. Before he made up his mind.

179

So dry and crisp was the cold night air that it seemed it could be crumbled between the fingers with a faint, brittle sound. Which Yoel so longed for that for a moment he could somehow almost hear it. But apart from bugs that fled from his light, he discovered no signs of life in the shed. Just some vague sense that everything was not really awake. That he was walking around, thinking, sleeping, eating, "having it off" with Annemarie, watching television, working in the garden, putting up new shelves in his mother-in-law's bedroom, all in his sleep. That if he had any hope left of deciphering something, or at any rate of formulating a searching question, he must wake up at all costs. Even at the cost of a disaster. An injury. An illness. A complication. Something must come and shake him until he woke up. Thump and smash the soft, greasy jelly that had closed around him like a womb. Blind panic seized him and he almost leaped out of the shed into the darkness. Because the flashlight got left behind. On a shelf. Switched on. And Yoel was totally unable to force himself to go back inside and pick it up.

For a quarter of an hour or so he walked around the garden, around the house, feeling the fruit trees, treading down the soil in the flower beds, trying in vain the hinges of the gate in the hope that they would squeak and he would be able to oil them. There was no squeaking, so he resumed his wandering. Eventually he was struck by a decision: tomorrow, the day after, or maybe at the weekend, he would go into Bardugo's Nurseries at Ramat Lotan junction and buy some gladiolus and dahlia tubers and some sweet pea and snapdragon seeds and some chrysanthemum plants, so that when springtime came everything would flower again. He might erect a pretty wooden pergola over the place where the car stood, and train vines over it, instead of the ugly corrugated-iron roof supported on iron columns that had rusted and would go on rusting however much he repainted them. Perhaps he would take a trip to Qalqilya or Kafr Kassem, buy half a dozen huge pots and fill them with a mixture of red soil and compost and plant them with different varieties of geranium that would spill over and trail around them and blaze in a riot of brilliant color. The word "brilliant" once more afforded him a sort of vague thrill; he felt like someone who has despaired of some endlessly protracted dispute when suddenly his vindication arrives unshakably from some totally unexpected quarter. When the light finally went out behind Netta's shutter he drove to the seashore and sat at the wheel very close to the edge of the cliff to wait for the trough of low pressure that was creeping in off the sea and was due to hit the coastal plain tonight.

36

He sat at the wheel of the car until almost two o'clock in the morning, with the doors locked, the windows rolled right up, the lights out, the radiator grille almost projecting over the edge of the cliff into the void. His eyes, once they were accustomed to the dark, were spellbound by the breathing of the pelt of the sea, swelling and sinking again and again with the expansive yet restless respiration of a giant whose slumbers are periodically punctured by nightmares. At times a sound escaped like an angry gust. At times it sounded like feverish panting. And again there rose the sound of breakers in the night, gnawing at the coastline and retreating with their booty to the deep. Here and there ripples of foam glistened on the dark pelt. Occasionally a pale milky beam passed high above among the stars, perhaps the quivering of a distant coast guard searchlight. As the hours passed Yoel had difficulty distinguishing between the murmur of the waves and the throbbing of the blood inside his skull. How thin was the crust that divided inside from outside. At moments of deep tension he experienced a sensation of having the sea inside his brain. Like that stormy day in Athens, when he had to draw a gun to frighten off an idiot who was trying to scare him with a knife in a corner of the bus terminal. And in Copenhagen, the day he finally managed to photograph the notorious Irish terrorist at the pharmacy counter with a miniature camera concealed in a cigarette pack. That night, asleep in his room at the Viking Pension, he heard several shots fired nearby and he lay down under his bed; even though all was quiet he preferred not to come out until daylight showed through the cracks of the shutters. Only then did he go out on the balcony and check it inch by inch, until he discovered two tiny holes in the plaster of the outside wall, which might have been caused by bullets. He ought to have continued the investigation until he found the answer, but because he had concluded his business in Copenhagen he did not bother, but packed in haste and left the hotel and the city. From some impulse that he still did not understand, before checking out he carefully filled the two holes in the wall outside his room with toothpaste, without knowing if they really were bullet holes and if so whether they had any connection with the sounds of shooting he had imagined he heard in the night, or if shots were fired, whether they had any connection with him. Once he had filled them in it was almost impossible to spot anything. What is there? he asked himself, and he looked out to sea but saw nothing. What was it that made me rush around for twenty-three years from square to square from hotel to hotel from terminal to terminal in night trains howling through forests and tunnels, the yellow headlight raking the fields of darkness? What made me run? And why did I fill the little holes in that wall and why didn't I make the slightest report? Once, she came into the bathroom at five o'clock in the morning when I was in the middle of shaving and she asked me, Where are you running to, Yoel? Why did I answer with just four words: It's the job, Ivria, immediately adding that there was no hot water again? And she, in her white clothes but barefoot, with her fair hair falling mainly over her right shoulder, nodded her head pensively four or five times, called me a poor fool, and left.

If a man in the middle of the forest wants to find out once and for all what is going on and what has happened and what might have been and what is a mirage, he has to stand still and listen. What is it, for instance, that makes a dead man's guitar produce soft cello music through the wall? What is the dividing line between longing and lunar-astral illness? Why was it that his blood froze the moment Le Patron uttered the word "Bangkok"? What had Ivria meant when she said several times, always in the dark, always in her quietest and most abstract voice, I do understand you? What really happened all those years ago among the taps at Metullah? And what was the point of her death in the arms of that neighbor in a shallow puddle in the yard? Is there a problem with Netta or isn't there? And if there is, which of us did she get it from? And how and when did my betrayal really begin, if the word has any real meaning in this particular case? Surely all this is meaningless unless we accept the supposition that there exists a precise, profound evil constantly at work in everything, an unselfish, impersonal evil that has no motive or purpose other than the cold thrill of death, and this evil is gradually dismantling everything with its watchmaker's fingers. It has already taken one of us to pieces and killed her, and which of us will be its next victim there is no way of knowing. And is there some way of protecting oneself, not to mention a chance of mercy or pity? Or possibly not protecting oneself but getting up and running away. But even if a miracle were to occur and the tormented predator were to free itself from the invisible nail, the question still remains of how and where an eyeless creature can leap. Above the water a little reconnaissance plane with a hoarse piston engine buzzed its way slowly northward, flying fairly low, with green and red lights flashing alternately at its wing tips. But it was quickly lost to sight, and there was only the silence of the water blowing against the windshield. Which had misted up, on either the inside or the outside.

Can't see anything. And it's getting colder. Soon the promised rain will be here. Let's get out and wipe the windows, run the engine and the heater for a while, put the defroster on, turn around and drive to Jerusalem. Just to be on the safe side, we'll park around the corner. Under the cloak of mist and darkness we'll penetrate as far as the second floor. Without switching on the light on the stairs. With the help of a bent wire and this little screwdriver we'll get the lock to give without making the slightest sound, and so, barefoot and silent, we'll creep into his bachelor apartment and materialize before them, quiet, sudden, and controlled, with a screwdriver in one hand and a bent wire in the other. Sorry, don't let me disturb you, I haven't come to make a scene, my wars are all over, just to ask you to let me have the lost woolen scarf and also the copy of *Mrs. Dalloway*. And I'll mend my ways. I've already begun to improve a little. As for Mr. Eviatar, hello there, Mr. Eviatar, if you wouldn't mind, would you play us an old Russian song we used to love when we were little, "We've lost forever that which was most dear / And it will never reappear." Thank you. That's all we wanted. And sorry for bursting in, we're already on our way. *Adieu. Proshchai.*

It was a little after two o'clock when he parked his car again, in the dead center of the carport, reversing it in as usual so the nose was pointing toward the street, ready to make a quick getaway. Then he conducted a final reconnaissance patrol around the front and back gardens, checking to make sure there was nothing on the clothesline. For a moment he was terrified because he thought he saw a faint flickering light under the door of the garden shed. But then he remembered that he had left his flashlight there, still on, and apparently the battery was not dead yet. Instead of putting his key into the keyhole of his own front door, as he had intended to do, he inserted it by mistake into his neighbors'. For several minutes he tried to open it, alternating gentleness with cunning and with force. Until he realized his mistake and started to retreat. But at that moment the door opened and Ralph roared in a bearish voice, drowsily, Come in, please, come in, come in, just look at yourself, first thing—drink, you look frozen right through and as pale as death.

37

After pouring him a drink in the kitchen, and then another one,
straight whisky this time instead of Dubonnet, the large pink man
who resembled a Dutch farmer in an advertisement for classy
cigars insisted on not giving Yoel a chance to apologize or to
explain. Never mind. I don't care what brings you here like this
in the middle of the night. After all, everybody has enemies and
everybody has worries. We've never asked you what you do—
and by the way, you haven't asked me either. But maybe one day
you and I will have a nice job together. I've got a suggestion. Not
now in the middle of the night, of course. We'll talk about it
when you're ready for it. You'll find that I can do anything you
can, dear friend. Now, what can I offer you? Some supper? A hot
shower? Very well then, now it's bedtime even for big boys.

In a kind of sleepy submissiveness that fell upon him suddenly, from fatigue or mental distraction, he allowed Ralph to
take him to the bedroom. There, by the vague green underwater
light, he saw Annemarie sleeping on her back like a baby, with
her arms spread out by her sides and her hair spread out on the
pillow. Next to her face lay a little rag doll with long eyelashes.
Fascinated and exhausted Yoel stood by the bookcase watching
the woman, who seemed less sexual than touchingly innocent.
And as he watched he felt too tired to resist when Ralph began
to undress him in a firm yet gentle, fatherly way, undoing his belt
and loosening his shirt, then hurriedly unbuttoning it, releasing
Yoel's chest from his undershirt, bending over and untying his
shoelaces and removing the socks from the feet that Yoel obedi-

ently held out, unzipping his trousers, easing them down, pulling off the underpants too, and then, with his arm around Yoel's shoulder, like a swimming instructor leading a hesitant pupil to the water, taking him to the bed and raising the blanket and, when Yoel was lying, also on his back, next to Annemarie, who did not wake up, tenderly covering the two of them, whispering good night, and withdrawing.

Yoel raised himself on his elbow and gazed at the face of the pretty baby in the faint watery light. Gently, lovingly he kissed her, almost without his lips touching her skin, on the corners of her closed eyes. She put her arms around him, in her sleep, and focused her fingers on the back of his neck until his hair bristled slightly. As he closed his eyes, he picked up for a moment the sound of a warning from somewhere inside himself, Careful, man, check the escape routes, and at once he replied with the words, The sea doesn't run away. With that he began to devote himself to her pleasure as though pampering an abandoned child, almost ignored his own flesh, and in this way he had his pleasure. Until his eyes filled suddenly. Perhaps because, as he was sinking into sleep, he felt or guessed that her brother was adjusting the blanket over them.

38

It was not yet five o'clock when he got out of bed and dressed silently, pondering again, for some reason, what he had heard the neighbor Itamar or Eviatar say about the Biblical words *shebeshiflenu* and *namogu,* namely, that the former had a Polish sound, whereas the latter demanded to be pronounced in an indubitably Russian way. Unable to resist the temptation, he murmured softly to himself, *namogu,* indubitably, *shebeshiflenu.* But Annemarie and her brother went on sleeping, one in the double bed and the other in the armchair in front of the television, so Yoel tiptoed out without waking them. The promised rain had indeed arrived, even though it was only a gray drizzle in the darkness of the little street. Yellow puddles of mist formed around the street lamp. The dog Ironside came up and sniffed his hand, pleading for a caress, which Yoel granted him while reconstructing in his thoughts:

> Boyfriends
> breakers
> the sea.
> So youthful and pure
> rest in peace
> and they shall become one flesh.

Just as he opened his garden gate there was a vague brightening at the end of the street; the needles of rain were illuminated by a kind of murky whiteness, and for a moment it seemed again as though the rain were not falling but rising from the ground. Yoel darted forward and clung to the window of the old Susita at the moment the delivery man opened it a narrow crack and was about to throw the newspaper. When the man, who was old, possibly a pensioner, with a thick Bulgarian accent, insisted that he wasn't paid to get out of his car and bother with mailboxes, and, anyway, to put the paper in the mailbox he'd have to switch off the engine and leave the car in gear so it wouldn't run down the slope, since the hand brake was useless, Yoel cut him short, pulled out his wallet, and placed thirty shekels in his hand, saying that at Passover he'd get another thirty, and so he put an end to the problem.

But when he sat down in the kitchen, warming his hands on his coffee cup and poring over the newspaper, it dawned on him, as a result of connections he made between a short news item on page two and a death announcement, that the newscaster had been wrong at the end of last night's TV news. The mysterious accident had taken place, not in Taiwan, but in Bangkok. The man who had been killed and whose next of kin had been informed was not a businessman, but Yokneam Ostashinsky, known to some of his friends as Cockney and to others as the Acrobat. Yoel closed the newspaper. He folded it in half and carefully folded it in half again. He put it down on a corner of the kitchen table and took his coffee cup over to the sink, poured its contents away, rinsed it out, wiped it clean, rinsed it out again, and washed his hands too, in case they were black with ink from the newspaper. Then he dried the cup and spoon and put them both away. He left the kitchen and went to the living room, but not knowing what to do there he walked down the hall past the closed doors of the children's rooms where his mother and mother-in-law were sleeping and that of the master bedroom, and stood by the door of the study, afraid to disturb anyone. With nowhere else to go he went into the bathroom and shaved and was delighted to discover that this time there was plenty of hot water. Accordingly he stripped and got into the shower cubicle and washed his hair and soaped himself thoroughly from his ears to his toes and even

189

stuck a soapy finger inside his anus and rubbed it, then carefully washed the finger several times. He got out and dried himself, and before dressing dipped the finger in his after-shave as an extra precaution. It was ten past six when he left the bathroom, and until six-thirty he busied himself preparing breakfast for the three women, getting out the jam and honey, slicing the bread, and even preparing a finely chopped salad dressed with oil and dried hyssop and black pepper and sprinkled with little cubes of onion and garlic. Then he put fresh coffee in the percolator and set out plates and knives and forks and teaspoons and paper napkins on the table. So he passed the time until his watch showed quarter to seven, and he called Krantz and asked him if he could borrow their second car again, because Avigail might need the car and he had to go into town today, and might even have to go out of town. Krantz said immediately: No problem. He promised that he and Odelia would be around in convoy within half an hour with their two cars and leave him, not the little Fiat, but the blue Audi, which had been serviced only two days ago and was running like a dream now. Yoel thanked Krantz and sent his regards to Odelia and remembered the moment he replaced the receiver that there was no Lisa or Avigail; they had gone to the Winter Festival on Mount Carmel the day before yesterday and wouldn't be back till tomorrow. It was all for nothing that he had set the table for four and troubled Krantz and his wife to come around in convoy. But in accordance with some stubborn logic Yoel decided, Why not? I did them a big favor yesterday, so it won't hurt them to do me a little one today. From the telephone he returned to the kitchen and removed two place settings from the table, leaving only one for himself and a second for Netta, who woke up by herself at seven o'clock, got dressed, and appeared in the kitchen, not in her baggy pants and tentlike shirt, but in her school uniform, dark-blue skirt and light-blue blouse, and at that moment she seemed to Yoel pretty, attractive, and almost womanly. As she left she asked, What's up? And he delayed replying, because he hated lying, and finally he said only: Not now. I'll explain some other time. And then apparently I'll also have to explain why Krantz and Odelia are pulling up outside now, bringing me their Audi, even though there's nothing wrong with our car. That's the trouble, Netta: once you start explaining, it shows that something's already screwed up. You'd better go now, or you'll be late. Sorry I can't take you today. Even though I'll soon have two cars at my disposal here.

The moment the door closed behind his daughter, whom the Krantzes offered to take to school in their little Fiat on their way into town, Yoel rushed to the phone. He bumped his knee on the stool in the hall, and when he furiously kicked the stool, the telephone, which had been standing on it, fell off. It rang as it fell, and Yoel snatched the receiver, but he heard nothing. Not even the dial tone. Evidently the kick had damaged the instrument. He tried to fix it by raining blows on it from different directions, but to no avail. So he ran, panting, to the Vermonts', but as he got there he remembered that he had installed an extension phone in Avigail's bedroom so the old women could phone from there. To Ralph's astonishment therefore, he mumbled, Sorry; I'll explain later. And right outside their front door he turned around and raced home and finally called the office and discovered that he needn't have rushed: Tsippy, Le Patron's secretary, had got to work "right this very second." If Yoel had called two minutes earlier she wouldn't have been there. She'd always known that there was a kind of telepathic bond between them. And anyway, ever since he'd left— But Yoel interrupted her. He had to see his brother as soon as possible. Today. This morning. Tsippy said, Wait a moment, and he waited at least four minutes before he heard her voice again. And then he had to order her to stop apologizing and tell him what she'd been told. It emerged that Teacher had dictated his reply, word for word, and instructed her to repeat the message to Yoel without changing or adding a word: There's no hurry. We cannot arrange a meeting for you in the near future.

Yoel listened and restrained himself. He asked Tsippy if they knew yet when the funeral would be. She asked him to wait again, and this time he was made to hang on even longer than the first time. Just when he was about to slam the receiver down she said to him: It hasn't been arranged yet. He asked when he should call again, but he already knew that she would not answer him without a further consultation. Finally the reply came: You should watch for the announcement in the paper. That's how you'll find out.

When she asked him in a different voice, When are we going to see you at last? Yoel answered her softly: You'll be seeing me quite soon. He limped out favoring his injured knee, started Krantz's Audi at once, and drove straight to the office. For once he had not washed and dried their breakfast plates. He'd left everything, including the crumbs, on the kitchen table. No doubt to the astonishment of a couple of winter birds that were used to picking up the crumbs from his breakfast when he shook the tablecloth out on the lawn.

39

"Angry," said Tsippy, "isn't the right word. He's—what should I say?—mourning."

"Naturally."

"No, you don't understand: he's not mourning just for the Acrobat. He's mourning for the two of you. If I were you, Yoel, I wouldn't have come here today."

"Tell me. What happened in Bangkok? How did it happen? Tell me."

"Don't know."

"Did he tell you not to say anything to me?"

"I don't know, Yoel. Don't press me. It's not only you who finds it hard to live with."

"Who does he blame? Me? Himself? The bastards?"

"If I were you, Yoel, I wouldn't be here right now. Go home. Listen to me. Go."

"Is there anyone in there with him?"

"He doesn't want to see you. And that's putting it mildly."

"Just let him know I'm here. Or, rather"—Yoel suddenly laid his hard fingers on her soft shoulder—"wait. Don't tell him." In four paces he had reached the inner door and entered without knocking, and as he closed it behind him asked, How did it happen?

Teacher, portly, well groomed, with the face of a discriminating culture-consumer, his gray hair cut with precision and good taste, his fingernails carefully manicured, his plump pink cheeks smelling effeminately of after-shave, looked up at Yoel, who took

193

care not to lower his eyes. At that instant he saw that yellow cruelty like an overfed cat's glinting in the small pupils.

"I asked how did it happen."

"It doesn't matter how," the man replied with a singsong Gallic lilt, which on this occasion he chose to exaggerate, as though it gave him a malicious pleasure.

Yoel said:

"I have a right to know."

And the man, with no interrogative tone and with no ironic emphasis:

"Indeed."

"Look," said Yoel, "I have a suggestion to make."

"Indeed," the man repeated. And he added: "It won't help, comrade. You'll never know how it happened. I shall personally see to it that you never find out. You'll just have to live with it."

"I'll have to live with it," Yoel said. "But why me? You shouldn't have sent him. You sent him."

"In your place."

"I," Yoel said, fighting back the upsurge of mingled sorrow and anger, "would never have stepped into that trap. I didn't buy the whole story from the outset. That whole replay. I didn't believe it. The moment you told me that the girl was asking for me to come, letting fly all sorts of personal clues about me, I had a bad feeling. It smelled fishy. But you sent him."

"In your place," Le Patron repeated, this time very slowly, pronouncing each word separately. "Now—" and as though by prearrangement the ancient square Bakelite telephone on his desk began to ring hoarsely and the man cautiously raised the cracked receiver and said: Yes. Then, for ten minutes or so, he sat back and listened motionlessly and without making a sound except that he twice repeated: Yes.

So Yoel turned and walked over to the only window. Through which he could see a thick, almost porridgelike, gray-green sea, framed by two tall buildings. He remembered that it was less than a year ago that he had been thrilled by the prospect of inheriting this office when Teacher moved out to his colony of nature-loving philosophers in Upper Galilee. In his mind he sketched again that pleasing little scenario. He invites Ivria here on the pretext of consulting her about redecorating the room. Changing the furniture. Fixing up the gloomy office, which is beginning to look shabby. He sits her down there, facing him, on the chair he himself was occupying a moment ago. Just like a child amazing his mother after years of gray mediocrity. You see, from this Spartan office your husband controls a service that is considered by some to be the most efficient in the world. And now the time has come to change the prehistoric desk flanked by two metal file cabinets, to get rid of the coffee table and those ridiculous wicker chairs. What do you think, my dear? Maybe we should replace this bric-a-brac with a push-button telephone with automatic memory. Throw out the tattered curtains. Should we or shouldn't we leave the views of the walls of Jerusalem by Litvinowsky and the alley in Safed by Rubin hanging there as a reminder of bygone days? Do you see any point in keeping the National Fund collection box with its inscription "Bring Redemption to the Land," and its map of Palestine from Dan to Beersheba dotted with flyspecks indicating the tracts of land purchased by the Jews up to 1947? What shall we keep, Ivria, and what shall we throw out forever? And all of a sudden, as though with a faint quivering in the loins heralding the renewal of desire, it occurred to Yoel that it still wasn't too late. That in fact the Acrobat's death had brought him closer to his goal. That if he wanted it and if he calculated carefully, if he thought out his moves without making any mistakes, a year or two from now he would be able to invite Netta here on the pretext of asking her advice about redecorating the room, to sit her down precisely there, facing him across the desk, and explain to her modestly: You could describe your father as a sort of nightwatchman.

When he thought of Netta he was hit by the sharp, blinding realization that it was thanks to her that his life had been saved. That it was she who had not let him go to Bangkok this time, even though in his heart of hearts he had longed to go. That if it had not been for her obstinacy, her capricious intuition, the alarm raised by the sixth sense that came from her lunar-astral illness, he would be lying now in place of Yokneam Ostashinsky in the sealed lead coffin, perhaps in the hold of a Lufthansa jumbo jet making its way at this moment from the Far East over Pakistan or Kazakhstan in the dark toward Frankfurt and from there to Ben-Gurion Airport and from there to that rocky cemetery in Jerusalem, to the catarrhal voice of Nakdimon Lublin drawling the memorial prayer with comical mistakes in the Aramaic words. Thanks to Netta alone he had been saved from making that journey. From the seductive webs that woman had woven for him. And from the fate that the rotund, cruel man whom he sometimes, for purposes of emergency communication, called his brother had reserved for him. Now here he was, saying, "Yes. Thank you," putting the receiver down, and turning to Yoel and resuming his sentence at the precise point at which he had broken it off ten minutes earlier, when his shabby telephone had croaked:

". . . it's all over. And I must ask you to leave."

"Just a minute," said Yoel, running his finger as usual between his neck and his shirt collar. "I said I have got a suggestion to make."

"Thank you," said Le Patron. "It's too late."

"I'm offering"—Yoel chose to ignore the insult—"to go to Bangkok to find out what happened. Tomorrow. Even tonight."

"Thank you," said the man, "but we have all we need." In his accent, which was still more marked, Yoel thought he detected a trace of mockery. Or restrained anger. Or maybe just impatience. He spoke with a coquettish emphasis that sounded like a parody of a French immigrant. He stood up and concluded:

"Don't forget to tell my beloved Netta to call me at home about the matter she and I have been discussing."

"Wait a moment," said Yoel. "I also wanted to let you know that I'm prepared to consider returning to work now. Maybe on a part-time basis. Let's say in Operations Analysis. Or in Training."

"I've already told you, we have all we need."

"Or even in Archives. I don't mind. I think I can still be of some use."

In less than two minutes, when Yoel had left Le Patron's office and was walking along the corridor whose stained walls had finally been soundproofed and covered with cheap imitation-wood sheeting, he suddenly recalled the Acrobat's mocking voice telling him here not long ago that curiosity killed the cat. So he stepped into Tsippy's office and said only: "Excuse me a minute; I'll explain later," and he grabbed the intercom on her desk and, almost in a whisper, asked the man on the other side of the wall, "Tell me, Yirmiyahu, what have I done?"

Slowly, with didactic patience, the man stated: "You want to know what you've done." Then he continued as though dictating an official summary for the record: "By all means. You'll have your answer. An answer that you know already. You and I, comrade, are both refugees. Holocaust kids. They risked their lives to save us from the Nazis. They smuggled us here. And on top of that they fought and were maimed and killed to make a state for us. They handed it to us on a tray. They picked us up out of the shit. And after that they also did us an enormous honor. They let us work in the inner sanctum. In the heart of hearts. That puts an obligation on us, doesn't it? But you, comrade, when you were needed, when you were sent for, you wriggled out of it and got someone else sent in your place. One of them. And he was sent. So now just you go home and live with that. And don't call us three times a day to know when the funeral is. It'll be in the papers."

Yoel limped outside to the parking lot, because of the injury to his knee that morning when it collided with the stool. For some reason he was tempted, like a punished child, to exaggerate the limp, as though he had a serious injury. So he limped up and down for twenty or twenty-five minutes, passing every car three or four times, looking in vain for his own. At least four times he returned to the spot where he had parked. He could not imagine what had happened. Until he had a minor brainstorm and realized that he did not bring his own car, but Krantz's blue Audi, which was parked precisely where he had left it. With a kindly winter sun splitting into a thousand dazzling flashes on its rear window. And so he came to terms, more or less, with the realization that this chapter was now closed. That he would never again set foot in this old, unimposing building, surrounded by a high wall and hidden by thick cypress trees, shut in by many modern buildings of glass and concrete, all much taller. At that moment he felt a little pang of regret for something he could never do now: often during his twenty-three years here he had felt an urge to reach out and check once and for all whether anybody occasionally dropped a coin through the slit of the blue National Fund collection box in Le Patron's office. Now this question too would have to remain open. As he drove Yoel thought about the Acrobat, Yokneam Ostashinsky, who could not have been less like an acrobat. If anything, he had resembled an old Labor Party apparatchik, a quarry worker who in the course of time had become a regional boss in the construction cooperative. A man in his sixties with a tight drumlike belly. Once, seven or eight years ago, he had made an embarrassing mistake. Yoel had come to his rescue, and succeeded in extricating him from the consequences of his error without having to resort to a lie. Unfortunately, it subsequently transpired that, as often happens with the beneficiary of a favor that cannot ever be repaid, Ostashinsky nurtured petty spite against Yoel, and spread the word that he was a condescending prig. Yet, thought Yoel as he crawled along in the heavy traffic, if it is possible to use the word "friend" in my case, he was my friend. When Ivria died and Yoel was summoned back from Helsinki and arrived in Jerusalem only a few hours before the funeral, he discovered that all the arrangements had been made. Nakdimon Lublin drawled that he had had nothing to do with it. After a couple of days Yoel went in to clear up how much he owed and to whom, painstakingly checking the receipted bills for the funeral expenses and the announcement in the newspaper, and everywhere he found the name Sasha Schein. So he called the Acrobat to ask how much he had spent, and Ostashinsky, in an offended tone, swore at him in Russian and told him to fuck off. Once or twice, after a fight, late at night, Ivria had whispered to him: I understand you. What did she mean? What did she understand? What was the extent of the resemblance or difference between people's secrets? Yoel knew that there was no way to know. Even though the question of what people really know about each other, especially people who are close to one another, had always been an important one for him and had now become an urgent one. She almost always wore a white blouse and white linen pants. In winter she also wore a white sweater: a sailor whose fleet had set sail without her. She had worn no jewelry apart from the wedding ring on the little finger of her right hand. It was impossible to get it off, although her thin, childlike fingers were always cold. Again Yoel longed for their cool touch on his bare back. Just once, the previous autumn, on the kitchen balcony in Jerusalem, she had said to him: Listen. I'm not well. When he has asked what sort of pain she had, she had replied, No, you're wrong; it's not something physical. I'm just not well. And Yoel, who was waiting for a phone call from El Al, had answered, to evade the issue, to free himself, to cut short what was likely to develop into a long saga, It'll pass, Ivria. It'll be all right; you'll see. If he had responded to the call and gone to Bangkok, Le Patron and Ostashinsky would have taken on the task of looking after his mother, his daughter, and his mother-in-law. Every betrayal he had ever committed would have been forgiven and forgotten if he had gone and not come back. A cripple born without arms and legs was almost incapable of doing evil. And who could do evil to him? One who had lost his arms and legs could never be crucified. Would he never get to know what really happened in Bangkok? Maybe it was just a trivial accident at a pedestrian crossing or in an elevator? And would the members of the Israel Philharmonic Orchestra be informed one day that it was the man who at this moment was lying in a sealed lead coffin in the hold of a Lufthansa jumbo jet flying in the darkness over Pakistan who a few years ago, by his wisdom and courage, and with his gun, had saved them from massacre in the middle of their concert in Melbourne? At that moment Yoel felt an upsurge of rage at the secret joy that had been coursing through his chest all day: So what? I got rid of them. They wanted me dead and now they're dead themselves. He died? It shows he failed. She died? So she lost. Too bad. I'm alive. It proves I was right.

Or perhaps not. Maybe it's just the wages of treachery, he said to himself as he left the city and charged wildly past a line of four or five cars on his left, tore up the empty right-hand lane and cut in four inches in front of the nose of the front car in the line at the very split second the lights changed. Instead of going straight home, he turned off in the direction of Ramat Gan, pulled up outside the shopping center, and entered a large store selling women's clothing. After an hour and a half of reflection, comparison, examination, and fine reasoning he left, carrying an elegant package containing a daring, almost naughty dress for his daughter for saving his life. He was never wrong about sizes or about the fashions or about the quality of material or about colors and cut. In his other hand he held a bag containing, in separate packages, a shawl for his mother, a belt for his mother-in-law, a cute scarf for Odelia Krantz, a nightdress for Anne-marie, and half a dozen expensive silk handkerchiefs for Ralph. There was also a package done up with a bow and containing a handsome, conservative sweater as a parting present for Tsippy: one could not simply disappear without a trace after all those years. Although, on second thought, why not just slink away without leaving any mark behind him?

40

Netta said: "Are you crazy? I wouldn't wear that to save my life. Why don't you try giving it to the cleaner; she's my size. Or let me give it to her."

Yoel said:

"OK. Whatever you like. Only, try it on first."

Netta went out of the room and came back wearing the new dress, which had magically eliminated her skinniness and made her look erect and lithe.

"Tell me something," she said: "is that what you've always wanted me to wear, but never dared to ask?"

"What do you mean never dared?" Yoel smiled. "After all, I chose it myself."

"What's wrong with your knee?"

"Nothing. I bumped it."

"Let me have a look."

"What for?"

"I could put a bandage on it for you."

"It's nothing. Forget it. It'll go away."

She disappeared and returned to the living room five minutes later wearing her old clothes. She did not put the sexy dress on again in the weeks that followed. But she did not give it away to the cleaner either, as she had said she would. Yoel sometimes sneaked into the master bedroom when she was out and checked that it was still hanging in the closet, waiting. He saw this as a limited success. One evening Netta put a book in his hands, *Anx-*

ious Relations by Yair Hurvitz. On page 47 he came upon a poem called "Responsibility," and he said to his daughter:

"I like that one. Though how do I know if what I think I understand is what the poet meant?"

He did not go back into Tel Aviv. Not even once, up to the end of that winter. Sometimes at night he stood facing the fence around the citrus grove at the end of the street, with its smell of moist earth and trees heavy with foliage, and stared for a while at the glare that seemed from the distance to be hanging over the city. Its color was sometimes a brilliant blue and sometimes gold or pale yellow or even reddish-purple, and at times it reminded him of the poisoned sickly color of a chemical flame.

Meanwhile he had abandoned his nocturnal drives to the Carmel range, the Trappist monastery at Latrun, the limit of the coastal plain, and the hill country near Rosh Ha'ayin. He no longer whiled away the small hours in conversation with the night-shift Arabs at gas stations, or crawled slowly past the highway whores. Nor did he visit the garden shed in the deepest darkness. But he did find himself every four or five evenings standing before the neighbors' front door, and recently he had taken to bearing a bottle of whisky or a well-known liqueur. He was always careful to get home before dawn. Occasionally he came across the old Bulgarian who delivered the newspapers; so he took the paper from his hand through the window of the battered Susita and spared him the trouble of getting out and putting it in the mailbox. Several times Ralph said, We're not rushing you. Take your time, Yoel. Who shrugged and said nothing.

Once, Annemarie suddenly asked:

"Tell me, what's the matter with your daughter?"

Yoel reflected for almost a full minute before replying:

"I'm not sure I understand the question."

Annemarie said:

"Well. I always see you together but I've never seen you touching one another."

Yoel said:

"Yes. Maybe."

"Won't you ever tell me anything? What am I to you, some kind of kitten?"

"It'll be all right," he said absentmindedly, and poured himself a drink. What could he tell her? I murdered my wife because she was trying to murder our daughter who was trying to do away with her parents? Even though there was more love among the three of us than was permissible. Like the verse that says, From thee to thee I flee. So he said:

"Let's talk about it some other time." And he drank and closed his eyes.

A delicate, precise carnal kinship gradually deepened between him and Annemarie. Like a long-standing experienced pair of tennis partners. Lately Yoel renounced his habit of making love with her as though he were bestowing favors on her and denying his own flesh. Slowly he began to trust her and hint at his weaknesses. He began to make secretive physical demands on her which all those years he had been too embarrassed to reveal to his wife and too delicate to impose on passing women. Annemarie would concentrate with her eyes closed, straining to catch the faintest note. She would bend over and play tunes for him that he himself did not know how much he was longing for her to play. Sometimes she seemed to be not so much making love to him as conceiving and bearing him. And the moment they finished, Ralph would burst in, bearlike, overflowing with joy and kindness, like a coach whose team has just won a victory, serving his sister and Yoel glasses of hot punch spiced with fragrant cinnamon, holding out a towel, changing the Brahms for a quiet country-music record, turning down the sound and the green submarine light, whispering good night and fading away.

Yoel bought gladiolus corms and dahlia tubers and gerbera bulbs at Bardugo's Nurseries, and planted them for spring. He also bought four dormant vine shoots, as well as half a dozen large pots and three sacks of enriched compost. He did not go as far as Qalqilya. He set the pots in the corners of the garden and planted different-colored geraniums in them, so that in the summer they would pour in a blaze over the sides. At the beginning of February he went to the local shopping center with Arik Krantz and his son Duby, and bought wooden beams and long bolts and metal catches and angle irons at a builders' supply store. In ten days, with the enthusiastic support of Arik and Duby but also, to his surprise, with Netta's help, he had dismantled the old carport with its corrugated-iron roof and replaced it with a beautiful wooden pergola, which he painted with two coats of weatherproof brown varnish. He planted the four vine shoots so that he could train the vine over the pergola. When he came across an announcement in the paper of his friend's funeral in Pardes Hanna, Yoel decided not to go. He stayed at home. Whereas for the memorial service in Jerusalem on the sixteenth of February, the anniversary of Ivria's death, he went with his mother and his mother-in-law, and it was Netta who once again decided not to go, but to stay behind and look after the house.

When Nakdimon intoned his faulty version of the kaddish in his nasal drawl, Yoel leaned toward his mother and whispered to her, The best thing is the way his glasses make him look like an educated horse. A religious horse. Lisa hissed in an angry whisper: Shame on you! And at the graveside too! You've all forgotten her! Avigail, stiff and aristocratic-looking in the black scarf that covered her head and shoulders, signaled to them, Stop it. And Yoel and his mother did instantly stop whispering.

Later that day all of them, including Nakdimon and two of his four sons, went to the house in Ramat Lotan. They found that Netta, with the help of Ralph and Annemarie, had extended the Spanish dining table for the first time since they had moved in and had spent the day preparing a meal for ten people. With a red tablecloth and candles, and spicy turkey scallops, boiled vegetables, steamed rice and mushrooms, and piquant tomato soup served cold in tall glasses with a slice of lemon riding astride the rim of each one. It was the soup that her mother had been in the habit of surprising visitors with, on the rare occasions when they had visitors. Netta had even devised a carefully thought-out seating plan, putting Annemarie next to Krantz, Nakdimon's sons between Lisa and Ralph, Avigail next to Duby Krantz, and Yoel and Nakdimon at the ends of the table.

41

The next day, the seventeenth of February, was a gray day and the air seemed to be congealed. But it was not raining and there was no wind. After taking Netta to school and his mother to the foreign-language lending library, he drove on to the gas station; he filled the tank and went on pressing until the pump cut out automatically, then he checked the oil and water and the battery and the tire pressures. When he got home he went into the garden and pruned the rosebushes, as he had planned. He spread manure over the lawns, which were yellowing owing to the winter rain and the cold. He also mulched the fruit trees in readiness for the approaching spring, mixing the manure in with the leaves that were moldering under the trees, then spreading the mixture with a fork and a rake. He repaired the irrigation basins and weeded the flower beds a little, with his fingers, bending over as though prostrating himself, and removing the first shoots of couch grass, wood sorrel, and bindweed. It was from this deep crouching position that he saw her blue flannel dressing gown coming out of the kitchen door; he could not see her face, and he shrank back as though he had received a well-aimed punch in the solar plexus or as though some kind of collapse had occurred in his stomach. Instantly his fingers stiffened. Then he gained control of himself, stifled his anger, and said: "What's happened, Avigail?" She burst out laughing and replied: "What's the matter, did I startle you? Just look at your face. You look as though you're about to kill somebody. Nothing's happened. I just came out to ask you if you'd like your coffee out here or if you're coming in soon." He said: "No. I'm just coming," and then he changed his mind and said: "Or, rather, bring it out here, so it doesn't get cold." Then he changed his mind again and said in a different voice: "Never, do you hear me, don't you ever put her clothes on again." What Avigail heard in his voice made her broad, bright, placid Slavic peasant's face turn a deep red: "It's not her clothes. This is a dressing gown she gave me five years ago when you bought her a new one in London."

Yoel knew he ought to apologize. Only a couple of days earlier he had pleaded with Netta to wear the nice raincoat he had bought for Ivria in Stockholm. But his rage, or perhaps his anger at the appearance of this rage, made him not apologize, but hiss grimly, almost menacingly: "It makes no difference. This is my house and I won't put up with it."

"Your house?" Avigail inquired in her pedagogic tone of voice, like a tolerant headmistress of a liberal school.

"My house," Yoel repeated quietly, wiping the damp soil off his fingers on the seat of his jeans. "And here in my house you're not to wear her things."

"Yoel," she said, after a moment, in a tone of sadness tinged with affection, "would you mind my saying something to you? I'm beginning to think that your condition may be as bad as your mother's. Or Netta's. Except that of course you're better at concealing your problems, and that makes your condition even worse. In my opinion, what you really need is—"

"OK," Yoel cut in, "that'll do for today. Is there some coffee or isn't there? I ought to have gone inside and made it myself instead of relying on favors. It won't be long before we have to send in the antiterrorist troops."

"And speaking of your mother," Avigail said, "you know very well that we have a meaningful relationship, the two of us, but when I see—"

"Avigail," he said, "the coffee."

"I understand," she said, going indoors and returning with a mug of coffee and a grapefruit on a plate, carefully peeled and opened out like a chrysanthemum. "I see. Talking hurts you, Yoel.

I should have sensed it myself. Seemingly everybody has to bear his affliction in his own way. I want to say I'm sorry if I hurt you."

"All right, let's drop it," said Yoel, suddenly filled with loathing because of the way she said "see-eemingly." He wanted to think about something different, but there suddenly floated into his mind the image of Shealtiel Lublin, the policeman, with his walrus mustache, his rough kindness, his clumsy generosity, his jokes about sex and other bodily functions, and his habitual smoke-scorched sermons on the subject of the tyranny of the gonads or the community of secrets. He found that the loathing welling up inside him was directed against neither Lublin nor Avigail, but against the memory of his wife, against her icy silence and her white clothes. With difficulty he forced himself to take a few sips of coffee, like someone bending over sewage, and immediately handed the mug and the grapefruit-flower back to Avigail. Without another word he prostrated himself once more over the cleared flower bed, and resumed his hawk-eyed search for signs of sprouting weeds. He decided to put on his black-framed glasses to help him in his search. After twenty minutes, however, he went into the kitchen, and saw her frozen in a stiff sitting position, with her widow's scarf draped around her shoulders, looking the very picture of the unknown bereaved mother, staring unmovingly through the window at the precise spot in the garden where he had been working a moment before. Unthinkingly he followed her gaze with his eyes. But the spot was empty. He said:

"All right. I've come to apologize. I didn't mean to upset you."

Then he started the car and went back to Bardugo's Nurseries.

Where else could he go during these days at the end of February, after Netta had already been twice to the recruiting center, at a week's interval, and they were waiting for the results of her physical. He took her to school every morning, always at the last minute. Or later. But on her visits to the recruiting center it was Duby, one of Arik Krantz's two sons, who accompanied her, a skinny, tousled lad who for some reason made Yoel think of a

Yemeni newsboy from the early years of the state. It turned out that his father had sent him, and apparently also instructed him to wait outside on both occasions until she was finished and then drive her home in the little Fiat.

"Tell me something. Do you happen to collect thistles and sheet music too, by any chance?" Yoel asked this Duby Krantz. And the young man, totally ignoring the irony or incapable of detecting it, replied softly: "Not yet."

Besides driving Netta to school, Yoel also drove his mother, for regular checkups, to Dr. Litwin's private clinic not far from Ramat Lotan. On one of these trips she suddenly asked him, without any warning or connection, whether the business with the neighbor's sister was serious. And without thinking he answered her with the same words that Krantz's son had used to answer him. He often spent an hour or more at Bardugo's Nurseries in the middle of the morning. He bought various window boxes, large and small flowerpots of earthenware or synthetic material, two different types of enriched potting compost, a tool for loosening the soil, and two sprays, one for watering and another for pesticides. The whole house was filling up with plants. Especially ferns, which hung from the ceilings and doorframes. To put them up, he had to bring his electric drill with its extension cord back into service. Once, when he was on his way home from the nursery at half past eleven in the morning, with his car looking like a tropical jungle on wheels, he noticed the Filipino maid from the house down the street pushing her loaded shopping cart up the steep slope a quarter of an hour's walk from their street. Yoel stopped and made her accept a lift. Even though he was unable to engage her in conversation beyond the necessary expressions of politeness. After that he lay in wait for her on several occasions at the corner of the parking lot by the supermarket, alert behind the wheel and hidden behind his new sunglasses, and when she emerged with her cart he drove up sharply and managed to waylay her. It turned out that she knew a little Hebrew and a little English and made do for the most part with three- or four-word answers. Without being asked, Yoel

volunteered to improve the shopping cart: he promised to fit rub-
ber-rimmed wheels in place of the noisy metal ones. He did go
into the builders' supply store in the shopping center and, among
other things, bought some wheels with rubber rims. But he never
managed to bring himself to the front door of the strangers the
woman worked for, and on the occasions when he succeeded in
waylaying her with her cart on the way out of the supermarket
and taking her home in his car, he could hardly stop suddenly in
the middle of the street in the middle of the neighborhood in full
view and start emptying the shopping out of the heavily laden
cart, turning it upside down, and changing its wheels. And so it
was that Yoel did not keep his promise, and even pretended he
had never made it. He hid the new wheels from himself in a dark
corner of the garden shed. Even though in all his years in the
service he had always been particular about keeping his word.
Apart, perhaps, from his last day at work, when he had been
summoned back in a hurry from Helsinki and had not managed
to keep his promise to get in touch with the Tunisian engineer.
When this occurred to him, he discovered to his amazement that
even though the month of February had just ended, and so it was
a year or more since the day he had seen the cripple in Helsinki,
the telephone number that the engineer had given him was still
engraved on his memory. He had memorized it at the time and
never forgotten it.

That evening, when the women had left him alone in the living room to watch the last news and the snowflakes that filled
the screen afterward, he had to fight against the sudden temptation to dial the number. But how could someone with no limbs
pick up the receiver? And what could he say? Or ask? As he got
up to switch off the uselessly flickering television set, it dawned
on him that the month of February had indeed ended the day
before, and that consequently today was his wedding anniversary. He picked up the big flashlight and went outside into the
dark garden to check the state of each and every sapling and
seedling.

One night, Yoel, after love, and over a glass of steaming punch, heard Ralph ask if he could offer him a loan. For some reason Yoel got the impression that Ralph was asking him for a loan and he had asked him how much, and Ralph had said "Up to twenty or thirty thousand" before Yoel figured out that he was being offered the money, not asked for it. He was surprised. Ralph said: "Whenever you like. Be my guest. We won't rush you." Suddenly Annemarie, clutching the red kimono to her slight body, intervened, saying: "I object to this. There'll be no business before we find ourselves."

"Find ourselves?"

"I mean: all of us straighten out our lives a little."

Yoel looked at her and waited. Ralph did not speak either. Some dormant sense of survival stirred suddenly deep inside Yoel and warned him that it would be best to interrupt her at once. Change the subject. Look at his watch and say good night. Or at least join Ralph and make fun of what she had said and what she was about to say.

"Musical chairs, for instance," she continued, and burst out laughing. "Who remembers how to play?"

"That will do," Ralph urged, as though he sensed Yoel's anxiety and saw reasons to share it.

"For instance," she said, "there's an old man living across the street. From Romania. He talks to your mother in Romanian for half an hour at a stretch over the fence. And he also lives by himself. Why shouldn't she move in with him?"

"But what for?"

"Why, then Ralphie can move into your house with the other mom and live with her. At least for a trial period. And you could move in here. What do you say?"

Ralph said: "Like Noah's ark. She pairs everyone off. What's the matter? Is there a flood coming?"

Yoel, taking care not to sound angry, but amused and good-natured, said: "You've forgotten about the child. Where do we put her in your Noah's ark? Can I have some more punch?"

"Netta," said Annemarie, so softly that her voice was almost inaudible and Yoel almost missed the words and the tears that filled her eyes at that moment. "Netta is a young woman. Not a child. How long will you go on calling her a child? I think, Yoel, you've never known what a woman is. You don't even understand the word. Ralph, don't interrupt me. You've never known it either. How do you say 'role' in Hebrew? I wanted to say that you always either make us play the role of a baby or act it out yourselves. Sometimes I think, What a sweet little, nice little baby, but we have to kill the baby. I'd like some more punch too."

42

During the days that followed, Yoel thought about Ralph's offer.
Particularly once it became clear to him that the new lines of
battle set him and his mother, the objectors, against his mother-
in-law and Netta, who supported the idea of renting the penthouse
apartment on Karl Netter Street. Even before the approaching
examinations. On the tenth of March, Netta received a notifica-
tion from the army computer saying that her call-up would be in
seven months' time, on the twentieth of October. From this Yoel
deduced that she had not informed the doctors at the recruiting
center about her problem, or perhaps she had but the tests had
revealed nothing. At times he asked himself if his silence was not
irresponsible. Was it not his clear duty, as a single parent, to
contact them on his own initiative and bring the facts to their
attention? The findings of the doctors in Jerusalem. On the other
hand, he thought, which of the divided opinions was it his duty
to present to them? And would it not be wrong and irresponsible
to initiate such a step behind her back? To stamp her for the rest
of her life with the stigma of an illness that was the butt of all
sorts of superstitions? Was it not a fact that Netta's problem had
never manifested itself outside the home? Not once. Since Ivria's
death there had been only one solitary occurrence even within
the home, and that had been some time earlier, at the end of
August, and since then there had been no further sign. In fact,
what had happened in August had involved at the least a slight
ambivalence. So why should he not go to Karl Netter Street in
Tel Aviv, check out the room that allegedly had a view of the

sea, investigate the neighbors, find out discreetly about the apartment mate, this classmate named Adva, and if it turned out that everything was aboveboard, she would receive a hundred and twenty dollars a month, or more, and in the evenings he could stop in for coffee and so make sure day by day that everything was OK. And what if it really turned out that Le Patron was seriously intending to offer her a minor clerical job in the office? Some sort of junior secretarial work? He could always decide to exercise his veto and frustrate Teacher's schemes. On second thought, why should he forbid her to work a little in the office? It would spare him the need to pull strings, to reactivate old contacts, to release her from her call-up without making use of the pretext of defective health and without branding her with the stigma of having been exempted on medical grounds. Le Patron could easily arrange to have her work in the office recognized as a substitute for military service. Moreover, it would be splendid if he, Yoel, with a few well-thought-out moves, could rescue Netta both from the army and from the stigma that Ivria had sometimes insanely accused him of trying to brand his daughter with. Moreover, shifting his ground on the question of the apartment in Karl Netter Street might bring about a change in the balance of power in the house. Though it was clear to him that the moment his daughter was on his side once more, the alliance between the two old women would be renewed. And vice versa: if he managed to recruit Avigail to his camp, his mother and his daughter would join ranks across the barricade. So what was the point of bothering? So he left the matter for the time being, without doing anything about either the call-up or the apartment. Once more he decided that there was no rush, tomorrow was another day, and the sea would not run away. In the meantime, he repaired the landlord, Mr. Kramer's, broken vacuum cleaner, and spent a day and a half helping the cleaner to remove every last speck of dust from the house, just as he had done every spring in their apartment in Jerusalem. So immersed was he in the operation that when the phone rang and Duby Krantz asked when Netta would be home, Yoel announced curtly that they were in the middle of spring-cleaning and could he please call back another time. As for Ralph's suggestion that he invest money in a discreet fund linked to a consortium in Canada that would double his investment in eighteen months, Yoel examined the proposition in relation to a number of other ideas that had been put to him. For instance, the hint his mother had dropped several times concerning the large sum of money she was keeping to start him off in the business world. And the fabulous rewards that his ex-colleague from the service promised him if he would only agree to go in with him in a private investigation agency. And Arik Krantz, who never stopped begging him to share his adventure: twice a week put on a white coat and spend four hours on a night shift as a volunteer auxiliary in the hospital where he had earned the devotion of Greta the volunteer; and where Krantz had earmarked two other volunteers, Christina and Iris, for Yoel, and he could choose between them or choose them both. But the fabulous rewards said nothing to him. Nor did the tempting investments or Krantz's volunteers. Nothing stirred in him, beyond a vague but constant feeling that he was not really awake: that he was walking about, brooding, looking after the house and the garden and the car, making love to Annemarie, driving backward and forward between the nursery, the house, and the shopping center, cleaning the windows for Passover; that he had nearly finished reading the biography of Chief of Staff Eleazar—all in his sleep. If he still retained a hope of deciphering something, of understanding, or at least of formulating the question clearly, he must get out of this thick fog. He must wake up at all costs from this slumber. Even if it needed a disaster. If only something would come and slice away the soft fatty jelly that was closing in around him from every direction and stifling him like a womb.

Sometimes he would recall the sharp, vigilant moments of his career, when he would steal down the streets of a foreign city as though slipping through a narrow crack between two razors, physically and mentally acute, as when hunting or making love, when even simple, trivial, everyday things yielded hints to him of the secrets they enfolded. The evening lights reflected in a puddle.

The folds of a passerby's sleeve. A glimpse of the daring cut of a woman's underwear under a summer dress. Sometimes he even managed to guess something several seconds before it actually happened. Like a breeze starting up, or which way a cat crouching on a wall would leap, or the certainty that a man coming toward him would stop, tap his forehead, turn around, and retrace his steps. His perceptional life had been so sharp in those years, and now everything was blunt. Slowed down. As though the glass were clouding over, and he had no way of discovering whether the mist was on the outside or the inside, or whether, worse than that, it was neither of these, but the glass itself was suddenly discharging the opaque, milky element into itself. And if he did not wake up and smash it now, it would go on clouding over, the somnolence would deepen, the memory of the moments of alertness would gradually fade, and he would die unaware, like a wayfarer falling asleep in the snow.

At the optician's in the shopping center he purchased a powerful magnifying glass. When he was alone in the house one morning he finally inspected the strange spot by the entrance to one of the Romanesque abbeys in the photographs that had belonged to Ivria. He scrutinized it intensely for a long time, with the help of a focused beam of light and his glasses and Ivria's family doctor's glasses and the magnifying glass he had just bought, now from one angle and now from another. Until he began to feel inclined to accept the hypothesis that it was neither an abandoned object nor a stray bird but some sort of flaw in the photographic plate. Perhaps a tiny scratch that had occurred during the developing. The words of Jimmy Gal, the one-eared regimental commander, about the two points and the line connecting them, struck Yoel as correct beyond any doubt, but also trite, and evincing, ultimately, a measure of intellectual dullness that he deemed himself not free from, though he still hoped he might rid himself of it.

43

Suddenly spring exploded in the humming of swarms of wasps and flies, and eddies of scents and colors that struck Yoel as almost overdone. All of a sudden the garden seemed to be overflowing and discharging a mass of blossom and seething vegetation. The fruit trees came into flower and three days later they were aflame. Even the cactuses in their flowerpots on the porch erupted in scarlet and flaming orange-yellow, as though trying to talk to the sun in its own tongue. There was a kind of swell, which Yoel imagined he could hear foaming if he listened hard enough. As though the roots of the plants had turned into sharpened claws that were ripping at the earth in the blackness and drawing from it dark juices that were shooting upward in the tunnels of the trunks and stems and being proffered in the unfolding of the blossoms and foliage to the blinding light. Which tired his eyes again, despite the sunglasses he had bought himself at the beginning of the winter.

Standing beside the hedge Yoel reached the conclusion that the apple and pear trees were not enough. But ligustrum and oleander and bougainvillea, and even hibiscus bushes, struck him as boring and vulgar. He therefore decided to do away with the stretch of lawn at the side of the house, under the windows of the two children's rooms where the old women slept, and plant figs and olives and perhaps pomegranates. In due course the vines that he had planted around the new pergola would also spread to this part, so that in ten or twenty years there would be a perfect miniature replica of a thick dark Biblical orchard such as he

217

had always envied around the homes of Arab villagers. Yoel planned it down to the last detail: he shut himself away in his room and studied the relevant chapters of the agricultural handbook, drew up a table of the advantages and drawbacks of different varieties, and then went outside and measured the space there would be between the saplings, marked the positions with small pegs, telephoned Bardugo's every day to see if his order had arrived. And waited.

On the morning of Passover Eve, when the three women had gone off to Metullah leaving him alone, he went into the garden and dug five nice square holes where the pegs were. He lined the bottom of each hole with a layer of fine sand mixed with chicken dung. Then he drove to Bardugo's Nurseries to collect his saplings, which had just arrived: a fig, a date palm, a pomegranate, and two olives. He drove back in second gear all the way so as not to upset the plants, and found Duby Krantz sitting on the front doorstep, looking thin, curly, and dreamy. Yoel knew that both the Krantz boys had finished their military service, yet this young boy looked as if he were no older than sixteen.

"Did your father send you over to bring me the sprayer?"

"Well, it's like this," said Duby, drawing out the syllables as though he had difficulty parting with them, "if you need the sprayer, I can go back and get it. No problem. I've got my parents' car here. They're away. Mum's abroad and Dad's gone to Eilat for the festival and my brother's gone to stay with his girlfriend in Haifa."

"What about you? Have you locked yourself out?"

"No. It's something else."

"Like what?"

"The fact is, I came to see Netta. I was thinking, maybe tonight—"

"It's a pity you were thinking, friend." Yoel burst out laughing, surprising himself and the boy. "While you were busy thinking, she went off to the other end of the country with her grannies. Can you spare five minutes? Come and help me unload these trees."

For three-quarters of an hour they worked without talking, apart from essential words like "Hold this" or "Straighter" or "Pack it down well but carefully." They cut away the metal containers and managed to release the saplings without disturbing the ball of earth around the roots. Silently and meticulously they performed the burial ceremony, including filling in the holes and tamping down the soil, building a ring of earth around each tree for irrigation water. Yoel was pleased with the young man's work, and he began to appreciate his shyness or reticence. One evening at the end of an autumn day in Jerusalem—it was a Friday evening and the sadness of the hills was filling the air—he had gone out for a walk with Ivria, and they had gone into the Rose Garden to watch the sunset. Ivria said, You remember when you raped me under the trees in Metullah? I thought you were dumb. And Yoel, who knew that his wife rarely joked, at once corrected her and said: That's not right, Ivria. It wasn't rape; if anything, it was the opposite: seduction. That's point number one. But then he forgot to say what point number two was. Ivria said: You always file every detail away in that awesome memory of yours, you never lose the slightest crumb. But you always process the data first. After all, that's your profession. But on my side it was love.

When they had finished, Yoel said, Well, what does it feel like planting trees at Passover as if it were Tu Bishvat? He invited the boy into the kitchen for a cold orangeade because they were both pouring with sweat. Then he made some coffee too. And quizzed him a little about his army service in Lebanon, about his political views, which according to his father were extremely left-wing, and about his current activities. It turned out that the boy had served in field engineering, that he thought Shimon Peres was doing quite a good job, and that right now he was studying mechanics. It happened to be his hobby, and now he'd decided to make it his career too. He believed, though he had not had a lot of experience, that the best thing that could happen to a man was when his hobby filled his life.

Yoel intervened here, jokingly:

219

"Some people say that the best thing in life is love. Don't you agree?"

And Duby, intensely serious, with an emotion he managed to overcome so successfully that all that remained was a glint in his eye, said:

"I don't pretend to understand all that yet. Love and so on. When you look at my parents—you know them, after all—you might think the best thing is to keep feelings on a back burner. No. The healthy thing is to do something that you do well. Something that somebody needs. That's the two most satisfying things. Anyway, the two most satisfying things for me: to be needed, and to do a good job."

And since Yoel was in no hurry to reply, the boy made a further effort and added:

"Excuse my asking: is it true you're an international arms dealer, or something like that?"

Yoel shrugged, smiled, and said: "Why not?" Suddenly he stopped smiling and said:

"That was a joke. The fact is, I'm nothing more than a government employee. On a kind of extended leave at the moment. Tell me something: what exactly are you looking for in Netta? An introduction to modern poetry? A crash course on the thistles of Israel?"

With this, he managed to embarrass and frighten the boy. Duby hurriedly put the coffee cup he was holding down on the tablecloth, then picked it up again and put it carefully on the saucer, chewed his thumbnail for a moment, instantly thought better of it, and stopped, and said:

"Nothing special. We just chat."

"Nothing special," Yoel said, spreading on his face for a moment the stony, frozen-eyed feline cruelty he had employed at will to frighten punks, small-time crooks, creatures crawling out of the dirt. "If it's nothing special, you've called at the wrong address, friend. You'd better try somewhere else."

"All I meant was—"

"Anyway, you'd better keep away from her. Haven't you

heard? She's not a hundred percent. She has a minor health problem. But don't you dare breathe a word about it."

"I did hear something like that," said Duby.

"What!"

"I heard something. So what."

"Just a minute. I want you to repeat it. Word for word. What did you hear about Netta?"

"Forget it." Duby spun the words out. "All sorts of rumors. Trash. Don't get upset over it. I had the same thing once. Rumors buzzed around, something about nerves and so on. Let them buzz; that's what I say."

"You have a problem with your nerves?"

"Hell, no."

"Listen carefully. I can easily check, you know. Do you or don't you?"

"I did once. I'm OK now."

"That's what you say."

"Mr. Ravid?"

"Yes."

"Can I ask you what you want with me?"

"Nothing. Only don't start filling Netta's head with all sorts of nonsense. She's got enough of that already. So have you, by the sound of it. Have you finished your coffee? So there's nobody at home? Do you want me to make you a snack?"

Afterward the boy said good-bye and drove off in his parents' blue Audi. Yoel got under a very hot shower, soaped himself twice, rinsed in cold water, and got out muttering: Suit yourself.

At four-thirty Ralph arrived to say that he and his sister realized that he wouldn't be celebrating the festival, but seeing that he was all alone, would he like to join them for supper and watch a comedy on the VCR? Annemarie was making a Waldorf salad, and he was trying an experiment with veal stewed in wine. Yoel promised to come, but when Ralph came over to get him at seven o'clock, he found him sleeping, fully dressed, on the living-room sofa surrounded by pages from the special supplement of the newspaper. He decided to let him sleep. Yoel slept long and deeply in the empty, dark house. Only once, after midnight, did he get up and grope his way to the bathroom without opening his eyes and without switching on the light. The sounds of the television or the VCR next door were mingled in his sleep with the balalaika of the truck driver who might have been a kind of lover of his wife's. Instead of the bathroom door, he found the kitchen door, and he groped his way out into the garden and pissed with his eyes closed; returning to the sofa in the living room with his eyes still closed, he wrapped himself in the checked bedspread and sank back into sleep, like an ancient stone sinking into the dust, until nine o'clock the following morning. So that night he missed a mysterious sight taking place right overhead: vast flights of storks, in a broad stream, one after another without a break, sailing northward under a full spring moon, in a cloudless sky, thousands, perhaps tens of thousands of lithe silhouettes floating over the earth with a silent swishing of wings. It was a long, relentless, irrevocable, yet delicate movement, like masses of tiny white silk handkerchiefs streaming across a vast black silk screen, all bathed in a luminous silvery lunar-astral glow.

44

When he got up at nine o'clock on Passover morning he padded to the bathroom in his crumpled clothes, shaved, took another long, thorough shower, put on clean white sports clothes, and went outside to see how his new plants, the pomegranate, the two olive trees, and the date palm, were feeling. He gave them a light watering. He plucked out, here and there, tiny tips of new weeds that had apparently sprouted during the night, after his careful search of the previous day. While the coffee was percolating he dialed the Krantzes' number to apologize to Duby for possibly treating him rather rudely. At once he realized that he would have to apologize twice, the second time for waking him up from his holiday sleep-in. But Duby said, It's nothing, it's only natural you should worry about her, it doesn't matter, though you ought to know that actually she's quite good at worrying about herself. By the way, if you need me again for the garden or anything, I've got nothing special to do today. It was nice to you to call, Mr. Ravid. Of course I'm not angry.

Yoel asked when Duby's parents were due back, and when he learned that Odelia was expected back from Europe the following day and that Krantz was returning from his sortie to Eilat that same evening in order to be home in time to turn over a new leaf again, Yoel thought that the expression "a new leaf" was unsatisfactory, because it sounded flimsy, like paper. He asked Duby to tell his father to give him a call when he got back; there might be a little something for him.

Then he went into the garden and looked at the bed of carnations and snapdragons for a while, but he could not see what else he could do there, and he said to himself: Enough. On the other side of the fence the dog Ironside, sitting in the street in a formal pose, with his legs together, was trying to follow with a speculative gaze the flight of a bird whose name Yoel did not know but which thrilled him with its brilliant blue color. The truth is that there can be no new leaf. Only perhaps a prolonged birth. And birth is a form of parting, and to part is hard, and anyway who can part all the way? On the one hand you continue being born to your parents for years upon years, and on the other hand you start giving birth even before you have finished being born, and so you get caught up in disengagement battles to the front and the rear. It suddenly occurred to him that there was reason to envy his father, his melancholy Romanian father in the brown striped suit, or his unshaven father in the filthy ship, both of whom had vanished without a trace. And what was it that stopped you from vanishing without a trace too, during all those years, assuming the identity of a driving instructor in Brisbane or living as a trapper and fisherman in a forest north of Vancouver, in a log cabin you built for yourself and the Eskimo mistress who so annoyed Ivria? And what is it that prevents you from vanishing now? "What a fool," he said affectionately to the dog, who had suddenly decided to cease looking like a china ornament and become a hunter, standing on his hind legs and resting his front paws on the fence, presumably in the hope of catching the bird. Until the middle-aged neighbor opposite whistled to him and took the opportunity to offer Yoel the season's greetings.

All of a sudden Yoel felt sharp hunger pangs. He remembered that he had eaten nothing since lunch the previous day, because he had fallen asleep fully dressed. And he had had nothing but coffee this morning. So he went next door and asked Ralph if there was any of last night's veal left, and if he could have the leftovers for breakfast. "There's some Waldorf salad left too," Annemarie said cheerfully, "and some soup. But it's very highly seasoned, and it might not be a good idea to have it first thing in the morning." Yoel chuckled, because he remembered right then one of Nakdimon Lublin's rhymes, "Muhammad said: Make no mistake, When my belly's empty I could swallow a snake." Without troubling to reply he simply gestured Bring out whatever you've got.

It seemed as though there was no limit to his eating capacity on that festival morning. Having demolished the soup and the leftover veal and salad, he did not hesitate to ask for breakfast as well: toast and cheese and yogurt. When Ralph opened the door of the refrigerator for a moment to get out the milk, Yoel's well-trained eyes spotted a pitcher of tomato juice and he shamelessly asked if he could demolish that too.

"Tell me something," Ralph Vermont began. "Heaven forbid that I should try to rush you, I just wanted to ask."

"Ask ahead," said Yoel, with his mouth full of cheese on toast.

"I wanted to ask you, if you don't mind, something like this: Are you in love with my sister?"

"Right now?" Yoel muttered, startled by the question.

"Now too," Ralph specified, calmly but with clarity, like a man who knows where his duty lies.

"Why are you asking?" Yoel hesitated, as though playing for time. "I mean to say, why are *you* asking instead of Annemarie? Why isn't she asking? Why does she need a go-between?"

"Look who's talking," said Ralph, not sarcastically, but blithely, as though amused by the sight of the other's blindness. And Annemarie, almost devoutly, with her eyes nearly closed, as though in prayer, whispered:

"Yes. I am asking."

Yoel ran his finger slowly between his neck and his shirt collar. He filled his lungs with air and let it out slowly. Shame, he thought, shame on me, for not gathering any information, not even the most basic details, about these two. I haven't got a clue who they are, where they sprang from or why, what they're after here. But he refrained from telling a lie. The true answer to their question he did not know yet.

"I need a little more time," he said. "I can't give you an answer right away. It needs some more time."

"Who's rushing you?" Ralph asked, and for a moment Yoel thought he saw a swift flash of paternal irony cross his middle-aged schoolboy's face, which life's sorrows had left no trace on. As if the placid face of an aging child was only a mask, and for an instant a bitter or sly expression had been revealed underneath it.

Still smiling affectionately, almost stupidly, the overgrown farmer took Yoel's broad, ugly hands, which were brown as bread with garden soil under the fingernails, between his own pink, abundantly freckled hands, and placed each of them slowly and gently on one of his sister's breasts, so accurately that Yoel could feel the stiffened nipple in the exact center of each hand. Annemarie laughed softly. Ralph sat down clumsily, with a chastened air, on a stool in a corner of the kitchen, and asked sheepishly:

"If you do decide to take her, do you think I . . . that there'll be some room for me? Around the place?"

Then Annemarie released herself and got up to make the coffee, because the water was boiling. While they were drinking it, the brother and sister suggested that Yoel watch the comedy that they had seen the previous evening on the VCR, and he had missed because he had fallen asleep. Yoel stood up and said, Perhaps in a few hours' time. I've got to go and take care of some business right now. He thanked them and left without explaining, started the car, and drove out of the neighborhood and the city. He felt good, well, inside, within his body, within the sequence of his thoughts, as he had not for a long time. It might have been because he had satisfied his huge appetite by eating a lot of delicious things, or because he knew exactly what he had to do.

45

On the way along the coast road he recalled the various details he had heard here and there over the years about the man's private life. He was so deep in thought that the Netanya interchange caught him by surprise, heaving suddenly into view barely past the northern exit from Tel Aviv. He knew that his three daughters had been married for some time; one was in Orlando, Florida, one was in Zurich, and the last was, or at least had been a few months ago, on the staff of the embassy in Cairo. It followed that his grandchildren were scattered over three continents. His sister lived in London. His ex-wife, his daughters' mother, had been married for upward of twenty years to a world-famous musician, and she too lived in Switzerland, not far from the middle daughter and her family, perhaps in Lausanne.

The only member of the Ostashinsky family left in Pardes Hanna, if his information was correct, was the old father, who must now, Yoel calculated, be at least eighty. Perhaps closer to ninety. Once, when the two of them had waited all night in the Operations room for a message that was supposed to be coming in from Cyprus, the Acrobat had said that his father was a fanatical, mad chicken breeder. More than that he had not said, and Yoel had not asked. Everyone has his own shame in the attic. Although now, as he drove along the coast road north of Netanya, he was surprised to see how many new houses were being built with pitched roofs and storage space in the attic. Until a little while before, cellars and attics hardly existed in Israel. Yoel reached Pardes Hanna soon after hearing the one o'clock news on the car radio. He decided not to visit the cemetery, because the village was already subsiding into the calm of a festival-day siesta, and he did not want to cause a disturbance. He asked twice before he discovered where the house was. It was set apart somewhat, near the edge of an orange grove, at the end of a muddy track overgrown with thistles that reached up to the car's windows. After parking, he had to force his way through a thick hedge that had run wild and almost grown together from each side of a path of broken and uneven paving stones. He therefore prepared himself to encounter a neglected old man in a neglected old house. He even entertained the possibility that his information was out of date, and that the old man had passed away or been moved into an institution. To his surprise, when he emerged from the overgrowth he found himself standing before a door painted psychedelic blue surrounded by standing, hanging, and hovering pots of petunias and white cyclamens blending into the bougainvillea that trailed over the front of the house. Among the flowerpots masses of little china bells hung from intertwined strings, making Yoel think he detected the hand of a woman, and a young woman at that. He knocked five or six times, pausing between knocks and knocking harder each time, because it occurred to him that the old man might be hard of hearing. And all the time he felt embarrassed to be disturbing the still, small silence of the vegetation that filled the place by making such an impertinent noise. He even felt, with a pang of longing, that he had been in a place like this once before, and that it had been good and pleasant. The memory was heartwarming and dear to him, though in fact there was no memory, since he was unable to focus his feeling and locate the place.

Since there was no answer, he went around the bungalow and tapped at a window that was framed by white curtains draped in a pair of rounded wings, like the curtains painted at the windows of the symmetrical houses in children's books. Between the two wings he could see a tiny but pleasant and extremely clean and neat living room, a Bukhara rug, a coffee table made from the stump of an olive tree, a single deep armchair and also a rocking chair in front of a television set on which stood a glass jar of the kind yogurt used to be sold in thirty or forty years ago, containing a bunch of chrysanthemums. On the wall he saw a painting of snow-capped Mount Hermon with the Sea of Galilee below, wreathed in bluish early-morning mist. Out of professional habit, Yoel identified the painter's vantage point, apparently on the slope of Mount Arbel. But what was the explanation for the increasingly painful feeling that he had been in this room before, and not only been there, but had lived there, a life full of powerful, forgotten joy?

He went around to the back of the house and knocked on the kitchen door, which was painted the same dazzling blue and was also surrounded by masses of petunias in flowerpots amid china bells. But there was no answer here either. Pressing down the handle, he discovered that the door was not locked. Beyond it he found a tiny, splendidly clean and neat kitchen, painted pale blue, though all its furnishings and equipment were ancient. Here too Yoel saw the same kind of old yogurt jar on the kitchen table, except that here it was sprouting marigolds instead of chrysanthemums. From another jar, which stood on the old refrigerator, a sturdy, attractive sweet-potato plant trailed along the wall. It was only with difficulty that Yoel resisted the sudden desire to sit down on the rush stool and settle here in this kitchen.

Finally he left, and after a slight hesitation decided to inspect the outbuildings before coming back and penetrating deeper into the house. There were three matching henhouses, well kept, enclosed by tall cypress trees and with small squares of lawn decorated in the corners with cactuses growing in rock gardens. Yoel observed that the henhouses were air-conditioned. And in the doorway of one of them he saw a skinny, small-framed, compressed-looking man standing, squinting at a test tube that was half full of a cloudy liquid. Yoel apologized for his unannounced visit. He introduced himself as an old friend and colleague of the man's late son. Of Yokneam.

The old man stared at him in amazement, as though he had never heard the name Yokneam in his life. For a moment Yoel's confidence was shaken: had he come to the wrong old man after all? He asked the man if he was Mr. Ostashinsky, and whether he was disturbing him. The old man wore neatly pressed khaki clothes with wide military pockets, which might have been an improvised uniform from the time of the War of Independence; the skin of his face looked as rough as raw flesh, and his back was slightly hunched and bent, vaguely suggesting a nocturnal predator, a badger or pine marten, but his little eyes flashed sharp blue sparks that matched the doors of his house. Without responding to Yoel's outstretched hand, he said in a clear tenor voice and the accent of the early settlers: "Yeis. You are disturbing me. And yeis again, I am Zerach Ostashinsky." After a moment, slyly, with a shrewd wink, he added: "Ve didn' see you et de funeral." Once more Yoel had to apologize. He almost uttered the excuse that he had been abroad at the time. But, as ever, he avoided telling an untruth. He said:

"You are right. I didn't come." He added a compliment to the old man on his excellent memory, which the man ignored.

"And for vy hef you come here today?" he asked. As he did so he looked not at Yoel but, squinting sideways against the daylight, at the spermlike liquid in the glass test tube.

"I've come to tell you something. And also to see if there's some way I can be of help. But, if it's possible, perhaps we could talk sitting down?"

The old man thrust the stoppered test tube with the opaque liquid in it like a fountain pen into the pocket of his khaki shirt. He said:

"I'm sorry. I'm not free." And: "Are you also a secret agent? A spy? A licensed killer?"

"Not any more," said Yoel. "Couldn't you spare me just ten minutes of your time?"

"Vell, five then," the old man compromised. "Please. Begin. I am all ears." But with these words he spun around and quickly entered the dark henhouse, obliging Yoel to follow on his heels, almost running after him as he darted from battery to battery adjusting the water taps attached to the metal troughs that ran along the cages. A constant quiet cackle, like busy gossip, filled the air, which was heavy with the smell of dung and feathers and chicken feed.

"Speak," said the old man. "But keep it short."

"It's like this, sir. I came to tell you that your son actually went to Bangkok instead of me. I was the one who was told to go first. And I refused. And your son went instead of me."

"Nu? So vot?" the old man said without surprise. And without interrupting his brisk, efficient progress from battery to battery.

"You might say that I have some responsibility for the disaster. Responsibility, though naturally not guilt."

"Nu. So it's nice of you you should say det," declared the old man, still darting along the alleys in the henhouse. Occasionally he would disappear for an instant and reappear on the other side of a battery, leading Yoel to suspect that he had a network of secret passages.

"It's true that I refused to go," Yoel said as though arguing, "but if it had been up to me, your son would also have stayed at home. I would never have sent him. I wouldn't have sent anyone. There was something there that I didn't like right from the start. It doesn't matter. The truth is that to this day it isn't clear to me what really happened."

"Vot heppened. Vot heppened. Dey kilt him. Det's vot heppened. Vid a revolver dey kilt him. Vid five bullets. Vould you hold dis please?"

Yoel held the rubber hose with both hands at the two points indicated by the old man, who suddenly, as quick as lightning, drew a flick-knife from his belt, made a small hole in the hose, and at once fitted a sparkling metal tap in it, tightened it, and pressed on, with Yoel at his heels.

"Do you know," Yoel asked, "who killed him?"

"Who kilt him. Who kilt him. De Jew-haters kilt him. Vy, who did you tink, de students of Greek philosophy?"

"Look here," Yoel said, but at that instant the old man vanished. As though he had never existed. Or as though he had been

231

swallowed up by the ground, which was covered here with a layer of pungent-smelling chicken droppings. Yoel began hunting for the old man between the rows of batteries, peering underneath the cages, walking faster and faster, breaking into a run, peering down the alleys to left and right, mixing them up, as though lost in a maze, retracing his steps, going up to the entrance and returning by a parallel alley, until he finally gave up in despair and shouted at the top of his voice: "Mr. Ostashinsky!"

"It seems your five minutes are over," replied the old man, suddenly springing up behind a small stainless-steel counter immediately to Yoel's right, this time holding a reel of fine wire.

"I wanted you to know that they ordered me to go, and your son was sent only because I refused."

"Det I heard you say already."

"And I would never have sent your son. I wouldn't have sent anyone."

"Det also I heard you say. Vos dere something else?"

"Did you know, sir, that your son once saved the lives of the Philharmonic Orchestra, when they were about to be massacred by terrorists? May I tell you that your son was a good man? An honest man? A brave man?"

"Nu? So, for vot do ve need an orchestra? Vot good can orchestras do for us?"

A lunatic, Yoel decided, peaceable, but definitely certifiable. And I was mad too, to come here.

"Well, anyway, I share your grief."

"After all, in his own vay he vos a terrorist himself. And if any man seeks his own private death, de death det suits him, den in de fullness of time he vill surely find it. And vot is so special about det?"

"He was a friend of mine. Quite a close friend. And I would like to say, seeing that, if I have understood correctly, you are alone here . . . maybe you'd like to come and be with us? To stay? To live? Even maybe for quite a long time? We are, I should say, an extended family . . . a sort of urban kibbutz. Almost. And we could easily—how should I put it?—absorb you. Or maybe there's something else I can do for you? Something you need?"

"Need? Vot do I need? 'And purify our hearts to serve Thee in truth'—det's vot ve all need. But in dis you don' help and you don' get help. It's every man for himself."

"Still, I wish you wouldn't turn it down just like that. Think whether there isn't something I can do for you, Mr. Ostashinsky."

Again the slyness of a badger or a pine marten flashed across the old man's rough face, and he almost winked at Yoel as he had winked at the cloudy liquid in the test tube when he had held it up to the sunlight.

"Did you hef a hend in my son's death? Have you come here to buy yourself forgiveness?"

And as he made his way to the electrical control panel by the entrance to the henhouse, walking fast and weaving slightly, like a lizard crossing an exposed patch of ground between two shadows, he suddenly turned his shriveled face and transfixed Yoel, who was running behind him, with his glance:

"*Nu*? So who did?"

Yoel did not understand.

"You told me it vosn' you det sent him. And you asked me vot I need. So, vot I need is I should know who did send him."

"Of course," Yoel said keenly, as though he were trampling the divine name underfoot with vindictive glee or righteous zeal. "Of course. For your information. It was Yirmiyahu Cordovero who sent him. Le Patron. The head of our office. Our Teacher. The famous mystery man. The father of us all. My brother. He sent him."

The old man surfaced slowly from behind his counter, like a drowned corpse rising from the deep. Instead of the gratitude Yoel was expecting, instead of the absolution he imagined he had rightfully earned by his candor, instead of an invitation to tea in the house that glowed with the magic of a childhood he had never known, in the little kitchen that had won his heart like a promised land, instead of the open arms, came a blow. Which somehow, secretly, he had been expecting. Even waiting for. The father suddenly erupted, puffed himself up, bristled like an attacking pine marten. And Yoel recoiled from the spit. That never came. The old man merely hissed at him:

"Traitor!"

As Yoel turned to effect his retreat, with measured steps yet inwardly in headlong flight, the old man shouted after him again as though stoning him:

"Cain!"

It was important to him to avoid the house and its charms and to cut straight through to his car. So he plunged among the overgrown bushes that had once been a hedge. Very soon a bristly darkness, a thick, humid coat of ferns, closed around him. Gripped by claustrophobia, he began to trample on branches, to flail, to kick out at the dense foliage, which simply absorbed his kicks; bending stems and twigs, scratched all over, panting hard, his clothes covered with burrs and thorns and dry leaves, he seemed to be sinking in the folds of thick, soft, twisted, dark-green cotton wool, struggling with strange pangs of panic and seduction.

He cleaned himself up to the best of his ability, started the car, and reversed rapidly down the dirt track. He only came to his senses when he heard the sound of the taillight being crushed as the car hit the trunk of a eucalyptus that was leaning across the track. Yoel could have sworn it was not there when he arrived. But the accident restored his self-control and he drove carefully all the way home. When he reached the Netanya interchange, he turned on the radio and managed to hear the end of an old piece for harpsichord, although he did not catch the name of it or of the composer. Then there was an interview with a Bible-loving woman who described her feelings about King David, a man who often in his long life received news of a death, and each time tore his clothes and uttered heartrending lamentations, even though in fact each news of a death was good news to him, because it brought him relief and sometimes even rescue. So it was in the case of the death of Saul and Jonathan at Gilboa, of Abner son of Ner, of Uriah the Hittite, and even of his son Ab-

234

salom. Yoel turned off the radio and parked the car expertly, in reverse gear, with the front toward the street, dead in the center of the new pergola he had constructed. Then he went indoors to take a shower and change.

As he was getting out of the shower the telephone rang; he picked it up and asked Krantz what he wanted.

"Nothing," said the real-estate agent. "I thought you left a message for me, with Duby, to call you the moment I got in from Eilat. So now here I am, back with that chick, and now I've got to clear away the evidence because Odelia's flying back from Rome tomorrow and I don't want to have any trouble with her first thing."

"Yes," said Yoel, "I remember now. Listen. I've got some business to talk over with you. Could you drop around tomorrow morning? What time does your wife get in? Hold on a minute. Actually, tomorrow morning is no good. I've got to take the car in to be mended. I've smashed a taillight. And the afternoon's no good either, because my women are coming back from Metullah. How about the day after tomorrow? Have you got the whole week off for Passover?"

"What the hell, Yoel," said Krantz. "What's the problem? I'll come around right away. I'll be with you in ten minutes. Put the coffee on and stand by to repel boarders!"

Yoel made coffee in the percolator. He'd have to go and see about the insurance tomorrow too, he thought. And spread some fertilizer on the lawn, because spring was here.

46

Arik Krantz, suntanned, in high spirits, wearing a shirt covered with flashing sequins, regaled Yoel, as they drank their coffee, with detailed descriptions of what Greta had to offer and what there was to see in Eilat when the sun came out. He begged Yoel again to come out of his monastery before it was too late, and let himself go. Why not start, let's say, with one night a week? You come to the hospital with me as a volunteer from ten to two in the morning. There's almost no work to do, the patients are asleep, and the nurses are awake, and the female volunteers even more so. And he went on to sing the praises of Christina and Iris: he was reserving them for Yoel, but he wouldn't be able to keep them indefinitely, and if it was too late, it was too late. He still hadn't forgotten that Yoel had taught him to say "I want you" in Burmese.

Then, since they were both alone for the evening, Yoel let Krantz inspect his refrigerator and get them a bachelor supper of cheese and yogurt and a sausage omelette, while he made out a shopping list for the next morning, so that his mother, his mother-in-law, and his daughter would find the refrigerator full when they got back from Metullah in the afternoon. He reflected that mending the taillight would cost several hundred shekels, and this month he had already spent several hundred on the garden and the new pergola, and there were still some items on the agenda, such as a solar water heater, a new mailbox, a rocking chair or two for the living room, and after that some lighting for the garden.

"Duby tells me he helped you with your gardening. Well done. Can't you tell me the magic word that makes him work, so I can get him to do something in our garden too?"

"Listen," Yoel said after a moment, changing the subject without noticing, as he often did. "What's the situation with apartments at the moment? Is it a buyers' or a sellers' market?"

"Depends where."

"In Jerusalem for instance."

"Why?"

"I want you to go to Jerusalem for me and find out what I can get for a two-bedroom apartment with a living room, and actually it's got a little study too; in Talbiyeh. It's rented at the moment, but the lease comes up for renewal soon. I'll give you the particulars and the papers. Wait. I haven't finished. We've got another apartment in Jerusalem, two rooms, in the middle of Rehavia. Find out what the market value of that one is at the moment too. I'll refund all your expenses, of course, because you might have to spend a few days in Jerusalem."

"What the hell! Yoel, you ought to be ashamed of yourself. I wouldn't dream of taking a penny from you. We're friends. But tell me, really, have you decided to sell everything you've got in Jerusalem?"

"Wait. I haven't finished yet. I want you to find out from that friend of yours, Kramer, if he's willing to sell me this house."

"Tell me, Yoel, is anything the matter?"

"Wait. I haven't finished yet. I want you to go into Tel Aviv with me one day this week to look over a penthouse apartment. On Karl Netter Street. The city at your fingertips, as you put it."

"Just a minute. Give me time to breathe. Let me try to understand. You're planning to——"

"Wait. Apart from all that, I'm interested in renting a room somewhere around here with all conveniences and a separate entrance. Something with privacy guaranteed."

"Girls?"

"Only one. Maximum."

The agent, in his sequined shirt, with his head on one side

and his mouth slightly open, stood up. Then he sat down again even before Yoel had time to tell him to. Suddenly, taking a small flat metal box out of his rear pocket, he popped a tablet in his mouth, put the box back in his pocket, and explained that the tablets were for heartburn, the fried sausage in the omelette had brought on a slight attack; would Yoel like one? Then he chuckled and said in a surprised tone, more to himself than to Yoel:

"Boy—a revolution!"

They had another cup of coffee and talked over the details. Krantz called home to tell Duby to get one or two things ready for his mother's return, because he would be staying late and might be going straight from Yoel's to his volunteer shift at the hospital, and would he wake him at six the next morning, because he wanted to take Mr. Ravid's—Yoel's—car to Guetta's Garage. Yoav Guetta would fix his taillight without making him wait and he'd charge him only half-price. So don't forget, Duby—"Just a minute," said Yoel, and Krantz stopped and covered the mouthpiece with his hand. "Tell Duby to come over some time when he's free. I've got something for him."

"Should he come right away?"

"Yes. No. Let him come in half an hour. So you and I can finish working out a plan for my musical apartments."

When Duby arrived half an hour later in his mother's little Fiat, it was time for his father to leave for his volunteer shift at the hospital, which he would spend, he announced, in a horizontal position in a cubicle behind the nurses' station.

Yoel sat Duby down in the comfortable armchair in the living room, and sat facing him on the sofa. He offered him a hot or cold drink or something stronger, but the curly-haired, skinny, short boy, who with his matchlike arms and legs looked more like a sixteen-year-old than someone who had served in a combat unit, politely declined. Yoel repeated his apology for being so rude the day before, and thanked him again for helping with the planting. He engaged Duby in light political discussion and then turned the conversation to cars. Duby, realizing at last that Yoel

238

was having difficulty getting to the point, found a tactful way of helping him out:

"Netta says you're working terribly hard on yourself to be the perfect father. That you've made it your, well, your ambition. In case you're dying to know what's going on, it's no problem for me to tell you that Netta and I talk to each other. We're not exactly going out together. Yet. But if she likes me, there's no problem. Because I like her. A lot. And that's all there is to it at this stage."

Yoel spent a moment or two checking these things in his head, and however hard he tried he could find no error in them.

"All right. Thank you," he said at last, with an uncharacteristic fleeting smile on his face. "Just remember that she's—"

"Mr. Ravid. There's no need. I haven't forgotten. I know. Forget it. You're not doing her a favor."

"What did you say your hobby was? Mechanics, is that it?"

"It's my hobby and it's going to be my career. And you, when you said you were a government employee, you meant some sort of classified work?"

"More or less. I used to assess certain types of merchandise, and merchants, and sometimes I used to buy as well. But that's all over, and now I've got a period of leisure. Which doesn't prevent your father's deciding that it's his duty to save me time by taking my car to the garage for me. Well, so be it. I wanted to ask you a favor. Something connected with mechanics, in a way. Look here. Take a look at this object: have you got any explanation of why it doesn't fall over? And how this paw is attached to the base?"

Duby stood for a while with his back toward Yoel and the room and his face toward the shelf over the fireplace, saying nothing. Yoel suddenly noticed that the boy was slightly hunchbacked, or else his shoulders were not the same height, or his spine was slightly twisted. It's not exactly James Dean we're getting here. But on the other hand we're not exactly offering Brigitte Bardot, either. Ivria might have been quite pleased with him, actually. She was always saying that hairy muscle men of all sorts disgusted her. Between Heathcliff and Linton, she apparently preferred the latter. Or else she wanted to. Or she was only working on herself to. Or she was only deceiving herself. And Netta, and me. Unless not all our secrets are ultimately identical, as that pain in the neck of an electricity-inventing Pushkin from the North Galilee police used to say. He may really have believed right up to the end that I caught his daughter near the irrigation taps in the dark and raped her twice until she agreed to marry me. And after that he used to come and wave his story in my face about my lacking three things that are the foundation of the world: desire, joy, and pity, which according to Nakdimon's theory come as a package, and if you're missing, say, number two then you haven't got numbers one and three, and vice versa. And if you try to say to them, Look, there's also love, they put a thick finger to that bag of flesh hanging under their beady eyes, and they draw the skin slightly downward and say to you with a sort of bestial mockery: Sure. What else?

"Is it yours? Or was it here before?"

"It was here before," said Yoel, and Duby, still with his back turned to the man and the room, said softly:

"It's beautiful. There may be some flaws, but it's beautiful. Tragic."

"Is it right that the animal is heavier than the base?"

"Yes, it is."

"So how come it doesn't fall over?"

"Don't take offense, Mr. Ravid. You're asking the wrong question. The laws of mechanics. Instead of asking how come it doesn't fall over, we should simply take note: if it doesn't fall over, that proves the center of gravity is over the base. That's all."

"And what's holding it? Do you have a miraculous answer to that too?"

"Not really. I can think of two ways. Maybe three. There may even be more. Why is it important to you to know?"

Yoel was in no hurry to reply. He was used to weighing his

answers, even to such simple questions as How are you or What did it say on the news. As though words were personal possessions that one should not part with. The boy waited. Meanwhile he inspected Ivria's photograph, which had reappeared on the shelf, as mysteriously as it had vanished. Yoel knew that he ought to find out who had taken it away and who had put it back and why, but he also knew that he would not do it.

"Netta's mother? Your wife?"

"She was," Yoel specified punctiliously. And he replied belatedly to the previous question: "Actually it doesn't make much difference. Forget it. It's not worth breaking it just to find out how it's held together."

"Why did she kill herself?"

"Who told you such a thing? Where did you hear that?"

"That's what people say. Even though no one knows exactly. Netta says—"

"Never mind what Netta says. Netta wasn't even there when it happened. Who would have thought that rumors would start here? In point of fact, it was an accident, Duby. An electric cable broke. After all, they spread all sorts of rumors about Netta too. Tell me something: do you have any idea who Adva is, the girl who wants to rent Netta a room that apparently she inherited from her grandmother, on the roof somewhere in old Tel Aviv?"

Duby turned and scratched his curly hair. Then he said quietly:

"Mr. Ravid. I hope you won't be angry at me for what I'm going to say to you. Stop spying on her. Stop following her around. Leave her alone. Let her live her own life. She says you're always working to be the perfect father. It would be better if you stopped. Excuse me for, well, for being frank. But I don't think you're doing her a favor. Well, I've got to go now, I've got one or two things to do at home because my mother's coming back from Europe tomorrow and my dad wants everything to be shipshape and above suspicion. Actually it's good that we had this talk. Good night now."

And so, a fortnight later, the day after the first of her examinations, when Yoel saw his daughter in front of the mirror adjusting the dress he had bought her the day he heard about the disaster in Bangkok, which smoothed out her bony angles and made her look erect and lithe, he decided to keep his mouth shut for once. He did not say a word. When she got in from the date at midnight he was waiting for her in the kitchen and they chatted a little about the imminent heat wave. Yoel made up his mind to accept the change and not stand in her way. He felt it was his right to make this decision on his own behalf and on Ivria's. He also decided that if his mother or his mother-in-law attempted to interfere by so much as a word he would react so strongly that they would both lose any desire to interfere again in Netta's affairs. From now on he would be tough.

A few days later, at two o'clock in the morning, he finished reading the last few pages of the book about the Chief of Staff, and instead of turning the light out and going to sleep, he went to the kitchen to have a drink of cold milk, and he found Netta sitting there in an unfamiliar dressing gown reading a book. When he asked her, And what is your ladyship reading, she answered him with a half-smile that she was not exactly reading, but reviewing for an exam, going over her work on the history of the Mandate period. Yoel said:

"That's one subject that I can actually help you with a little, if you like."

Netta replied:

"I know you can. Shall I make you a sandwich?" And without waiting for his reply, without any connection to her question, she continued:

"Duby gets on your nerves."

Yoel thought for a while and replied:

"You'd be surprised. I think he's bearable." To which Netta replied in a voice that, to his astonishment, almost sounded happy:

"You'd be surprised, Dad, but that's just what Duby said about you. Almost the same words."

On Independence Day the Krantzes invited him, his mother, his mother-in-law, and his daughter for a barbecue in their garden. Yoel surprised them by not being evasive, simply asking if he could bring along his neighbors, the brother and sister. Odelia said, Sure. Toward the end of the evening Odelia informed Yoel, in a corner of the living room, that during her European trip she had actually fooled around a little, twice, with different men, and she had seen no reason to keep it secret from Arye; and actually, since she had told him, their relationship had improved and you could say that for the time being they were relatively reconciled. No small thanks to you, Yoel.

For his part, Yoel remarked modestly:

"What did *I* do? All I wanted was to get home safely."

47

At the end of May the very same cat had another litter of kittens on the same old sack in the garden shed. There was a fierce quarrel between Avigail and Lisa; they did not speak to each other for five days, until Avigail nobly undertook to apologize to Lisa, not because she admitted she was in the wrong, but purely out of consideration for Lisa's condition. Lisa in her turn consented to a truce, but not before she had a slight attack and was taken to Tel Hashomer Hospital for two days. Although she did not say it, and even said the contrary, it was clear that she believed the attack had been caused by Avigail's cruelty. The middle-aged doctor took Yoel into the consulting room and told him that he agreed with Dr. Litwin's opinion that there was a certain, not very significant, deterioration. But Yoel had long since despaired of understanding their language. The two old ladies, after their reconciliation, resumed their joint voluntary activities in the mornings as well as their evening yoga classes, and they also took on a new involvement, with the Brother to Brother Association.

Then, in early June, right in the middle of the matriculation examinations, Netta and Duby moved together into the rented room in the penthouse apartment on Karl Netter Street. One morning the closet in the master bedroom was empty, the pictures of poets were gone from the walls, Amir Gilboa's skeptical smile stopped provoking in Yoel a constant urge to repay the face in the picture in its own coin, and the collections of thistles and sheet music had vanished from the shelves. If he had trouble sleeping at night and he found himself making his way to the kitchen in search of a glass of cold milk, he was reduced to drinking it standing up and going right back to bed. Or picking up the big flashlight and going outside to see how his plants were growing in the dark. After a few days, when Duby and Netta had settled in, Yoel, Lisa, and Avigail were invited to see the sea from their window. Krantz and Odelia came too, and when Yoel happened to see, under a vase, the check that Krantz had left for Duby, in the sum of two thousand shekels, he locked himself in the bathroom for a moment and wrote a check made out to Netta for three thousand and slipped it underneath Krantz's when no one was looking. Later that afternoon, when he got home, he moved his clothes, papers, and bedding from the stiflingly small study to the empty master bedroom, which also had the benefit of air-conditioning, like the grannies' bedrooms. The unlocked safe was left behind in Mr. Kramer's study. It did not make the move with him to his new bedroom.

In the middle of June he learned that Ralph had to return to Detroit in the early autumn but that Annemarie had not yet made up her mind. Give me another month or two, he said to the brother and sister, I need a little more time. He could barely conceal his surprise when Annemarie replied coolly, Sure, you can decide whatever you like whenever you like, but then I have to ask myself if I am interested in you, and if so, in what capacity. Ralph is dying for us to get married and then to adopt him as our child. But I'm not so sure right now that it's my cup of tea, a setup like that. And you know, Yoel, you're the opposite of a lot of men: you're very considerate in bed but out of it you're rather boring. Or else you're beginning to find me a little boring. And you know that for me the most precious man is Ralphie. So let's both give it some more thought. And then we'll see.

It was a mistake, thought Yoel, to see her as a child-woman. Even though she, poor thing, obediently acted out the role that I imposed on her. And now it turns out that she's really a woman-woman. Why is it that this realization makes me recoil? Is it really too difficult to reconcile desire with respect? Is there really a contradiction between the two, which is why I could never have had that Eskimo mistress? Maybe, in point of fact, I was lying to Annemarie, without lying to her. Or else she was lying to me. Or we both were. Let's wait and see.

Sometimes he remembered how he had received the announcement that winter night in Helsinki. When precisely did it begin to snow? How he broke his promise to the Tunisian engineer. How he disgraced himself by failing to notice whether the cripple was coming toward him in a motorized wheelchair or whether there was someone pushing him: he had made a fatal and irreparable slip by failing to discover who, if anyone, was moving the wheelchair. Only once or twice are you granted a special moment that everything else depends on, the moment for which you have been trained and prepared throughout those years of activity and cunning, a moment that might allow you, if you seize it, to discover something about the matter without knowledge of which your whole life is merely a sterile sequence of arrangements, organization, evasions, and troubleshooting.

Sometimes he thought about his eye fatigue and attached to it the blame for that missed opportunity. About why he had stumbled for two blocks in the snow that night instead of simply phoning from his hotel room. And how the snow showed blue and pink like a skin disease wherever the glow of the street lamps fell on it. And how he could have lost the book and the scarf, and what foolishness it was to shave while climbing Mount Castel in Le Patron's car, merely to arrive home without stubble. If he had insisted, if he had been really stubborn, if he had had the courage to risk a fight, even a rift, Ivria would probably have given up and agreed to name the child Rakefet. Which was the name he had wanted. On the other hand, there are times when you have to give up. Not every time, though. How much, then? What is the limit? "A good question," he suddenly said aloud, as he put down the hedge clippers and wiped away the sweat that was running into his eyes from his forehead. His mother said: "There you go again, Yoel, talking to yourself. Like an old bachelor. You will end up going mad if you don't do something with your life. Or else you'll be sick, heaven forbid, or you'll start to pray. The best thing is, you should go into business. For business you do have some talent, and I give you a little money to get started. Should I bring you some soda water from the refrigerator?"

"Idiot," Yoel said suddenly, not to his mother, but to Ironside, who had burst into their garden and started to run around ecstatically, describing rapid loops on the lawn, as though the joy-producing sap had overflowed inside him. "Silly dog! Get away with you!" And to his mother he said:

"Yes. If it's not too much trouble, get me a big glass of ice-cold soda. Better still, bring the bottle out here. Thanks." And he went on clipping.

In the middle of June too, Le Patron telephoned: Not to tell Yoel what had come to light about the disaster in Bangkok, but to ask after Netta. No difficulties, he trusted, about her call-up? Had she had any more medical examinations recently? At the recruiting center, for example? Should we—that is to say, should I—get in touch with the manpower branch of the military? Well, do you mind telling her to get in touch with me? At home, in the evening, not at the office. I've had a thought about giving her something to do here. In any case, I'd like to see her. Will you tell her that?

Yoel nearly said, without raising his voice, Go to hell, Cordovero. But he controlled himself and refrained. He chose to replace the receiver without saying a word. Then he poured himself a brandy, followed by another, though it was only eleven o'clock in the morning. Maybe he's right—that I'm just a refugee kid, nothing but soap fodder, and they rescued me and created a state and built this and that, and even took me into the heart of the heart. But he and they will not be satisfied with less than my whole life, with everybody's whole life, including Netta's, and I'm not giving them that. And that's flat. If your whole life is devoted to the sanctity of life, then that's not life, it's death.

At the end of June, Yoel ordered garden lighting and a solar water heater, and at the beginning of August, even though negotiations with Mr. Kramer, the El Al manager in New York, were still under way he hired workmen to widen the living-room window that looked out on the garden. He bought a new mailbox. And a rocking chair to place in front of the television. And a second television set, with a small screen, for Avigail's room, so that the old ladies could spend the evening there while he and Annemarie made themselves a dinner *à deux*. Ralph had started visiting the Romanian neighbor, Ironside's master, who, Yoel discovered, was also some kind of chess genius. Or the Romanian neighbor would visit Ralph for a return game. Yoel examined all these things several times, and could find no error in them. By the middle of August he knew that what he could get from selling the apartment in Talbiyeh would be almost exactly enough to buy Kramer's house in Ramat Lotan, provided the man agreed to sell it. Meanwhile he was beginning to behave proprietorially. Arik Krantz, whose duty it was to keep an eye on the house on behalf of Mr. Kramer, eventually found the courage to look Yoel in the eye and say: "Listen, Yoel, in a word, I'm your man, not his." As for the self-contained one-room apartment he had been thinking of renting, with a separate entrance and guaranteed privacy, so that he and Annemarie would have some space for themselves, he decided that he might not need it now after all, because Avigail had been invited to return to Jerusalem the following year to serve in a voluntary capacity as secretary of the Society for the Promotion of Tolerance. He put off the actual decision almost to the eve of Ralph's departure for Detroit. Maybe because one evening Annemarie said to him: Instead of all this, I'm going to Boston to lodge an appeal and put up one last fight for my daughters by my two lovely marriages. If you love me, why don't you go with me? You might even be able to help me. Yoel had not replied, but, as usual, had run his finger slowly between his neck and his shirt collar and held his breath for a while before releasing it slowly through a narrow gap between his lips.

Then he had said to her:

"That's not easy."

And also:

"We'll see. I don't think I'll go." That night, when he woke

248

up and padded toward the kitchen, he saw clearly before his eyes, in his mind, with all the details of the colors, an English country gentleman of a century earlier, slim, pensive, tramping in boots along a winding muddy path, holding a double-barreled shotgun, walking slowly, as though deep in thought, and running in front of him a flecked gundog, which suddenly stopped and looked up at its master with its doggy eyes so full of devotion, wonder, and love that Yoel was filled with pain, longing, the grief of eternal loss, because he realized that both the pensive man and his dog were now enclosed in earth and would remain so forever, and only the muddy path still wound to this day, empty of people, between gray poplars under a gray sky with a cold wind and a drizzle so fine it could not be seen, only felt. And in a moment the whole scene vanished.

48

His mother said:

"In your blue shirt with the checks, you lost a button."

Yoel said:

"OK. I'll sew it on this evening. Can't you see I'm busy now?"

"You won't sew it on this evening, because I've already done it for you. I'm your mother, Yoel. Even if you've forgotten that a long time ago."

"That's enough."

"The same like you forgot her. Like you forget that a healthy young man needs to work every day."

"All right. Look. I've got to go now. Shall I bring your medicine out for you?"

"No, bring me some poison instead. Come. Sit next to me. Tell me something: where are you going to put me? Outside in the garden shed? Or in an old people's home?"

So he carefully put the pliers and the screwdriver down on the table, wiped his hands on the seat of his jeans, and after a moment's hesitation sat down on the end of the glider, next to her feet.

"Don't get worked up," he said. "It doesn't help you to get better. What's happened? Have you had another fight with Avigail?"

"What did you bring me here for, Yoel? What do you need me for at all?"

He looked at her and saw her silent tears. It was a mute, babylike weeping that took place only between her open eyes and her cheeks, without her making any sound, without her covering her face, without contorting her face into a crying expression.

"That's enough," he said. "Stop it. No one's going to put you anywhere. No one is abandoning you. Who on earth put that ridiculous idea in your head?"

"Anyway, you can't be so cruel as to do it."

"Do what?"

"Abandon your mother. Already you abandoned her when you were so big. When you started to run away."

"I don't know what you're talking about. I've never run away from you."

"All the time, Yoel. All the time running away. If I didn't grab first thing this morning your blue check shirt, even a button you wouldn't let your poor mother sew on for you. There's this story about little Yigor, who has a hunch growing on his back. *Cocoşat.* Don't interrupt me in the middle. Silly little Yigor starts to run to escape from his hunch what is growing on his back, and so he is running around all the time. Soon I will die, Yoel, and then afterward you'll want to ask me all sorts of questions. Wouldn't it be better you should start asking now already? Things what I know about you, nobody else knows."

So Yoel, by a concentrated effort of willpower, laid a broad, ugly hand on the skinny, birdlike shoulder. Just as in his childhood, disgust was mingled with compassion and other feelings, which he did not know and did not want to, and after a moment, in an invisible panic, he withdrew his hand and wiped it on his jeans. Then he stood up and said:

"Questions. What questions? Good. All right. I'll ask questions. But some other time, Mother. I haven't got time now."

Lisa said, with her voice and face suddenly old and shriveled, as though she were his grandmother or great-grandmother rather than his mother:

"All right then. Never mind. You go."

When he had gone a little way in the direction of the back garden, with a kind of internal wringing of hands, she added, with only her lips moving:

"Lord have mercy on him."

Toward the end of August it emerged that he could buy Kramer's house right away, but that he would have to add nine thousand dollars to the price Krantz would get for him for the apartment in Talbiyeh, which the heirs of their old neighbor Itamar Vitkin were interested in buying. He therefore made up his mind to go to Metullah and ask Nakdimon for this amount, either as an advance on his and Netta's share of the income from the property that Lublin had left them, or through some other arrangement. After breakfast he took his travel bag, which he had not used for a year and a half, down from the top shelf in the closet. He packed shirts and underwear and shaving things, because he thought that he might have to stay over in the old stone house at the northern end of the town if Nakdimon raised difficulties or placed obstacles in his way. Indeed, he almost discovered a desire to spend a night or two there. When he unzipped the side pocket of the bag, he found an oblong object and was startled for a moment; was it an old box of chocolates that he had absentmindedly left to rot there? Cautiously he pulled it out and found it was wrapped in yellowing newspaper. When he placed it gently on the table, he saw that it was a Finnish newspaper. After a moment's hesitation he decided to open it by a special method he had been taught during a course he had taken. But it turned out to be nothing more than *Mrs. Dalloway*. Yoel placed it on the bookshelf next to its double, which he had purchased in the shopping center in Ramat Lotan the previous August, erroneously supposing that this copy had been left behind in his hotel room in Helsinki. So it happened that he abandoned his intention of going to Metullah that day and contented himself with a telephone conversation with Nakdimon Lublin, who, after a moment, grasped the sum he was talking about and the purpose for which he required it and at once interrupted Yoel with the words: "No problem, Captain. It'll be in your bank account in three days' time. I know the account number already."

49

This time he followed the guide through the tangle of narrow alleys without hesitation and without the slightest suspicion. The guide was a slim, delicate man with a perpetual smile on his face and rounded gestures, who was constantly bowing politely. The damp sticky heat spawned a cloud of flying insects out of the misty swamp. They crossed and recrossed fetid canals, treading on rickety bridges whose planks were eaten away by the moisture. The thick water in the canals stood almost motionless, steaming. And in the crowded streets throngs of quiet people moved unhurriedly in a cloud of decomposition and incense from household shrines. The odors mingled with the smoke of damp wood. It was amazing to him that he did not lose his guide in the dense crowd, in which almost all the men looked like his man, the women did too, and in fact it was hard to tell the difference here between the sexes. Because of a religious prohibition on taking life, there were leprous dogs sprawling in yards, in streets, and in the dust of the rough alleys, rats as big as cats crossing the road unconcernedly and unhurriedly in convoys, mangy, boil-ridden cats, gray mice that flashed sharp red eyes at him. Again and again there was a dry crunch under his shoes as he trod on cockroaches, some of which were as big as hamburgers. They were so lazy or indifferent that they made barely any effort to escape their fate, or perhaps they were afflicted with some kind of orthopteran plague. As they were crushed, a jet of fatty murky-brown juice squirted underfoot. From the water rose the stench of open sewers and dead fish and frying and rotting seafood, a ferocious blend of the odors of reproduction and death. The heady rotting effervescence of the hot damp city, which always attracted him from a distance and yet when he arrived always made him want to leave and never return. But he clung to his guide. Or perhaps it was not his first guide, but a second or a third, a casual passerby out of the crowd of comely, womanish men, or perhaps it really was a girl in boy's clothing, a slender, elusive creature among thousands of identical creatures moving like fish in the tropical rain that poured down from a height here as though tubs of used water were being simultaneously emptied from all the upper stories, water that had been used for washing or cooking fish. The whole city stood on a marshy delta whose water frequently, with or without the river rising, flooded whole quarters, whose residents could be seen standing up to their knees in water inside their own hovels, bending over as though in deep prostration, fishing with tin cans in their own bedrooms for the fish that had come in with the floodwater. In the streets there was a perpetual roaring and a stench of burned engine fuel because the masses of ancient cars had no exhaust pipes. Among disintegrating taxicabs moved rickshaws drawn by young boys or old men, and pedicabs. Skeletal, half-naked men passed carrying buckets at either end of a flexed yoke. The hot, filthy river traversed the city bearing on its murky water a slow-moving, congested traffic of cargo boats, barges, dinghies, and rafts laden with bleeding raw meat, vegetables, and heaps of silvery fish. Among these craft bobbed wooden flotsam and bloated corpses of drowned beasts both great and small, buffalo, dogs, and monkeys. On the skyline, in the few places where there was a gap between the dilapidated hovels, rose palaces, towers, and pagodas sparkling with delusive gold turrets set alight by the sun. On the street corners shaven-headed monks in saffron robes held empty brass bowls, waiting wordlessly for offerings of rice. In the yards and by the doors of the hovels stood tiny spirit houses, like dolls' houses, with miniature furniture and gilt ornaments, where the spirits of the dead dwelt near their living dear ones, watching over all their doings and receiving daily offerings of a few grains of rice and a thimbleful of rice beer. Small, apathetic twelve-year-old prostitutes, whose bodies fetched ten dollars here, sat on walls and sidewalks, playing with rag dolls. But nowhere in the whole city had he ever seen a couple embracing or linking arms in the street. And here they were outside the city, with the warm rain falling relentlessly over everything and the guide, treading as daintily as a dancer even though he was not dancing, seemingly levitating; no longer bowing politely, no longer smiling or even troubling to look back to make sure his customer had not got lost; and the warm rair falling relentlessly on the buffalo drawing a cartload of bamboo, on the elephant laden with crates of vegetables, on the square paddy fields flooded with murky water, and on the coconut palms looking like monstrous women with dozens of soft heavy breasts growing all over their chests and backs and thighs. Warm rain on thatched roofs of houses constructed on widely spaced wooden piles planted astride the water. Here and there a village woman dressed in layers of clothes, washing almost up to her neck in a filthy canal, or laying fish traps. And the suffocating blast. And silence within the miserable rustic temple, and then a minor miracle: the warm rain did not cease, but fell relentlessly, somehow, even inside the chambers of the temple, which were partitioned by mirrors in order to mislead unclean spirits, which are able to move only in straight lines, which is why everything made of circles, curves, and arches is beautiful and good, whereas the opposite invites tribulation. The guide had vanished and the pockmarked monk, who might have been a eunuch, rose and declared in curious Hebrew: Not yet ready. Not yet enough. The warm rain did not cease until Yoel was forced to get up and take off his clothes, in which he had fallen asleep on the living-room sofa; naked he turned off the flickering television, switched on the airconditioning in the bedroom, took a cold shower, and went outside to turn off the sprinklers, then went indoors again and lay down to sleep.

50

On the twenty-third of August, at half past nine in the evening, he inserted his car carefully and precisely between two Subarus in the visitors' parking lot, ready to go, with its nose pointing toward the exit, checked that the doors were locked, entered the reception area which was lit by a gloomy, flickering neon light, and asked how to get to Orthopedic Ward C. Before he entered the elevator, he checked, as had been his habit all these years, the faces of the people already inside with a rapid but severe and detailed glance. And found that everything was correct.

In Orthopedic Ward C, by the desk at the nurses' station, he found his way barred by a middle-aged nurse with thick lips and misanthropic eyes who hissed at him that visiting was totally out of the question at such an hour. Yoel, hurt and embarrassed, nearly retreated, but managed to mumble meekly, Excuse me, sister, but I think there must be some misunderstanding. My name is Sasha Schein, and I haven't come to visit a patient, I've come to see Mr. Arye Krantz, who was supposed to be waiting for me now at this desk.

Immediately the cannibal's face lit up, her thick lips parted in a warm smile, and she said, Oh, Arik, of course, what a dunce I am, you're Arik's friend, the new volunteer. Welcome. Wonderful. First of all, can I make you a cup of coffee? No? All right then. Take a seat. Arik left word that he'll be free shortly. He's just gone downstairs to get an oxygen tank. Arik is our ministering angel. The most devoted and wonderful and humane volunteer I've ever had. One of the Thirty-six Righteous Men. Meanwhile

I can give you a quick guided tour of our little kingdom. By the way, I'm Maxine. How about you? Sasha? Mr. Schein? Sasha Schein? Is that some kind of joke? What kind of a name have you been saddled with? Yet you look like a native—this is the special unit for seriously ill patients—like a battalion commander or a managing director. Just a minute. Don't say anything. Let me guess. Let's see: you're a police officer? Is that right? You've committed some disciplinary offense, and the hearing or whatever it's called sentenced you to a period of voluntary public service? No? You don't have to answer. Let it be Sasha Schein. Why not? As far as I'm concerned, any friend of Arik's is a guest of honor here. Anyone who didn't know him, judging just by his style, might get the impression that Arik is just another little fart. But anyone with eyes in his head can tell that it's nothing but a façade. He just puts on a performance so that people won't see what a treasure he is really. Well, this is where you wash your hands. Use that blue soap and scrub them well, please. Paper towels over here. That's right. Now put on a gown—take one of those hanging over there. At least you could tell me if my guess was hot or cold or lukewarm. These door lead to the toilets for walking patients and visitors. The staff toilets are at the far end of the corridor. Ah, here's Arik. Arik, show your friend where the linen stores are, so he can start loading a cart with clean sheets and bedspreads. The Yemeni woman in number three has asked to have her bottle emptied. Don't rush, Arik; it's not that urgent; she asks every five minutes and as often as not there's nothing in it. Sasha? OK. As far as I'm concerned, you can be Sasha. Though if his real name is Sasha then I'm Jane Fonda. Good. Anything else? I must fly now. I forgot to tell you, Arik, that Greta called while you were downstairs to say she wouldn't be coming in tonight. She's coming tomorrow instead.

So Yoel began to work two half-nights a week as a volunteer auxiliary. As Krantz had been begging him to do for ages. And he soon discovered how the real-estate agent had lied to him. It was true he had a fellow volunteer named Greta. It was true that they would disappear together for a quarter of an hour or so at one o'clock in the morning. And Yoel did also notice a couple of student nurses named Christina and Iris, though at the end of two months he still could not tell them apart. Nor did he particularly try to. But it was not true that Krantz spent his nights in lovemaking. The truth was, the agent took his work as an auxiliary in deadly earnest. Devotedly. And with a cheerful glow that sometimes made Yoel stop and eye him covertly for a few seconds. There were times when he felt strange pangs of shame and an urge to apologize. Although he never managed to clarify what, precisely, he ought to apologize for. He just tried very hard not to lag behind Krantz.

The first few times he was mainly set to work on the laundry. The hospital laundry apparently functioned even during the night shifts. Two Arab laborers would arrive at two o'clock to collect the dirty linen from the ward. Yoel's job was to sort out what had to be boiled and what needed a delicate wash. To empty the pockets of the dirty pajamas. And to enter on the appropriate form how many sheets, how many pillowcases, and so forth. Bloodstains and filth, the acid smell of urine, the stench of sweat and other body fluids, traces of excrement on the sheets and pajamas, patches of dried vomit, medicine stains, the intense whiff of tormented bodies—all these aroused in him neither disgust nor loathing, but a powerful, if secretive, triumphant joy, which Yoel was no longer ashamed of and did not even attempt, in his usual fashion, to decipher. He yielded himself to it with silent elation: I am alive. Therefore I take part. Unlike the dead.

Sometimes he had an opportunity to see how Krantz, pushing a bed along with one hand and holding an IV bottle aloft with the other, helped the team from the Emergency Ward to bring in a wounded soldier who had been flown down from South Lebanon by helicopter and operated on earlier in the evening. Or a woman who had lost her legs in a road accident at night. Sometimes Maxine and Arik would ask him to help them move a man with a fractured skull from a stretcher to a bed. Gradually, as the weeks went past, they learned to trust his skill. He rediscovered in himself the powers of concentration and precision that

258

not long before he had tried to persuade Netta he had lost. He was able, if the regular nursing staff was under particular pressure and requests for help came simultaneously from several quarters, to adjust an IV or change a catheter bag. But his main discovery in himself was unexpected powers to soothe and pacify. He was capable of approaching the bed of a badly injured patient who had suddenly started screaming, and, laying one hand on his forehead and another on his shoulder, silencing the screams, not because his fingers had somehow pumped away the pain, but because even from a distance he had identified the screams as being caused not by pain but by fear. And this fear he was capable of allaying with a touch and with a simple word or two. Even the doctors recognized this power, and sometimes a doctor on night duty would call him over or send for him when he was sorting piles of filthy linen, to come and calm someone whom not even an injection could quiet. Yoel would say, for instance:

"What's your name, miss? Yes. It's burning. I know. It's burning terribly. You're right. Hellish pain. But it's a good sign. It's supposed to be burning now. It proves that the operation has been successful. Tomorrow it'll burn less, and the day after it'll only itch."

Or:

"Never mind, friend. Throw it all up. Don't hold back. It'll do you good. You'll feel better afterward."

Or:

"Yes. I'll tell her. Yes. She was here when you were asleep. Yes, she loves you a lot. It's plain to see."

In a strange way that Yoel again made no effort to understand or anticipate, he sometimes experienced some of the patients' pain in his own body. Or so he imagined. This pain thrilled him and put him in a state of mind that resembled pleasure. Yoel also was better than the doctors, better than Maxine and Arik and Greta and all the others, at calming desperate relatives who sometimes burst in screaming or threatening violence. He knew how to extract from himself an accurate combination of compassion and firmness. Of sympathy, sorrow, and authority. In the

259

way that the words "Unfortunately I don't know the answer to that" often emerged from his mouth, there was such an undertone of knowledge, albeit vague and concealed beneath layers of responsibility and reserve, that after a few minutes the desperate relatives were filled with a mysterious feeling that here was an ally who would fight cleverly and courageously on their behalf against disaster, and would not easily be defeated.

One night an unfamiliar young doctor, almost a boy, told him to go to another ward chop-chop and get him his bag, which he had left on the table in the consulting room. When Yoel returned a few minutes later without the bag, explaining that the room was locked, the young doctor shrieked at him, Then go and get the key from somebody, you nincompoop. Yet even this humiliating treatment did not humiliate Yoel; it almost gratified him.

If he happened to witness a death, Yoel would maneuver himself into a position from which he could observe the death throes and would absorb every particular with the whetted senses that his professional life had developed in him. He filed it all away in his memory and went on counting syringes, wiping toilet seats, sorting dirty linen, all the while playing back the death scene in slow motion in his mind's eye, freezing the picture and scrutinizing every tiny detail, as though he had been instructed to trace a strange misleading blip that might in fact have occurred only in his imagination or in his tired eyes.

Often Yoel had to take a senile, dribbling old man, hobbling on crutches, to the toilet, and help him lower his pants and sit down. He would kneel and hold the old man's legs while he painfully emptied his bubbling bowels; then he had to wipe away the excrement, mixed with blood from his hemorrhoids, carefully and very patiently, so as not to hurt him, and dry his behind. After that he would wash his hands thoroughly with soap and carbolic, take the old man back to his bed, and put the crutches away carefully by his bedside. And all in total silence.

Once, at one o'clock in the morning, nearly at the end of the volunteer shift, when they were drinking coffee in the little cubicle behind the nurses' station, Christina or Iris said:

"You should have been a doctor."

Yoel hesitated before answering:

"No. I can't stand blood."

And Maxine said:

"Liar. I've seen all sorts of liars in my time, so help me, but I've never yet met a liar like this Sasha. He's a liar you can trust. A liar who doesn't lie. More coffee anybody?"

Greta said:

"To look at him, you'd think he was floating in another world. Seeing nothing, hearing nothing. Even now, when I'm talking about him, he looks as though he's not listening. But later it turns out that he's filed it all away. You watch out for him, Arik."

And Yoel, putting his coffee cup down very gently on the stained Formica table, as though fearful of hurting the table or the cup, ran two fingers between his neck and his shirt collar and said:

"The boy in room 4, Gilad Danino, had a nightmare. I told him he could sit in the nurses' station and draw for a while, and then I promised him an exciting story. So I'm off. Thanks for the coffee, Greta. Remind me, Arik, before the end of the shift to count the cracked cups."

At quarter after two, as they were both walking out, very tired and silent, to the parking lot, Yoel asked:

"Have you been to Karl Netter?"

"Odelia's been. She said you were there too. And the four of you played Scrabble. Maybe I'll drop by tomorrow. That Greta tires me out. Perhaps I'm getting too old for that sort of thing."

"Tomorrow is today," said Yoel.

Suddenly he also said:

"You're all right, Arik."

And the man replied:

"Thanks. You too."

"Good night. Drive carefully, friend."

And so Yoel Ravid began to give in. Since he was capable of observing, he grew fond of observing in silence. With tired but open eyes. Into the depth of the darkness. And if it was necessary to focus the gaze and remain on the lookout for hours and days, even for years, well there was no finer thing than this to do. Hoping for a recurrence of one of those rare, unexpected moments when the blackness is momentarily illuminated, and there comes a flicker, a furtive glimmer, which one must not miss, one must not be caught off guard. Because it may signify a presence which makes us ask ourselves what is left. Besides elation and humility.

BOOKS BY AMOS OZ AVAILABLE IN
HARVEST PAPERBACK EDITIONS

Elsewhere, Perhaps

The Hill of Evil Counsel

In the Land of Israel

A Perfect Peace

To Know a Woman

Touch the Water, Touch the Wind

Unto Death

9 780156 906807